Cowboy Up

Cowboy Up

A Tangled Up in Texas Romance

Michelle Beattie

TULE
PUBLISHING

Cowboy Up
Copyright © 2019 Michelle Beattie
Tule Publishing First Printing May 2019

The Tule Publishing, Inc.

ALL RIGHTS RESERVED

First Publication by Tule Publishing 2019

Cover design by The Killion Group

No part of this book may be used or reproduced in any manner whatsoever without written permission except in the case of brief quotations embodied in critical articles and reviews.

This is a work of fiction. Names, characters, places, and incidents are products of the author's imagination or are used fictitiously. Any resemblance to actual events, locales, organizations, or persons, living or dead, is entirely coincidental.

ISBN: 978-1-950510-49-8

Thanks

My thanks to Jan O'Hara, MD and fellow romance writer, not to mention friend, as well as Linda Taylor, RN, for all their expertise with the anything medical. Any errors or omissions were entirely my own.

Also my sincerest thanks to my editor, Sinclair Sawhney and the ever-talented Jane Porter. Thanks for brainstorming, for not giving up on this book and this series until we had it down. Your belief in me and my writing, and your collaboration to ensure it happened, means everything.

Dear Reader,

If you've followed my other books you know this is a big switch for me. Not the cowboys, but the genre. I've typically stayed with historicals but have always been told I had a modern voice in a historical setting. It was always my plan to switch to contemporary at some point. The idea for Dallas's book came to me about eighteen years ago. I loved the idea of a man with a bit of a chip on his shoulders being humbled into realizing he was wrong and that some of his prejudices were unfounded. I think at some point we've all judged unfairly. I know I have. So I liked the idea that he needed to be "knocked down" a peg or two. And who better to show him the error of his ways than the woman who steals his heart?

But Dallas's story wasn't ready to be told until now. I'm not one who writes fast nor can I work on multiple projects at once, so I had to tie up my historical series before I felt ready to move on. And now, I'm so pleased to bring you Dallas and Ashley's story. Life hasn't been easy for either, something I can relate to. What they have, they've had to fight tooth and nail to get. Something else I can relate to. As I think, most of us can.

Cowboy Up is the first in the *Tangled Up in Texas* series and introduces you to the Granger Brothers. It also takes you to the beautiful hill country of Texas. I hope you get lost not only in the beautiful landscape and the wonderful fictional town of Last Stand, but also in the lives and loves of the characters who live there. Who get up, every morning, no matter their struggles and Cowboy Up.

Saddle up. It's going to be a great ride!

My best to you always,
Michelle

Chapter One

"**Y**OU'RE SHITTING ME, right?"

It probably wasn't a good idea to talk to the San Antonio Police Department that way, but Dallas was so surprised by the officer's statement the words flew out of his mouth before he could stop them.

"Do I look like I'm kidding?"

The cop settled his hand on the butt of his holstered pistol. His steely gaze never wavered from Dallas's. His mouth was flat and hard. No semblance of a smile softened his face. Behind the officer's back, the red and blue lights of his police cruiser flashed ominously. No, he sure as hell didn't look like he was kidding. In fact, there wasn't anything humorous about the situation Dallas Granger currently found himself in.

"Look, officer, I explained what I was doing with the nail gun."

"A *stolen* nail gun," he corrected.

"Yeah, I'm not denying that. But *I* didn't steal it. I told you it was one of my guys. I'd sent him to the hardware store to get nails and, for whatever dumbass reason, he decided to steal the gun out of the bed of another customer's truck."

The officer jutted his chin toward the Granger Construction logo on the side of Dallas's white pickup.

"That customer ID'd this truck."

"No, he ID'd *one* of my trucks. You said yourself the witness didn't get a look at the driver."

"And you're saying it was your employee?"

"I'm telling you it was Vince Chapman."

"Because you caught him with it."

Dallas ground his teeth. Dammit, they'd gone through this already.

But he couldn't afford to lose his temper so he took a deep breath before continuing. "That's right. And it was a stroke of luck, if anything can be considered lucky in this situation. I wasn't supposed to be at my shop, but my office manager is pregnant and she wasn't feeling well. So, not long after I'd sent Vince for nails, she called to tell me she was going home. Normally, I'd have told her to lock up but we were expecting a delivery and someone had to be there to sign for it, so I went back to the office.

"When I heard someone drive in the yard, I thought it would be the delivery truck, but it was Vince. I went out to see what he was doing because he should have gone straight back to the jobsite. That's when I looked in the box of the truck and saw the nail gun.

"Since Vince lives in an apartment and wouldn't have need for one personally, I asked him what he was doing with it."

"And he admitted it he took it?"

"Yeah, eventually." After a little shoving and more than a few threats. "That's when I fired his ass."

The cop's gaze remained a mask of granite. If he was buying Dallas's story, it was anybody's guess.

"But you didn't call the police."

Dallas shook his head, rubbed the sweat off the back of his neck. Dammit, he knew how it looked. "No, that's when the delivery truck showed up. After that, I made some calls and by then it was pretty much time to close so I just figured I'd take it to the station myself." He sighed. "And that's when you pulled me over."

Hindsight was a bitch and Dallas could easily see his mistake. He should have forced Vince to come with him but he'd been so furious he'd just wanted the prick off his property and out of his sight. He shook his head in disgust. He'd been livid that not only had one of his employees stolen, but that he'd done it on company time, in a company truck. Both of which reflected poorly on Granger Construction. But who was the one pulled over by the cop?

He'd been about to drive out of the industrial park when the officer had lit up the cherries and swung in behind him. As it was just past five o'clock the road was busy with men and women leaving for the day. They all slowed and stared as they rolled past. Not exactly the kind of advertising he wanted for Granger Construction.

His dad would love this. Joe Granger had never approved of his son moving off the ranch and striking out on his own. But Dallas had other plans, other dreams that weren't his dad's. Selfish, Joe had called him. Among other things. Then he'd threatened to disown him. And if there was one thing his old man didn't do it was give idle threats.

Dallas rolled his shoulders. It was water under the damn bridge and he'd made it, dammit. He'd built Granger Construction. He'd left Last Stand and the Diamond G

Ranch and made something of himself in nearby San Antonio. And even though there were times he missed riding, missed the open spaces, and the smell of crisp clean air, he didn't regret leaving.

"So what happens now?" Dallas asked, shifting his attention back to the present.

"You'll be charged with possession of stolen property. If the video surveillance at the hardware store proves you didn't steal it, then there won't be any other charges. Otherwise you'll also be charged with theft. Either way, you'll have to go before a judge."

Dallas turned his head and swore. He wanted to punch something. God dammit, he hadn't done anything wrong. He jammed his hands into the pockets of his jeans before they curled into fists. Not that he'd ever hit a cop, but he didn't need the cop thinking he was a threat either.

"So I get charged even though I didn't do anything but try to return stolen property?"

The officer handed Dallas back his license and registration. "I don't write the law. If it's any consolation, you'll likely only get a fine and some community service, especially if you plead guilty."

Dallas shook his head. "Some consolation."

"You want to run that by me one more time?"

Dallas's probation officer—Justin Finkel, according to the cheap metal nameplate perched precariously on the edge of his cluttered desk—had the damn nerve to smile.

For a moment, the man's verdict was lost to Dallas as the wrinkles on Finkel's face multiplied with his grin until he resembled one of those wrinkly dogs. Only this guy wasn't tan colored. He wasn't colored at all. Bright white hair, pale white skin, and stiffly starched white shirt. The only bit of color was the large brown age spot that kept drawing Dallas's attention to the old man's forehead.

"It's really quite simple, Mr. Granger. The judge ordered you to pay a thousand dollar fine and—"

"Yeah, I heard that. I've got no problem paying the fine. Nor do I have an issue fulfilling my sixty hours of community service."

In the weeks since he'd been pulled over, Dallas had accepted what had happened. The officer was bound by the law and Dallas respected the man more for upholding it than he would have had he let Dallas go without consequence.

Besides, once the cop had verified through security footage that it was indeed Vince who'd stolen the nail gun, he'd tracked Dallas down to personally tell him that his ex-employee had been charged with theft.

Since Dallas had been sanding some cupboards in the shop at the time, the conversation had shifted to carpentry and by the time Officer Leman—Jack—had left, Dallas had the man's number and an appointment to meet him and his wife about new cabinets for their kitchen.

But as well as that had turned out, it didn't change Dallas's current predicament.

"The judge didn't specify where or how I had to spend those sixty hours of community service," Dallas reminded the older man.

"No, Mr. Granger. That's not his job. That's up to my discretion."

"So, can't your discretion find another place for me to work?" he pleaded.

Finkel folded his veiny hands on his desk. "Now why would I do that when I've found the perfect place for you? I've researched your company. Granger Construction has a great reputation here in San Antonio. I've read several reviews on you specifically." Light shone in the man's pale blue eyes. "You're very good at what you do, Dallas. Otherwise, I wouldn't put you on this project."

Great. His dad couldn't acknowledge his own son's skills, would rather cut out his tongue than ever praise Dallas, but this stranger was telling him he was so good he was getting assigned to a project he didn't want any part of.

"I may have the skills for this job, but that doesn't make me a good fit. I don't support this cause. Never have."

Finkel's jaw went so slack Dallas half expected the man's false teeth to fall out of his mouth.

"It's *Houses of Hope*," he stated as though that alone should be enough.

"I know what it is. A bunch of volunteers getting together to build houses that some people are going to get for free. Like I said, I don't support it."

Finkel pursed his lips. "What do you know about *Houses of Hope*, Mr. Granger?"

"I know I've busted my a—" He swallowed the word, started again. "I've busted my back to get what I have in life, Mr. Finkel. Nobody gave me a hand or a handout." Especially his own father.

"I see. Well, Mr. Granger, my decision stands. In fact, after listening to you, I'm even surer of my choice. And I think the recipient of this house won't be the only one benefitting from this project. You're in for a surprise, Mr. Granger."

So was the guy who jumped out of a plane only to find his parachute was broken. Surprise didn't always mean a good thing, but clearly there was no explaining that to Finkel.

Cheery as a bird first thing in the morning, his probation officer picked up a few sheets of legal-looking paper. As he passed them over to Dallas, his wrist bumped his nameplate off the desk. It clattered to the dull gray cement floor.

Dallas retrieved it for the man and set it back on the desk before taking the papers from Finkel's hand.

"The foreman on this project is Rick Redmond," the man began. "You'll have to set up your schedule with him. You're not the first person I've sent his way so he knows what he needs to do as far as paperwork goes.

"Make sure you have him sign or initial each day to verify the hours worked. You have ninety days to complete your assigned hours. Once you've finished, bring the forms back to me. As long as everything is in order your restitution to the state and the community will be considered complete. Good day, Mr. Granger."

Before Dallas could attempt another last-ditch argument, Finkel's phone rang. "Good afternoon, Justin Finkel speaking," he said into the receiver. He dismissed Dallas with a shooing motion of his bony fingers.

Knowing there was no changing Finkel's mind, Dallas

turned on the heel of his work boot and wove through the maze of cubicles and straight out the front door of the court building. Straight into a deluge.

Despite getting wet, Dallas was more than happy to leave the stale air, office chatter, ringing telephones, and muted conversations behind him.

He'd known from an early age that office work wasn't for him. School was a necessity and a means to an end but he'd always resented being contained inside four walls, chained to a chair. While construction work also required being inside, at least he was able to move about and he got more than his share of fresh air hauling in supplies or working on outside projects. And best of all it gave him the chance to use both his brain and his back.

Ranching had too, he remembered with a stab. And once upon a time he'd envisioned doing both. Not a large spread like the Diamond G, but a few horses, a small herd. Something he could manage while still pursuing his dream of owning his own construction business. But the more his dad had pushed him into ranching the more Dallas had come to resent it. Until he'd wanted no part of ranching at all.

He leapt over a growing puddle and dodged another handful before reaching his truck. Inside, he ran a hand through his wet hair then wiped the moisture onto his jeans. Respectfully, he'd kept his ball cap in his truck, but he hadn't bothered to dress up. This little meeting was already eating into his workday and he hadn't wanted to waste more time going back to his place to change before heading back to the jobsite.

Dallas turned over the engine, pushed the controls over

to defrost since his breath and the moisture from his wet hair were fogging the windshield.

He supposed it could have been worse. Finkel could have sent him on garbage picking duty, or graffiti cleanup. He could have had him scraping gum off the plastic walls of the bus shelters. At least the man had taken into account Dallas's skills.

With that in mind, Dallas clicked on his seat belt, flipped on his wipers, shoulder checked, and pulled away from the curb. He increased the volume when he recognized Luke Bryan's new song coming through the radio. But just as Luke hit a high note, the song was interrupted by an incoming call coming through his Bluetooth.

Dallas hit the button on the steering wheel to accept the call. "Granger Construction, Dallas here."

"Dallas, it's Ken. Richard just slipped off the ladder. He hurt his ankle pretty bad. Might be broken. Danny's taking him to the hospital now."

Dallas had three crews out at the moment and he knew which man worked at what site. Ken, one of his foremen, was working on a new garage in one of the more established areas of San Antonio. They were scheduled to start shingling the roof that day.

"It's pouring rain. What was he doing on a ladder?"

"That was my fault. They've been forecasting rain for days and nothing's come of it. I thought maybe we'd get lucky and it wouldn't happen today either. Or, if it did, we'd have time to get down before it got too wet and slippery. Dallas, I'm sorry, this was my call, but honestly, the sky just opened up."

Since he'd walked into Finkel's office dry and had gotten soaked within seconds of leaving, he couldn't argue.

Stopping for a red light Dallas said, "It's okay, Ken. Accidents happen. As long as Richard is getting looked after, that's all that matters."

Since Richard had just forked over a couple grand on car repairs and couldn't afford to be out of income Dallas asked, "You tell Danny to make sure he brings back a copy of the doctor's report?"

The sooner Sherry, his office manager, had it and sent it off to the worker's compensation board, the sooner Richard would get his benefits. And, in the meantime, if he needed it, Dallas could provide him with a loan.

"Yeah, I did," Ken answered.

"Okay then," Dallas said as the light turned green. "There's no point in you guys staying there now. Without shingles on, the insulation and drywall we were planning on installing would just get wet if the rain comes through the cracks."

Which meant there wasn't anything more they could do at that site today. And since another of the three projects on the go was building a large two-tiered deck off a bi-level, there was no point sending them there either. The third project in the works was a complete basement overhaul after the sewer had backed up in it.

"Sean with you?" Dallas asked of Ken's son. He was a university student and was working for Granger Construction for the summer.

"Yep."

"Take him and head to that basement job in Alamo

Heights. I'll meet you there. If it's too crowded I'll take some back with me to the shop. I can put some to work there."

While most jobs were on location, Dallas had a workshop along with his office in the industrial park. They did some prefab work there, like build cupboards, entertainment units, shelving units, as well as stain baseboards and doors. He could already think of a handful of jobs that needed doing.

"Sounds good. I'll see you there."

Dallas had no sooner disconnected the call when another came in.

"Mr. Granger, it's Lorne Shilling from the San Antonio Development Services Department. I was scheduled to come to one of your sites in Alamo Heights this afternoon."

Dallas's grip tightened on the wheel. It had nothing to do with the red traffic cones that converged the two-lane street into a one-lane road and everything to do with the tone of the inspector on the other end of the call.

"Yes, you were," Dallas confirmed. "And I hope you still are because with this rain I have three crews over there. The plumbing was approved yesterday but without your go ahead on the electrical we can't do anything else."

And then what the hell was he supposed to do with his men? He specifically always tried to have at least one inside project on the go at a time for this very reason. While he could use some men at the shop, there wasn't enough room or work for all of them there.

"I'm sorry, Mr. Granger, but an unexpected matter has arisen that I must attend to."

"And what about what I must attend to? I have men I

need to keep working not to mention clients who are tripping over themselves upstairs because what could be salvaged from their flooded basement is now stacked in their hallways, living room, and kitchen."

"I'm sorry, Mr. Granger, I really am. But there is nothing I can do about that today. I'll see you there tomorrow, you have my word."

The inspector hung up before Dallas could say anything else. Well, now what was he supposed to do?

If only it would stop raining. But Mother Nature had a nasty sense of timing and the black sky opened even further, forcing Dallas to slap his wipers on high speed while raindrops the size of pancakes hammered his windshield.

When his phone rang again, he was sorely tempted to ignore it. Unlike the other two calls he'd answered blindly, Dallas shifted his gaze to the display screen on his truck to see who was calling. And then did a double take when he saw it was Gage.

Though it wasn't unusual to get a call from one of his four brothers, it wasn't all that common either. The Granger brothers weren't exactly tight.

That Gage would call midmorning wasn't a good sign. Especially considering he worked as an EMT. Dallas's first thought was that it had something to do with their brother Hudson, who was serving overseas. But Ryker and their dad lived in Last Stand, and Cam still used it as a base between rodeos, so it could be about any of them as well.

Dallas's gut tightened. Somehow, he knew this call wasn't going to be good.

Anticipating that, he took a last-minute turn into a gas

station that appeared through the curtain of rain. The car behind him blared its horn as Dallas pulled to the side, shifted into park, and answered the call.

"What's up, Gage?"

Hearing sirens, Dallas turned in his seat and looked around. It took a moment to realize they weren't coming from the nearby street but rather through the speakers in his truck.

"It's Dad," Gage said. "He was just brought into the hospital. I don't know any details other than he's unconscious. Get down here, Dallas. Now. I'll call the others."

The line went dead and Dallas was left staring out into the wall of gray.

Chapter Two

DALLAS HAD A love/hate relationship with the Diamond G. Situated in the Hill Country of Southwest Texas, there was no shortage of beauty. No shortage of variety. Cliffs and plateaus. Rolling plains and prairies surrounded by craggy hills made of granite and limestone.

As a boy, he'd had canyons, rivers, and live oaks tall and thick enough to keep him and his brothers entertained and out of trouble. He had more than one scar from a tumble over rocks or a fall from a branch he shouldn't have reached for.

He'd loved it.

Loved riding his horse over the land, camping out with his brothers in the hills. Loved the nighttime campfires and lying beneath the stars while coyotes yipped nearby.

But then his mom got cancer and his dad had fallen apart. And no matter how much Dallas tried to keep the family together, to keep some semblance of normal, bitterness and resentment had sunk its teeth into the Diamond G. Anger at his dad for secluding their mom away into a bedroom where he wouldn't have to see her and the effects of her illness. For forcing Dallas into the role of guardian.

Then it was resentment from his brothers because it had been left to Dallas to be the hard-ass, the disciplinarian. The one who made sure there was no playing or partying until homework and chores were done. Which, more than once, had meant there was no going out at all. With only two years separating each of them, there'd been more than one fistfight over why they should have to listen to him.

His mom's death only made things worse. Their dad, who hadn't been any help during the illness, drove himself even harder. Distanced himself even more. The times Joe did deign to talk to them it was all criticism. They hadn't done this or that right. They were taking too long to get the work done.

But his brothers hadn't needed constant supervision and when the chores were done Dallas had needed something else to do. Something for himself, away from his brothers and father. Something that would allow him to relax, to quiet his thoughts. Something that fed his soul and mind.

Something that would allow him to be his own person instead of just the one struggling to keep the family together.

He'd found more than refuge in woodworking; he'd found his passion. What started out as small shelves for the barn, or a new desk for Gage, soon turned to big dreams of houses, sheds, decks. His own business.

And, somehow, despite his dad being absent for everything else, he'd caught on to Dallas's skills, to his desire for more. And he worked him that much harder so he'd have less time in the small shed he'd cleaned out to use as his workshop.

"The ranch puts food on this table. Don't you forget it," Joe had growled.

How could he? Joe reminded him at every meal. Reminded them all. Dallas put up with it as long as he could but eventually he'd felt trapped on the Diamond G, like he was slowly suffocating. He'd spent the bulk of his teen years tied to a ranch and a house, to responsibility he hadn't asked for but had taken on because it was needed.

Because he'd never abandon his brothers.

But when he hit twenty he was done. Gage, the baby of the bunch, had been twelve and with Ryker and Cam still at home, and Hudson about to graduate, Dallas felt they'd be fine without him. Besides, Joe was still there to work the ranch, so it wasn't like his brothers would be out of a home or have to go without food.

Dallas had tried talking to his dad but to Joe there wasn't anything but the Diamond G. At every turn, he belittled Dallas's dream, warned him if he left he could kiss the small acreage his dad had set aside for him goodbye. It didn't matter that Dallas had kept the family together when his dad failed to. None of that mattered to Joe. All that mattered was his eldest son wasn't willing to work the ranch.

So Dallas left. Oh, he visited on occasion, usually only around the holidays despite as stilted and cold those visits were. Not once did his dad ever ask how business was. Not once had he said he was proud of what Dallas had done.

Not once had the man ever thanked him for doing what he should have.

And that was where the hate came in.

Maybe hate was too strong a word, even if some days it didn't feel like it. However, those were usually the days he got to look at the Diamond G through his rearview mirror. A visit with his dad typically had that effect.

Not today, though. Not unless his dad was conscious.

Dallas slowed as he rolled into the town. He bumped across Hickory Creek and drove north on Laurel until he came to Gordon C. Jameson Hospital, or what the locals just referred to as Jameson Hospital, on his left. Seeing Ryker's dark blue pickup, he pulled in next to it.

He scanned the dusty pickups and shiny cars in the lot. Though the sky was a mass of dark gray clouds, Last Stand apparently hadn't gotten the deluge San Antonio had. Other than Ryker's, Dallas didn't see any other vehicles he recognized. Since he didn't see Gage's Jeep, he figured he'd gotten there in the ambulance. Dallas's gaze lingered on a souped-up copper-colored truck.

Four by four, shiny chrome trim, extended cab. The thing screamed new and expensive. Dallas smirked as he walked under the portico. Someone was compensating.

His smirk withered when the glass doors whooshed open. There was nothing more depressing than the smell of a hospital. Antiseptic. Sickness. Worry and grief.

Though Jameson Hospital had seen upgrades and modernization over the years, there wasn't enough pastel paint and potted green plants in the world to make an emergency room cheery. To make it anything but what it was—depressing. Though some of the art decorating the walls looked fancy enough to be in a gallery, Dallas wasn't in the mood to give it the appreciation it deserved.

He approached the emergency room desk.

"I'm looking for Joe Granger. I'm his son."

"The doctors are still with him. You'll have to wait there."

"There" being the waiting room. Dallas looked around. A couple held hands; the woman's head rested on her husband's shoulder. Another man sat forward, head bent, hands hanging between his spread knees. A woman rocked a crying baby. Though brash fluorescent lighting lit the room and sunlight filtered between the yellow plastic slats of the vertical blinds, gloom filled the space.

"You made good time."

Dallas turned. His brother was in full EMT uniform. Had he been the one to bring in their dad?

"You did tell me to get my ass over here right away."

Gage's gaze hardened. Since he and his brothers all hovered around six feet he looked Gage square in the eye.

"You aren't one for following orders. You're usually the one giving them."

It was an old argument and one Dallas refused to get into in the middle of the emergency department. Besides, he couldn't go back and change things and, even if he could, he'd do the same thing. Someone had had to step up and take care of the family when their dad had fallen apart. Dallas hadn't enjoyed it any more than his brothers had. In fact, he'd hated it.

More, he'd hated what it had done to his relationships with his brothers. They'd been close before their mom had gotten sick. Before Dallas had had to step in and be the hardass. That had ruined things between Dallas and his brothers.

And once Dallas had stood up to Joe to say he didn't want to work the ranch, it wasn't long until Cam and Hudson had done the same. Which had built fractures between the rest of them. Joe had told Dallas more than once it was all his fault.

A sentiment shared by his brothers.

Despite the fact his "defection" had made it easier for Cam and Hudson to do the same, it didn't stop them from resenting him for the dates he'd refused to let them go on, for the homework he'd forced them to do. For raising them, dammit, even when it was the last thing they'd all wanted.

Dallas blew out a long, troubled breath. This was exactly why he only visited when he had to.

"Were you the one that brought him in?"

Gage scrubbed a hand over his clean-shaven jaw. "No. I'd just gotten off shift when the call came in."

"Do we know what happened?"

"Looks like a heart attack or stroke right now. We won't know more until they finish running tests."

Which meant a shit ton of waiting. Great.

"All right, then. Why don't I go get us some coffee? Is the cafeteria still—"

Just as he was asking, Ryker came around the corner carrying two to-go cups. Like Dallas, he wore jeans, boots, and a T-shirt and, like Dallas, sported a hat head because he too must have left his hat in his truck. Although Ryker preferred a cowboy hat to Dallas's ball cap. But then they all did.

"Look who showed up," Ryker said as he ambled forward. His gaze stayed on Dallas as he handed Gage one of the cups he carried.

"Ryker. I saw your truck in the lot. Every time I see it I'm surprised you're still driving that old thing."

"Yeah, well, when something matters, you don't just walk away from it."

Figuring he might as well take all the punches at once he looked past Gage and Ryker.

"Any sign of Cam?" he asked.

"I left him a message," Gage said before taking a tentative sip of his coffee. "He was supposed to be heading this way, last I'd heard." He met Dallas's gaze over the rim of his plastic lid. "He promised to come help with the haying."

Which, of course, Dallas hadn't done. But then, he hadn't been asked.

"What about Hudson? Did you get word to him?"

"No point until we know more. He's only got six weeks left of his deployment. Hopefully, Dad will be all right and Hudson can finish it without taking an early leave."

Dallas nodded in agreement. "I guess I'll go get myself a coffee while we wait."

Despite there not being any warm feelings to rush back to the waiting room for, Dallas didn't linger in the cafeteria. Mostly because, even though it was midafternoon, the smell of lunch still hung thick in the room. It was a mixture of greasy burgers and tuna and it was enough to convince Dallas that if he was still here come supper, he was going to get takeout.

Cautiously, he took a sip of the coffee. If it tasted anything like what the rest of the room smelled like…

It was surprisingly good and strong and Dallas took a bigger drink. Maybe he could wander the halls for a bit, at least until he'd finished his drink. Then he could get another one before going to back to the waiting room. If he was going to sit with his brothers for the rest of the day he was going to need more than one cup of coffee.

He opted to call his foreman instead. "Ken, it's Dallas," he said when the call was answered. "Any word on Richard?"

"Yeah. X-rays came back. Luckily, it's just a bad sprain. They're still at the hospital, but Richard will be out of commission for four to six weeks."

He made a mental note to text Richard later, check in and reassure him he'd get his benefits ASAP, and if he was tight in the meantime, Dallas could advance him a loan.

"We'll make it work. Danny's got the paperwork?"

"Not yet, but he will. And he'll drive Richard home. Later, we'll get his car back to his place."

"Sounds good."

Dallas rearranged his work crews in his mind, shifted things until he had a plan to keep on target with his projects.

"Any word on your dad?"

Dallas walked to the window, looked out over the courtyard. The multicolored flowerbeds, ornamental trees, and park benches were a pretty sight. A shame they didn't open the windows. The floral smell and fresh air would go a long way to clearing the odor in the large room.

"No. Not yet. They're running tests."

"Whatever you need, let me know. I'm sure I can handle what comes up while you're with your dad."

"I know you could. But, hopefully, it won't be necessary. I'm still planning on being there in the morning."

"Okay. I'll see you then."

Dallas disconnected the call, slid his cell into his back pocket.

"You know most normal people don't work around the clock, right?"

Dallas turned from the window. The second youngest of the Granger boys, Cam, stood hipshot, his arms crossed over his button-down western-style shirt. His usual cocky grin was solidly in place.

"And most normal people grow up when they're approaching their thirties."

"Now where's the fun in that?"

Cam tipped up the brim of his cowboy hat. He was never without it. Like Burt Reynolds's character in *Smoky and the Bandit*, Dallas suspected Cam only ever took it off for one thing.

"It can't all be about fun, Cam."

"Well, you'd know. There hasn't been much fun about you in over a decade."

Dallas rubbed his forehead. He wasn't prone to headaches but every time he came to Last Stand he got them.

"Ryker and Gage didn't tell me you were here. I figured you were at some rodeo."

"I was. I was passing through Austin when I got Gage's call. I've actually been here for a while." His mouth curved into a shit-eating grin. "I would've gone straight to the emergency room but I bumped into an old friend and we had some catching up to do."

Dallas shook his head. "Of course you did."

Cam's laughter rang through the empty cafeteria. "I was just coming in for one of those." He tipped his chin toward Dallas's coffee. "Is it worth bothering or should I get a soda out of the vending machine?"

"Actually, it's decent."

"Great. Wait here and I'll get one."

With coffees in hand, they navigated the few short hallways back to the emergency room. The couple had gone, as had the mother and child, but the lone man remained. Only now he held a cup between his bent knees. Dallas cut his gaze to Gage. His brother's hands were empty. There was a reason Gage had gone into the line of work he had; he had an endless capacity of kindness. And while they weren't close anymore, Dallas had no doubt if one of them was ever truly in need, Gage would be the first to step up and offer help.

Cam's appearance didn't incite quite the same hostility Dallas's had, but then Cam was known to stop in between rodeos and give a hand on the ranch.

Figuring this was going to be a while, Dallas settled into one of the yellow vinyl chairs. One by one the others sat. Gage wandered out from time to time, checked in with nurses and doctors. He never had much to report other than their dad was alive and unconscious and they were waiting on test results. They'd sent Joe for an EKG and a CT scan and were running a grocery list of blood tests.

Dallas checked in with Sherry at four thirty. She sounded tired. He told her to lock up early, put the calls on forward to him, and go get some rest. Then, still planning on being at work come morning, Dallas told her he'd see her tomorrow.

Once he'd finished his calls, Dallas realized how hungry he was. He offered to run out and grab something to eat. For once, his brothers didn't take exception to his suggestion. But then, who in their right mind would if they had a choice of takeout or hospital food?

Dallas was back within the hour with takeout from

Hutchinson's BBQ Market, or The Hut for short. Dragging three chairs together, Dallas set out the containers of smoked brisket, beans, fried okra, dill pickles the size of hot dogs, and corn bread.

The smell of barbecue sauce filled the waiting room, which was now empty except for the four Granger brothers. The scrape of plastic knives on Styrofoam and the gulp from soda cans were the only sounds any of them made.

At the desk, doctors and nurses came and went. Files were read over and exchanged, calls were taken, and instructions were given. Finally, once all the containers were put in the trash and the cans into the recycling bin, the doctor came into the waiting room. The four of them came to their feet.

"I'm Doctor Fletcher," she said. "I'm the cardiologist on staff. Your father has been admitted into the ICU. He went into cardiac arrest earlier today. He's currently stable and resting, but remains in a coma. The good news is it doesn't sound as though he went too long without spontaneous circulation."

"English, please," Cam said.

"It means breathing on his own," Gage explained.

"That's right. It sounds as though he was revived very quickly and was here within the hour."

"Then why is he still unconscious?" Ryker asked.

"It's not uncommon for patients who suffered cardiac arrest to remain in a coma."

"For how long?" Dallas asked.

"Can be hours, days, weeks. There's no way of knowing. The good news is your father has many things working in his favor. He's under sixty, he's not overweight. The time between arrest and the restoration of spontaneous circulation was relatively short. He's also showing pupillary light response, which means brain damage due to anoxia should be minimal, if there is any."

"His eyes are dilating when they shine a light in them and his brain wasn't without oxygen long enough to cause severe brain damage," Gage summarized.

"Exactly." Dr. Fletcher turned to Gage. "You can see him, one at a time and just for a few minutes, but I'd say to go home and get some rest. I don't expect any changes tonight. If there is, we know how to contact you."

She left on silent rubber soles, leaving Dallas and his brothers standing in a semicircle.

"I'll go first, if that's okay," Dallas said. "Then I'm going to head out. Gage, if there's any change you'll—"

But it wasn't Gage who answered. It was Ryker. And he was pissed.

"You can't escape this, Dallas. Not this time. This isn't all just going to 'work out' because you want it to.

"I'm not running the ranch on my own." Ryker's narrowed gaze raked them all. "If something happens to Dad the Diamond G gets split five ways."

"Not five," Dallas corrected. "Just four."

Ryker ignored him. "It means we all have to pitch in. Not just me. And Gage on his days off. And Cam between rodeos. And you," he snarled at Dallas, "once or twice a year when you can fit it in."

Dallas's back went up. "It's not as though I live down the street. And I do have a business to run."

"Yeah, yeah. Same old shit. But guess what? I have a life

too. And I'm just as busy as you are so make the damn time, Dallas." Again his gaze raked everyone. "You all better make time. Because as of now, we're all working the Diamond G."

INSTEAD OF GOING first, Dallas ended up going last. By the time he walked past the nurse's station headed for his dad's room, he was the only one left in the emergency room. After each of his brothers had taken their turn, they'd filed straight past him and out the front doors.

That was fine. Dallas knew where to find them. Ryker had made it clear they were all to meet at the ranch after.

Dallas stopped at the door, which already bore his father's name on the nameplate next to it. Funny, he'd been sitting in a hospital most of the day and he hadn't prepared himself to see his dad lying in a hospital bed.

His dad had always been larger than life. Even when he'd shut down emotionally with his wife's illness and then death, he'd worked like a dog, putting in sixteen-hour days. He was strong as a mule and equally stubborn. Nobody told Joe Granger he couldn't do something.

Dallas scoffed. He supposed they had that in common.

Joe was robust and could work circles around most men. To think of him weakened to the state of coma was incomprehensible. And yet just on the other side of that door was proof of that.

He eased open the door. Though his mom had died at home, seeing his dad lying there was still eerily similar. His body lay as still as hers had been.

Although physically there were many differences. Hours working in the sun meant Joe's face wasn't as pale as hers had been. Though his work-roughened hands were limp at his sides, they still looked capable of lifting hay bales like Lego blocks. Muscles corded his forearms and his shoulders were still the width of a linebacker's.

Unlike his mom, who'd looked frail as an eighty-year-old, even though she'd only been in her mid-forties. There'd been no muscle tone left, nothing but papery skin over bones. She couldn't have weighed more than ninety pounds when she'd died. Lying there, she'd looked like a ghost.

He jumped when someone brushed past him.

"Sorry," the nurse said with a warm smile. "I just need to check his vitals."

Dallas stayed clear of the bed while she took Joe's temperature, blood pressure, and checked his eyes. She recorded everything into his chart before sliding it back in the slot at the foot of his dad's bed.

When they were alone again, Dallas moved to his father's side. He hadn't thought when he'd left at Easter that the next time he'd see his dad the man would be in a coma after suffering cardiac arrest.

Dallas dropped into the one chair in the room. Once again the weight of responsibility fell hard onto his shoulders.

Oh, it wasn't as though his brothers were children anymore. Even Gage, as the youngest, was in his mid-twenties. They could take care of themselves. He could always hire an extra hand or two to take his place.

But despite only pitching in at the ranch a few times a

year like Ryker accused him of, the truth was every time Ryker called to ask for help, Dallas showed up.

So though he had no idea how he was going to squeeze it in, and that working alongside his brothers in Last Stand was going to be anything but easy and enjoyable, Dallas was going to do it.

He just hoped at the end of it, his dad wasn't the only one to come out of this alive.

Chapter Three

DALLAS PARKED NEXT to Gage's Jeep, shut off his headlights, and stared at his childhood home. Though the sun had set a half hour ago, it wasn't full dark yet. Even still, light glowed bright through the kitchen window. His brothers would be there, fresh cups of coffee in hand.

Two things were a certainty in the Granger household. Any important discussion was had around the kitchen table and no matter the time of day, there was fresh coffee to be had. A good thing none of them were bothered by caffeine. They were all known to have a mug before bed and sleep without issues afterward.

Well, no issues caused by coffee. Speaking for himself, there'd always been something weighing on his mind, keeping him awake. To this day, he had difficulty turning his mind off at night. Tonight was sure to be the same.

Especially, when, for the life of him, he had no idea how he was going to squeeze in working on the ranch, not to mention the commute from San Antonio to Last Stand.

Might make more sense to pack an overnight bag on the days he was here.

Working and staying with his brothers? Yeah, that was going to go over well. About as good as finding a house filled with black mold. Might as well just shoot him now and get it over with.

"They'd love that," he muttered as he pulled his keys from the ignition and opened the door.

Gravel crunched under his boots as he aimed for the front door. He turned when he heard a vehicle's door slam behind him. It was just bright enough to recognize Cam strolling toward him. Dallas's lip curled when he recognized the copper-colored truck his brother had come from.

"I saw that truck at the hospital. My first thought was that whoever owned it was compensating for something."

The porch light caught Cam's grin. "Trust me. There isn't anything about me that needs to be compensated for."

"That's your ego talking."

Though Dallas would've sworn it was impossible, Cam's grin widened even more. "That's not what she said."

Laughing, Cam smacked Dallas on the back and strode up the wide porch. He left the door open behind him.

Dallas could almost hear his mom calling out, "Shut that door. You weren't raised in a barn."

Even after all these years, he missed the sound of her voice. Hated knowing when he walked into the kitchen she wouldn't be there waiting. Time didn't heal all wounds. It barely dulled them.

Keenly feeling her absence today, Dallas trudged inside, quietly closing the door behind him.

Exactly as expected, his brothers were gathered around the table. Before joining them, Dallas pulled a mug from the cupboard next to the sink and poured himself a steaming cup of coffee. He added some milk from the jug that had been left sitting on the counter before setting it back into the fridge.

The long oak table that dominated the room bore the scratches and small gouges of a household that had once been full of rambunctious boys. Like a book, each of those told a story and Dallas could, if asked, explain how most of those marks had come to be. They were part of the house's history. *His* history.

Pulling his gaze from the tabletop he finally took note of the seating placement around the table. Gage and Cam occupied one side. Ryker was at the head. The significance of that didn't escape Dallas. But that was fine. Dallas had no intention of taking over the helm. Taking his mug he sat by himself on the other side of the table.

Ryker didn't waste any time. He pulled the calendar he'd set on the corner of the table closer. Gripping the pen he looked over the squares.

"Okay, I already have Gage's schedule on here. Cam, I hope you didn't have any upcoming rodeos because you might have to cancel one or two."

Cam tipped his hat back, lounged back into the chair. His lips curved. "I've gotten lucky the last few. I can afford to miss one or two."

Ryker nodded then leaned forward, elbows braced on the table. He fixed his gaze on Dallas.

"What about you?"

His brother's confrontational tone raised Dallas's hackles. He knew, before he opened his mouth, whatever he was about to say wasn't going to be good enough for Ryker.

"I'll give you as much time as I can but I'll tell you right now it's not going to be close to what you're expecting from me."

Ryker sneered. "It never is."

"Ryker," Gage warned.

"What? I'm not allowed to speak the truth? That his precious company comes first."

With the tension mounting, Dallas got up and pulled the whiskey bottle from the liquor cabinet. He added some to his coffee, then set the bottle on the table.

"I have a business that needs running and that's a fact. I can only delegate so much. Besides, you have a ranch hand, Ryker. It's not like you're here by yourself."

Ryker's green eyes narrowed. "It's not like the Diamond G is swimming in money, which you'd know if you ever gave a rat's ass about this place. Brian is off because he couldn't ignore his hernia anymore and had surgery last week. So, yes, Dallas, without Dad here and when Gage is at work and Cam at a rodeo, I *am* here by myself."

"Why haven't you hired help before now?"

A muscle ticked in Ryker's stubble-covered cheek. "I've been trying, hot shot, but qualified help isn't exactly banging down the door."

"It's not just labor we need help with, either," Gage added. "We should probably take turns at the hospital, in case Dad wakes up."

"And there's the fact that Dad's office is a mess," Ryker said. "There's a couple weeks' worth of mail piled on his desk.

"Before you accuse me of not doing my job, the paperwork has always been Dad's responsibility and the last few times I offered to help him with it, he damn near bit my head off."

Dallas sipped his coffee and contemplated Ryker's words. The only person he knew who was qualified to do bookwork was his office manager but he couldn't very well ask Sherry to help out at the ranch. He didn't want a heavily pregnant women driving back and forth from Last Stand to San Antonio. Not to mention she wouldn't have the energy to work two jobs.

"I can put out some feelers in San Antonio. Maybe find a bookkeeper who can help with the office. I can make sense of spreadsheets and financial reports but I haven't got a clue how to put it all together."

He mostly kept all the figures in his head. His gaze skipped over his brothers. "Unless one of you knows how to do bookwork?"

With a united shake of their heads, Dallas pulled out his phone and entered a note to look for a bookkeeper.

"That better not be all you're willing to do," Ryker grumbled.

Dallas met his brother's scowl with one of his own. "Get the burr out of your ass, Ryker. I'll do the best I can but this couldn't have happened at a worse time."

"As if there's ever a good time with you."

Dallas finished his coffee and slammed the mug down. "How about you get all the facts before you jump down my throat?"

He clutched the mug until he feared it would break and cut up his hands. Then not only would he be useless to Granger Construction, he'd be useless to the Diamond G as well. Which would give his brothers yet one more thing to hold against him.

Dallas peeled his hands off the mug, set them on the table. "One of my guys stole a nail gun from the hardware store. Long story short, we both got charged. Him for stealing, me for getting caught taking it back. Because they couldn't prove that's what I was doing, I was charged with possession of stolen property because I knew it was stolen when I decided to drive it to the police station instead of calling it in."

"So," he added with a pointed stare at Ryker, "not only am *I* also down a man, two if you count the one who fell down a ladder this morning and sprained his ankle, I also now have sixty hours of community service to fulfill. On top of the business. On top of the ranch."

"Community service? That sucks," Cam supplied.

"So does the eleven hundred dollar fine."

Gage and Cam winced in sympathy. Ryker wasn't about to give Dallas a break, no matter how small.

Instead he placed the pen on the calendar and slid both Dallas's way. "Write on there when we can expect you."

Despite knowing exactly what his schedule looked like, Dallas opened the calendar app on his phone. He'd already rearranged things to add the community service. There wasn't a hell of a lot more he could squeeze in. Not if he intended to live on less than six hours sleep a night.

Dammit. He'd really wanted to finish the community service as fast as possible. But, as long as he finished in three months, he could afford to cut back the hours he'd allotted to work there and still get it done within the allowed time frame.

He deleted, did some shuffling and calculating in his head. Once he was satisfied, he lifted the pen and copied the hours he'd entered into his phone onto the calendar.

Sliding it back to Ryker he said, "Fifteen hours is as much as I can give you. In the meantime I'll look for a bookkeeper and see if I can't find a temporary ranch hand too."

Ryker balked. "I agreed to you looking for office help. I never said anything about you helping hire a ranch hand. That's my job."

Dallas stood. "You're the one who demanded I help. Now I'm helping. Next time, be careful what you wish for."

AFTER DOUBLE-CHECKING THE prices and totals from the invoice matched what she'd entered into the accounting program, Ashley Anderson shifted the mouse over the *post* button and clicked. With all the invoices and deposits entered, she closed the accounting program and set about shutting down the office.

The desk was the only part of Eugene's Small Engine Repair that was kept tidy and, to Ashley's mind, the only part that was organized. On the other side of the glass window that looked into the shop, was a veritable junkyard.

Shelves and bins of miscellaneous parts filled half of the concrete floor. The rest was filled with mowers, leaf blowers, chainsaws, and other small machines waiting to be serviced. The long workbench was a cluttered mess of parts, tools, and half-dismantled carcasses of the inner workings of an engine.

Or so she assumed. Other than a spark plug, Ashley couldn't identify anything else.

But clearly Eugene could, just as he always seemed to know where in the boxes and bins were the parts he needed at any given time. Old school, Eugene preferred to work with tools than computers and typically stayed clear of the office. If he had anything to tell her, he usually said it on her way in or out of the rolled-up garage door that signaled the shop was open for business.

Since he was currently zigzagging his way between machinery toward her, she set her purse back down and waited.

"I've left you a small deposit," she said, gesturing to the envelope perched on the corner of the desk.

He nodded. "Thanks."

"Something on your mind?" she asked when he simply stood there, gnawing on his lip.

"I don't know how else to tell you but to come right out and say it. I've gotten an offer on the building and business and I've decided to take it."

She heard what he said, but his words didn't make sense. "But it's not for sale."

"No, it wasn't."

"Then I don't understand."

His loud sigh filled the small room. "The plastics manufacturer next door is looking to expand and they want to use this lot. They want to buy me out."

"But, this is your life's work."

His dark eyes softened. "I'm sixty-three, Ashley. I'm ready to play more golf, spend more time with my wife and grandkids. I only ever kept at this because I couldn't afford to quit. With this offer I can."

Ashley grabbed the back of the chair. It might not have been a life and death situation but her life still flashed before her eyes. She needed this job. She needed *every* job she had. She had a daughter to raise. A car she was trying to keep pieced together. And the house that was currently under construction.

She dug her nails into the leather chair. She wasn't going to lose that house. Not after she'd fought tooth and nail to get it.

"How—" She stopped when her voice cracked, took a moment to control her rising emotions. "How soon?"

Eugene's eyes filled with regret. "I've had the offer for weeks. Both my lawyer and accountant say it's more than fair."

"Eugene, just say it."

He winced. "Next Friday."

Her jaw fell open. She only had just over a week to find another part-time job? Within an easy commute to the other jobs she worked? That was as flexible as this one? The slim chance of that made her feel sick.

"I know." He held up his work-roughened hands. "And I'm sorry. But other than taking some of my tools, there's nothing else I need to do. The deal is that they take everything. Because I haven't taken on any new projects since the offer came in and the two I have left will be done by Wednesday next week, there's no need to drag it out."

No. No reason. Other than Ashley couldn't afford to be without the job.

"You'll work Monday and Thursday like normal. I'll use

Friday to grab the few things that aren't in the deal."

What more could she say? He'd made his decision. Woodenly, she reached for her purse.

"Ashley, I'm sorry to do this to you. It was just one of those things that came up."

"It's fine."

But she didn't feel fine. In fact, she felt anything but fine.

WITH HER MIND still reeling from Eugene's news, Ashley drove to her apartment on autopilot. The good part about working different jobs in a single day was that she was rarely stuck in rush hour traffic. And since she'd specifically chosen jobs within a half hour commute from her home, she never had far to go. This afternoon, despite it being the time school was letting out, she made it home in twenty minutes.

Ashley grabbed her purse and hurried up the sidewalk. It was a small building; a four-story walk-up she often joked had been built before the invention of elevators. Days like today when she only had to carry her handbag up the three flights it wasn't so bad. But on grocery day it just plain sucked.

After letting herself into the small apartment, she rushed to her bedroom, changed out of her jeans and blouse into her uniform of black slacks and black T-shirt with *Coffee Time*'s logo embroidered in red over her left breast. In the bathroom, she brushed out her blonde hair, tied it into a messy bun, and seeing the bags under her eyes, dabbed on a little more concealer.

Unfortunately, there was no masking the worry in her eyes. She squeezed them closed to keep the threatening tears from falling. There wasn't time to fall apart now. She'd have to save that for later. Right now, she had another job to get to.

Since her daughter was also working tonight at the drugstore two blocks over, Ashley didn't need to start supper. She just grabbed an apple off the counter and, within ten minutes of entering her home, was once again out the door.

She'd been too shell-shocked leaving Eugene's to pay attention to the squeal under her hood that had developed in the last few days but there was no ignoring the screech when she turned over the engine this time. It sounded louder in the residential area where there wasn't as much traffic or industrial noise to muffle the sound. She'd hoped to get the squeal looked at in the next few weeks but until she found a job to replace the one she'd had at Eugene's, she didn't have a penny to spare.

Of course, even if she wasn't losing that job, she still didn't have a penny to spare.

Letting out a tired breath, Ashley put the car in drive and pulled away from the curb.

Twelve minutes later, all eyes were on her car when she pulled into the parking lot at *Coffee Time*, which was nestled between a subway sandwich franchise and a really good mom and pop burger place. Both of which were already seeing kids from the nearby high school strolling through their doors.

The smell of charbroiled meat taunted Ashley as she strode across the parking lot. Her mouth watered at the thought of a cheeseburger with all the fixings and her stomach gave an answering grumble. God, she couldn't remember the last time she'd had a hamburger or any meal she hadn't had to prepare herself.

But at least she had that. She knew for a fact there were people who didn't get to have home-cooked meals, even if was only mac and cheese and hot dogs. But so help her God if she ever won the lottery she'd never eat another frigging hot dog again in her life.

Ashley tossed her apple core into the trash bin hovering at the edge of *Coffee Time*'s small outside seating area and pulled open the door. Coffee beans were a great palate cleanser and within seconds of walking into the small shop the only thing Ashley smelled was fresh ground coffee. In the cramped staff room, Ashley secured her purse in one of the tiny lockers and donned her apron.

She grabbed the bottle of spray cleaner and a cloth and went through the small seating area, straightening chairs, wiping tables, and picking up trash. In no time at all she was back behind the cash register two minutes before her shift started.

Chelsea, the only other person other than the manager who'd been working there as long as Ashley, stepped back from the counter. Like Ashley, Chelsea was a single mother. But, unlike Ashley whose one child was old enough to look after herself and work part-time after school, Chelsea's twin boys were only in second grade and in an after-school program until their mother could pick them up. And thanks to child support from her ex-husband, Chelsea didn't need to work nights to make ends meet.

"Got any plans for the night?" Ashley asked.

"It's my night off," Chelsea grinned.

Every Thursday, Chelsea's ex picked up the boys from the after-school program, fed them supper, and took them to tae kwon do. Alternating Thursdays with his weekends with the kids, every other week they also slept over and he took them to school in the morning. Which meant Chelsea would have the entire night to herself.

Ashley sighed inwardly. A night to herself without work or worry? To have a bath with a glass of wine or indulge in the romance books she loved so much but was usually too tired to read more than a few pages of each night? It would be almost as good as winning the lottery.

And just as likely.

Chelsea untied her black apron. "I'm grabbing sushi on my way home and then putting on my pajamas and watching something on Netflix."

Though Ashley's heart sank with envy, she smiled at the woman. Mothers carried enough guilt. Chelsea didn't need any more.

"Sounds wonderful. Enjoy your night."

"Thanks, I will!"

Luckily, Ashley didn't have too much time to dwell on her jealousy. Customers kept a steady flow with moms or dads grabbing drinks on their way to watch their kids' activities. High school and university students came in to study, spreading their books and laptops over the tables. Then the monthly book club came in to discuss and dissect last month's assigned novel.

Things were winding down at nine thirty and Ashley was

feeling the effects of having been awake since six that morning when her best friend strolled in. She and Jess had been close since fifth grade when they'd attended the same elementary school. There, they'd bonded over their hatred of social studies and their love of the Backstreet Boys.

"Hey, you."

Ashley smiled as Jess approached the counter. Dressed in black leggings that hugged her long legs, knee-high boots, an asymmetrical hem on her peacock-blue tunic to match the asymmetrical pixie cut only someone with high cheekbones could pull off, Jess's entrance had caught more than one young man's attention.

"Just come from work?"

Jess was a hairdresser and Thursday nights were the one weeknight the salon stayed open until nine.

"Yeah. I stayed a little late, needed to trim my ends," she said, as she flicked her ringed fingers over her spiky blonde hair. "And now I'm ready for a nice cup of chai tea."

Knowing exactly how Jess liked it, Ashley rang it in, wrote her name on the to-go cup and handed it to the barista. With nobody behind her, Jess leaned against the counter.

"So, what are you doing for Brittany's sweet sixteen?"

Ashley smiled thinking of it, but just as she opened her mouth to say what she'd planned, her excitement plummeted.

"Damn," she muttered.

"What? What's wrong?"

"I had something planned but..." She shook her head and fisted her hands. Dammit, of all the times for this to happen.

"Ash, what is it?"

"I lost my job at the small engine repair shop today. He's selling his building to the company next door that wants to expand. After next week I'm down a job if I can't find another one right away.

"I've been saving for Brittany's birthday for months but if I can't find another job between now and her birthday next week, I'll need that money to buy groceries."

Or pay rent. Or fix her car. Or, or, or. There was never a shortage of "ors."

Jess reached over the counter and squeezed Ashley's hand. "What did you have planned and how much do you need?"

"Jess, I can't—"

"You can and you will. Now, what had you planned?"

"She's always wanted to go horseback riding, so I found a place out near Last Stand, the Cartwright Dude Ranch. They have an overnight trail ride package where they haul all their gear with them and sleep in tents. The plan was for her to go with her friends Maddy and Emily."

"Sounds fun."

"And she's so looking forward to it." And she'd be devastated if Ashley had to cancel.

"Thank you," Jess said when the barista handed her the tea. Then she faced Ashley once more. "Don't even think about cancelling this. I can pay for it—"

"Jess, no—"

"And you can pay me back when you find another job," Jess continued undaunted.

Ashley hated to do it. It made her feel like a failure to accept the help. But she rarely got to send her daughter back to school in more than one new pair of jeans. Most of her clothes came from the thrift store. Christmas was socks and necessities and rarely anything fun. Brittany had been looking forward to this for months and Ashley too. She couldn't bear to take it away from her.

"Okay," she conceded with a heavy breath. "If I need you to. But I'll start looking for another job when I get home. Hopefully, I'll find something."

Jess looked at her watch. "Ash, it's a quarter to ten. It'll be almost ten thirty before you get home. Just get some sleep. The jobs will still be there tomorrow."

Maybe. But it wasn't a chance Ashley could afford to take. Too exhausted to argue she simply answered, "Yeah, you're right. I'm pretty tired."

"It shows, sweetie. Get some sleep and keep me posted how the job search goes."

With a wave good night, Jess took her tea and left. Ashley saw out the last of the customers, wiped tables, swept, and mopped the floor. Then she hung up her apron and pulled her purse from the locker.

Just as her cell rang. Digging it out of her pocket she saw it from her manager, Jeff.

"Hello?"

"Oh, good, I'm glad I caught you. Listen, I know your schedule usually only allows you to work nights except for Sundays, but is there any chance you can work a day shift next week? Brent just texted me. That specialist appointment he was waiting for? It's next Thursday. He forgot to tell me when he was here earlier."

Thursday. Her busiest day of the week. Eight to twelve at the body shop, one to four thirty for Eugene and then five to ten at *Coffee Time*. There wasn't room in there for another shift. But with Brittany's birthday coming and her last shift at Eugene's that day…

"What time?" she asked.

"The morning. His shift was six to twelve but if you could manage say, seven to ten? I think we can manage the rest."

Like a block puzzle, Ashley moved the pieces around. If she went straight to the body shop from the morning shift at *Coffee Time*, she could still get in a couple hours work before she had to get to Eugene's. It wasn't ideal as it usually took her the full four hours scheduled, which meant she'd have to make up the hours somewhere else.

Ashley chewed her lip. The body shop was open Saturday. Much as that day was usually devoted to playing catchup on housework and groceries as well as fulfilling her longest stretch of volunteer hours, she could make up the time then.

All that mattered was that she needed the money and she'd make it work.

Somehow.

Chapter Four

ASHLEY FLIPPED THE last of the pancakes, then without having to do more than pivot on the balls of her feet, dove her hands into the soapy dishwater. After finishing the dishes, she stacked the last of the pancakes onto the plate, then grabbed the skillet and plunged it into the water. The resounding hiss filled the tiny pass-through kitchen.

Leaving the pan to soak, Ashley hurried to her bedroom and dressed for work. Since the garbage pickup company she worked at on Fridays subscribed to casual Friday, Ashley slipped on tan capris and a pink T-shirt. She was heading to the closet-sized bathroom when Brittany slogged out of her room. Shoot. She'd hoped to be done before her daughter needed it. An almost-sixteen-year-old girl was not fast in the bathroom.

"Morning, sweetie."

Brittany's hair was a few shades lighter blonde than Ashley's but it was thick as her mother's and she had to shove a tangled mass off her face to be able to look Ashley in the eye.

"Mornin'," she mumbled as she continued her shuffle toward the bathroom.

Ashley intercepted her. "Can I go in first? I was just about to do my makeup and brush my teeth." She smiled wide. "I made pancakes. You can eat while I finish getting ready."

"Yeah, fine. Whatever." With a scowl, she brushed past her mother.

Her daughter was generally a happy person and easy to get along with. Just not in the mornings. For the first hour upon waking Brittany was surly and miserable and God help anyone within a twenty-mile radius. Luckily, it didn't last all day. If it did Ashley would have lost her mind years ago.

In the bathroom, she had to move Brittany's things aside to make room on the miniscule counter. She knocked a brush and a bottle of hairspray onto the floor in the process, narrowly missing the toilet. With a frustrated sigh Ashley closed the lid. She didn't have time to fish anything out of the toilet bowl.

In the corner by the tub, Ashley dug through the small basket she kept her toiletries in and pulled out the little zippered pouch. Good thing she was low maintenance as there was hardly room to put her bag between Brittany's makeup, brushes, perfumes, and menagerie of hair products. Ashley couldn't have been in there more than ten minutes but Brittany was standing at the door, arms crossed, foot tapping, and scowl firmly in place when Ashley opened the door.

"So you're coming to help after school, right?"

"Yeah," Brittany grumbled. "But I can't be there all day tomorrow. I'm hanging out with Maddy in the afternoon."

"That's fine. As long as you come for a bit."

Her smile wasn't returned and soon she had a closed door in her face. Just as Ashley was putting away the food a loud clutter sounded from the bathroom. Judging by the sounds, she guessed all those hair products had hit the floor.

"Argh! I can't wait to have a real bathroom. And a real house. I'm so over this place!"

Since it wasn't a new rant, Ashley ignored her daughter as she shut the fridge door. But leaving the kitchen she tripped over the lifting rug in the hallway. She landed on her hands and knees, her left elbow slamming into the wall. Why they called it a funny bone she'd never understand. There was nothing humorous about the pain radiating from the joint. Ashley picked herself up, rubbing her elbow and scowling at the offending carpet as she did.

Brittany wasn't the only one over this place.

"AND, IF YOU can, write up a formal quote for this bathroom reno," Dallas said as he handed over the two lined yellow pages he'd ripped off his legal pad.

Sherry, the bookkeeper/office manager for Granger Construction took the notes, glanced over the figures.

"Make sense?" he asked, in case she couldn't make out his writing. "The email address you can send it to is there on the bottom."

"Seems pretty clear," she answered as she skimmed the page.

"I'll likely have some checks for you to sign later."

She patted the stack of bills. "If you're not back before I leave I'll set them on your desk with the envelopes ready to go. You can either pop them in the mail yourself or leave them for me to do on Monday."

"I can mail them. Just leave everything on my desk." He peered at her as his conscience tugged. "You're not overdoing it, are you? Because if you need to cut back on your hours—"

"No, I'm fine. It's mostly sitting and I have to do something. Can't just stare at the walls all day."

She seemed to mean it, but—

"Honestly, I'm fine. It's normal to feel tired, Dallas."

"Okay, but don't overdo it. Does Josh have the nursery ready yet?"

Sherry rolled her eyes. "No."

"I told him I'd help put those shelves up."

"I know. You and at least two of his other friends. He wants to do it by himself."

Dallas's lips twitched. "We could sneak out one day at lunch while he's at work and do them without him."

Her hazel eyes sparkled. "Ha! Yes, we could." But she shook her head. "He wants to do it. So I'll let him. Even if the baby will be in high school before he ever gets it done."

His phone beeped with an incoming text. Dallas read it quick, shot off a response, and slid it back into his pocket.

"I've gotta go. I don't think I'll be back today. I'm going to check and see how the crews are doing then I need to head over to that *House of Hope*. The project manager is expecting me."

Sherry leaned back in her high-backed chair, clasped her hands over her belly. He winced at the same time she did, only his wasn't a sympathy wince for whatever the little human inside her growing belly had just done. No, his was because there was no denying she was eight months pregnant and he had yet to line up a replacement. Like her husband with those shelves, Dallas really needed to get on that.

"Can't you just call and ask Ken and Dan how they're doing? Would save you some time."

"It would," Dallas agreed. "But with me having to go to Last Stand more it'll mean more responsibility for them too, and I'd like to tell them in person. Besides, I can spare some time to give a hand."

He'd learned early on that a boss working alongside his employees earned more respect than one who just barked out orders or worse, micromanaged. Plus, it wasn't a hardship to strap on his tool belt.

He loved to build things, to see the fruits of his labor take shape, and to stand back at the end of a project and think, "yeah, I built that." Which was a hell of a lot more satisfying than signing checks and doing paperwork.

"I was going to help shingle that garage. And if the inspector finally shows, we can start on the drywall in the basement."

He loved putting up sheetrock. Once the drywall started going up, suddenly the rooms took shape. While he had no problem seeing where each individual room was when the space was nothing but bare studs, most people couldn't get a clear picture until the actual walls were up. Dallas always got a kick out of seeing the pleasure light up their eyes when the vision they'd had in their head took that big leap forward toward being a reality.

Dallas fished his keys out his pocket. "I think that's it then. I'll swing by here on my way from the ranch Sunday, so if there's anything else just put it on my desk or if it can't wait, give me a call."

He'd missed the worst of rush hour and other than getting behind a street sweeper for three blocks, easily made his way to the jobsite. He swung into the subdivision and took a left down the back alley.

The garbage truck filled the narrow road but luckily was heading in the same direction as Dallas, so he just waited behind until he could swing onto the garage pad next to the other Granger Construction truck.

He might have been a born and bred Texan but the humidity still had the power to suck the air from his lungs. Knowing he wouldn't be able to once he reached the *House of Hope*, Dallas grabbed the hem of his T-shirt and yanked it over his head. He tossed it on the seat then reached across the cab and grabbed his hard hat off the passenger seat. He pulled his tool belt out of the box of the truck and buckled it on.

Since everyone was there and ready and Dallas had a full day and then some, he headed over to the packages of shingles stacked on the ground.

"Okay, let's get these on."

DRIVING UP AND seeing the house—*her* house—take shape never failed to give Ashley a thrill. It was no longer a pipe dream, something to buy if she won the lottery. It was no longer something she wished for in the quiet of night when life felt as though it were weighing her down. When it felt as though she'd never manage more than treading water for the rest of her life.

But since she'd been accepted as a candidate for *Houses of Hope*, she did, indeed, have hope. Even though she was about to lose one job, she had a lot to be grateful for.

Ashley pulled up behind the opened doors of the tan-colored utility trailer. Inside were boxes, tools, two ladders, lengths of two-by-fours, and some sort of plastic pipe. Coiled extension cords hung on the paneled inside walls. The foreman of the project, Rick Redmond, walked out of the trailer with one such coil draped over his shoulder. He waved when he saw her.

As Rick strode across the lumpy dirt that would one day be her front lawn, Ashley tucked her purse beneath the driver's seat. She grabbed her small insulated cooler bag, pocketed her phone, and locked the car. It was doubtful anyone would steal the outdated sedan, even if she left it unlocked with the keys dangling from the ignition.

Even her purse wasn't worth stealing. The little cash she had wouldn't be worth the effort and her credit cards were hovering around their limit. But replacing the ID and cards would take time and money and, since she had neither, she ensured her bag was hidden out of view and the car was locked.

The afternoon sun reflected off the white wrap covering her outside walls. Besides a new house, Ashley was also getting an education on house building and with each new step she learned something new. Rick had explained the purpose of house wrap was to keep moisture from penetrating through to the inside walls and studs.

It also acted as a barrier to the wind. And now that the windows and doors were in and the house wrap now complete, the vinyl siding could go on. She did a mental happy dance at the thought. She could hardly wait to see her house in the smoky blue siding she'd chosen.

Ashley let herself in through the front door. While the outside looked almost complete, the inside was just starting. And it was very much a construction zone. Stacks of two-by-fours lay on the plywood floor in the middle of what would be her living room. There were industrial lights mounted on tripods, though there was enough sunlight beaming in they weren't turned on. There were bags of nails, an air compressor, two kinds of saws, a few lunch boxes, and an assortment of empty water and juice bottles.

She breathed deeply the smell of fresh cut wood. With the exception of baking bread and campfire smoke, nothing beat the smell of new lumber. And though her ears would be throbbing by the time she left, she appreciated the thwacking sound of the nail gun, the loud rumbling of the generator that poured from the open window near where Rick and two other men were working on framing an inside wall. It all sounded like progress.

Ashley rubbed her still sore elbow. Progress couldn't come fast enough.

Three heavy-duty extension cords snaked out the window. Presumably to the generator chugging away in the backyard. She tracked one to the nail gun Rick was using. Another was attached to the compressor and the last to the saw. Since they were weeks away from getting electricity all the power needed to run the tools had to come from an outside source.

Because she'd wanted to be as much help as possible,

Ashley had spent many hours, when she should have been sleeping, searching the internet for how-to videos on home construction. She had a rough idea of the process and the order in which things were done.

She'd just put her little cooler down when Rick turned to her. With the air compressor running, he handed the nail gun to Jeff, one of the other contractors who'd been on-site since the beginning, and walked her way.

"Small crew today," Ashley commented.

"Yeah, that's the thing with volunteers. They can't be here all the time." He checked his watch. "But there's a new guy supposed to show up soon. He owns his own construction business so once he gets here, he and Jeff can start on the kitchen and living room while Kurt and I continue with bedrooms and bathrooms."

Bathrooms. She and Brittany would each have their own. She'd no longer trip over her daughter's things or have to rush in the mornings. Or have to worry about things falling in the toilet.

"Sounds good." She gestured to the empty bottles and take-out bags from their lunch. "You want me to start with cleanup?"

"Sure. And then you can go out back. They've starting on the siding. You can help pass the panels."

She grinned, excitement skimming along her nerves. "The siding is going on?"

Rick winked. "Go see for yourself."

She wanted to, more than anything, but she forced herself to wait. Instead, she grabbed a large black trash bag from the box next to the door and gathered the trash in one, recyclables in the other. Then she all but threw the bags on the ground as she rushed out the back door.

She pressed her palms to her cheeks. It was so pretty! Even with only a few rows done, it looked amazing. Her eyes went misty and she chuckled as she sniffled them back. Leave it to her to get teary-eyed over vinyl siding.

"What do you think?"

Recognizing the voice she didn't feel the least bit embarrassed when her eyes clouded over again. "It's perfect, Bob."

A recently retired shop schoolteacher, Bob had been on the project since the beginning. And, like most days, he wore a faded yellow T-shirt, jeans, and tan work boots. She imagined that was how he'd walked into his classroom, easy smile and welcoming deep brown eyes, ready and eager to get to work.

Hammer in hand, Bob came to stand beside her. His wife Joan, who volunteered a few afternoons a week, stepped to his side.

"Hi, Ashley."

"Hi, Joan. How was aquacize this morning?"

"Same as usual." The skin around her eyes crinkled as she smiled. "I was huffing and puffing by the end."

Ashley laughed. "I would be too."

Especially since most of her jobs entailed sitting at a desk. But she'd shoveled cement for the foundation and hauled two-by-fours for the frame and whatever other jobs Rick needed her to do and while she wouldn't profess to be an advertisement for physical fitness, she was proud of the muscles she'd gained since the ground breaking.

"So," she said, directing the conversation back to the

project. "I'll pass the slats and you two put them on?"

Bob and Joan exchanged a glance.

"With the first few rows done, it's easy. I'll show you how and then you and I can nail them in place," Bob said.

Excitement bubbled in her voice. "I can put on siding?"

"Trust me," Joan said, "it's easy."

Joan handed over her hammer. Bob took one end of a slat and Joan the other. Because siding started from the bottom and worked up, they squatted down to where they'd left off. They placed the slat in position overlapping the one below it.

Bob took a nail out of the pouch attached to his tool belt. "This is the flange," he said, referring to the top of the slat that had small horizontal holes running the length of the piece of siding.

"The trick is not to nail it too tight. It needs to be able to expand and contract with the weather. A general rule of thumb is if you can slide a dime between the slat and back of the nail head then you've left enough room."

He placed a nail in the middle of one of the holes. "You want to be dead center, and nail it in straight, not at an angle."

With three short taps he had the nail in place. He took another nail out of his pouch, handed it to her. Pointing to another hole he said, "Here, you do it."

Ashley was both nervous and excited. To her, a house was a big deal and needed to be done by professionals, not by people like her who could ruin it by making a mistake. But with Bob and Joan watching, Ashley took a deep breath, placed the nail in position, and tapped it home.

"See?" Bob said. "Not so hard." He scooted down a little, passed her another nail. "Do it again."

She did. And she loved it. With the starter plate level at the bottom all they had to do was position the slat to overlap the one below it and drive in the nails. They'd installed another four rows when Rick came out to have a look. He crouched, pulled on the slat. When it moved Ashley's stomach dropped, thinking she'd done it wrong. Until she remembered it was supposed to do that.

Rick nodded. "Looks good," he said before once again disappearing inside.

An hour later, Bob hooked his hammer into the notch on his tool belt and announced he had to leave.

"I have a dentist appointment and I've been waiting a week and a half to get in."

Since Bob and Joan came together, they left together as well. Unable to continue on her own, Ashley was about to go ask Rick what he wanted her to do next when a homeless man strolled up from the back alley. Her body tensed and automatically her hand tightened on the hammer she still held.

There were three men inside, she reminded herself and despite the constant rumbling of the generator, they'd hear her scream over the noise. She'd make sure of it.

Yet she held both her ground and her tongue as the man walked forward. Gray whiskers covered his chin and his hair looked about two months overdue for a cut. He wore worn sneakers and his T-shirt and jeans were streaked with dirt. Ashley suspected all his worldly possessions were tucked into the backpack he carried.

He stopped a safe distance from her, almost as though he knew moving any closer would send her running. He gestured to the siding.

"I like that color. Reminds me of the ocean at dusk." With a thin smile, he grabbed the empty boxes of siding and carried them back to the large dumpster.

Then, without another word, left as quietly as he'd come.

Ashley's breath came out in a long whoosh. It wasn't that she'd been scared exactly but there was no denying she'd been unnerved. She hated to admit it was stereotypical but having a homeless man approach her not knowing his intention—

"Are you all right?"

Ashley squealed at the tap on her shoulder and the voice directly behind her. Luckily, Rick stepped back before she whacked him with her hammer.

He held up his hands. "I called your name but you didn't answer. I didn't mean to scare you."

Ashley let the hammer fall to the dirt. She wiped her sweaty hands on her jeans. "No, it's fine. I just didn't hear you."

"No damage done. Thankfully." He picked up her hammer. "I saw Bob and Joan leave."

She accepted the tool he passed back to her. "I was about to come in and ask what you wanted me to do next when a homeless man walked up to me."

Rick looked past her but the alley was clear. "Did he say or do anything?"

"Other than compliment the color of the siding and toss the empty boxes in the dumpster? Not a thing."

"Well, clearly, he frightened you."

"Not frightened as much as made me uncomfortable. I've seen him around before too, just never that close. I wasn't sure what he was after."

"Far as I can tell, nothing. He's been around a few times. Mostly he just picks up some trash or debris and then leaves. Every time he could've taken something if he was so inclined."

"He never has?"

"Nope. But next time I see him I could threaten to call the police if he steps on the property again."

Ashley shook her head. "No, don't do that. I'm sure he's harmless."

But in case he wasn't, she'd make sure Brittany knew not to come out to the backyard alone.

Just then a white truck pulled up beside the dumpster.

"Ah, there he is," Rick said as he strode to meet the newcomer.

Since most volunteers parked out front and this truck had a company logo on the side, Ashley assumed this man was another tradesman. As she liked to thank everyone who worked on her house she stayed too.

The man stepped out of the truck.

Oh. My. God. He was gorgeous!

Ball cap, aviator sunglasses. A gray T-shirt that hugged his broad shoulders and defined his pecs. The short sleeves put his biceps on display and the snug jeans, well, they put *everything* on display. His sandy-brown scruff matched the short hair at the back of the cap and when he shook hands with Rick and introduced himself, Ashley heard nothing but a rasp that was every woman's fantasy.

And more than likely some lucky woman's husband or boyfriend. Which was fine. No problem. Because she didn't have time or energy to date. And she'd learned from the few attempts she'd made at dating over the years that men who looked that good, usually weren't as appealing once she got to know them.

If they weren't turned away by the fact she was a single mother, then they usually figured she must be lonely. So lonely she'd jump into bed with them after one or two dates. It had only taken two such men before Ashley had sworn off dating. She didn't need the aggravation or the disappointment.

But a little eye candy never hurt anybody and the man was definitely eye candy.

Of the yummiest variety.

Chapter Five

DALLAS DIDN'T CONSIDER himself a sexist man. Though he didn't know many women in the trades, he knew enough, had seen enough, to know they were just as capable. And seeing as how *Houses of Hope* were built by volunteers, it didn't surprise him to see the pretty blonde standing in the backyard. What did surprise him, however, was his reaction to her.

Maybe her petite stature did it. Or the fact that with her hair tied back in a ponytail, with her jeans, sneakers, and *Houses of Hope* T-shirt, she looked like she should be sitting in a university classroom, not out working a construction site. Not that he was disappointed.

Hell, no.

"Dallas Granger?"

Dallas shifted his gaze from the blonde to the man extending a hand toward him. Early sixties, if Dallas had to guess. Medium height and build. Gray just starting to lighten the man's brown hair, though mostly at the temples.

"That's me," Dallas answered.

The callouses and strength in the grip proved this was a man used to hard work. Dallas liked him immediately.

"I'm Rick Redmond. I'm heading this project. Justin Finkel told me to expect you. You brought me some paperwork?"

"Yeah."

Dallas cut his glance to the blonde before returning it to Redmond. Pretty as she was, she didn't need to know the reason he was really there. It was still a sore spot for him.

"But I'd prefer to go over it in private."

Rick turned to face the woman. "Ashley, why don't you wait for us inside. We won't be long."

Her cheeks darkened. "Oh. Yeah, sure. No problem."

With her ponytail swinging, the woman hurried through the back door. Dallas was sorry he'd embarrassed her but he felt like enough of a fool for what he'd done to get the community service. He didn't need his stupidity advertised.

Dallas waited until she was inside before reaching into his back pocket. He handed Redmond the paperwork.

"If you don't mind I'd like to keep my reason for being here between the two of us." He grimaced. "It's not exactly great advertising for Granger Construction."

"Probably not." Redmond's green eyes locked onto Dallas's. "But if that's what you're after you should probably come in another vehicle." He gestured to Dallas's truck. "One without your business's logo on it."

"It *is* good advertising if people think I'm just another volunteer. Besides, it's the only vehicle I own."

"Okay then." Rick tapped the envelope against his open palm. "Now that I have your paperwork, I have some of my own you need to sign. Follow me; it's in my truck out front."

Since Dallas hadn't bothered coming to see the site before now, he took a moment to note things as he followed Rick over the uneven ground. Windows and doors were in, so that meant the house was at lock-up stage. Shingles were in and siding was going on. He figured, given the rumbling generator, the cords snaking through the open window at the back, and the rhythmic thwack sound of the nail gun that framing was underway inside.

It wasn't a large house. About twelve hundred square feet. A modest three-bedroom bungalow. So maybe they only gave away reasonable homes. He'd half anticipated the house to be a sprawling two-story in excess of two thousand square feet.

On the tailgate of Rick's truck, Dallas looked over the necessary disclaimers and release of liability and scrawled his name on the line.

Rick added them to a folder with Dallas's name already on it, then sifted through the envelope Dallas had given him. He removed the time sheet, handed it back to Dallas.

"Fill in your time and make sure I sign it before you leave each day. If I'm not here, Jeff can do it."

Dallas tucked the sheet back into his pocket.

"Can you give me some sort of schedule you're able to be here?"

"Well, I was shooting for three hours a day on week days and a few hours on Saturday and Sunday mornings. But my dad was admitted to the hospital in Last Stand last night and now I also need to help my brothers run the family ranch. I can still manage the weekdays but I can only work Saturday mornings now. Sundays I'll be tied up in Last Stand."

Rick nodded. "Sounds reasonable."

He pulled his cell phone from his pocket. "Give me your contact information and that way you can text me if something changes."

After exchanging numbers, Rick pocketed his phone and stuffed the envelope Dallas had given him into the folder then locked it in the cab of his truck.

"Well, if you're all set, let's put you to work."

Instead of going inside like Dallas expected, he followed Rick around back again.

"I assume you've put on siding before?"

"I have."

"Good. Then I'll let you take over out here. I'm sure you have your own tools, but we have more than enough hammers to go around. The nails are all there." He gestured to the bags sitting on the dirt next to the boxes of vinyl. "I'll get Ashley to come back out and give you a hand."

Since he preferred his own tools, he went to fetch his tool belt out of his truck while Rick went inside. Dallas was just securing the belt when the woman stepped out the back door.

It had been a long time since he'd felt a hitch in his gut just looking at a woman, but it hadn't been so long he didn't recognize it when it hit him.

It didn't hurt that her gaze went to his tool belt first. Went and lingered. His lips twitched. He didn't know what it was, but uniforms and tool belts seemed to do it for women. Which was good news for him, Hudson, and Gage. Not nearly as good for Ryker and Cam. Although they had the whole cowboy thing going for them, so likely they weren't suffering either.

"I'm sorry if I was rude earlier. It's just that it was private business between me and Rick."

Her shoulder rose in a shrug. There was no anger or resentment in her eyes.

"You're entitled to your privacy. No need to apologize."

A sensible woman. Been a long time since he'd met one of those as well. Dallas closed the distance between them. Extending his hand he introduced himself.

"Dallas Granger."

"Ashley Anderson."

Her firm grip both surprised and impressed him. It was his experience that most women had a light touch and it usually felt like he was holding a delicate flower he was scared to hurt. But Ashley's was strong. Confident. Sexy as hell.

She reclaimed her hand sooner than he'd have liked and without a word plucked her hammer off the ground and took her position against the exterior wall. Since they were closer to the generator there, shouting over the rumbling wasn't conducive to conversation. Though he was a man who preferred to work in silence, it surprised him that he resented the fact he couldn't talk to her.

Before each new strip was added Dallas ensured the one below hadn't been nailed too tight. Again he was impressed, this time by the quality of her work. She didn't nail them in as fast as he did but she was accurate, and he'd take steady and right over hurried and wrong any day.

After they'd installed a dozen slats, he had enough confidence in her work that he didn't feel the need to oversee each one. But it gave him an excuse to get close enough to smell her citrusy perfume.

They continued until they couldn't go any higher without a scaffold to stand on. Right about then the generator sputtered and after a few wheezes, shuddered to a stop.

Ashley tipped her head back, closed her eyes, and sighed. "That's so much better."

Dallas hooked his hammer into his tool belt. "If the noise bothers you that bad you should wear earmuffs." He looked around but didn't see any.

"I tried. They kept falling off my head, no matter how much I tightened them."

Dallas walked to his truck. He lowered his tailgate and hopped up, aiming for the galvanized aluminum toolbox behind the cab. He pulled out a handful of plastic packages.

"Here, try these," he said when he returned. "They don't mask the sound as good as the muffs but they'll reduce it enough to make things more comfortable."

He handed her the individually wrapped pairs of purple and green foam earplugs. Since her hands were smaller than his, she made of bowl of her palms to hold them all. His fingers brushed her skin as he dropped the packages inside.

Heat sizzled up his arm. It only got hotter when her honey-gold eyes met his.

"Thank you."

He was the one who should be thanking her. For the first time in days he had something else to occupy his thoughts besides community service, his dad, and the ranch.

"You're welcome."

Rick stepped out the back door, eyed their progress.

He turned to Dallas. "Looks like you're ready for scaffolding on this side. I've got some in my trailer." He checked his watch. "Actually, let's not get into that today. I'll fuel up the generator and we can all go inside and work on framing."

His grin stretched his lips as he looked to Ashley. "Your master bath is all framed."

Dallas's jaw went slack. "This is *your* house?" he asked.

Rick turned his happy grin on Dallas. "Yeah. Did I forget to mention that when I introduced you?"

"You didn't introduce us, we introduced ourselves." Dallas locked his gaze on Ashley. "You didn't mention the house was yours."

"I didn't think it mattered."

Well, it did. It damn well did. And any interest he'd had toward her sputtered out just like the generator had moments ago.

Dallas wasn't getting involved with anyone who relied on charity or the hard work of another to get ahead. Not when he'd busted his balls to get where he was. Not when the only reason he was even standing there was because of Vince's lack of integrity.

Not when he'd already been used that way once before.

Aware both she and Rick were staring at him Dallas forced a smile.

"It doesn't," he stated. Then he turned to Rick. "Where's the fuel?"

"I've got a jerry can in my trailer but I can—"

"No, I've got it," Dallas said. And before Rick could beat him to the punch, he hurried off toward the front of the house.

Her house.

He shook his head. First pretty woman he'd seen in forever who'd stirred his interest, among other things. He should have known, given his luck of late, she was too good to be true.

IT MATTERED. HOWEVER he claimed otherwise the fact the house was hers bothered him. The fact that it did shouldn't concern her. But it did. It definitely did.

Darn it, it was why she'd waited so many years to apply for the project to begin with. Because even though it wasn't, sometimes it felt like charity and she hated that feeling. Hated feeling that no matter how many jobs she worked, how much she sacrificed, she couldn't quite do it all by herself. Hated that people like Dallas looked down on her for being a recipient. Hated that despite the fact she worked her butt off and it wasn't as though they were handing it to her on a silver platter, and—

What they think is none of your business.

Ashley shook her head and uncurled her tight fingers. No, it shouldn't be. And she shouldn't let it affect her. Which was all so much easier said than done. Especially since she'd felt people's judgments toward her since word had gotten out sixteen years ago that she was pregnant.

Especially when they were as blatant as Dallas had been. Still standing on the threshold of the back door, Ashley peered over her shoulder. Dallas had his back to her. Red gas tank in hand, he was bent over filling the generator with fuel.

Honestly, the man could be a walking ad for jeans. Unlike the young twenty-somethings who still thought it was cool to wear their jeans halfway down their butts, Dallas wore his just low enough that when he raised his arms a little his T-shirt crept up his back and exposed the thick black waistband of his underwear.

As though she was a teenager again with no control over her emotions, she felt hot all over. Her stomach jittered as her lower muscles clenched in a lust-filled fist.

Stop it. You are not that boy-crazy sixteen-year-old anymore!

No. No, she wasn't. Thank goodness. And a nice butt and sexy good looks weren't enough for her. Not anymore.

Even if it were, given his reaction to her being the recipient of the house, he wouldn't want anything to do with her. Which was just as well since she didn't need his judgment and superiority in her life.

There, problem solved. She mentally brushed him off her hands.

But it didn't stop her from checking out his butt one last time before finally going inside.

ASHLEY WAS CUTTING a piece of two-by-four with the electric saw when her phone vibrated in her back pocket. She finished the cut, turned off the saw, and carried the wood to Rick and Dallas, who were putting together a frame for another wall. The shorter pieces she'd just cut would be the braces that connected the doorframe to the ceiling. Once she'd handed the pieces over, she removed her safety glasses and pulled her phone from her pocket. It was a text from Brittany.

"Needed extra help from Mr. Sherman in chemistry. No

point coming now. I'll make up the time tomorrow. See you at home."

Ashley checked the time. It was almost five. No, there was no point in her coming since Rick liked to shut things down at six on Fridays and by the time her daughter took a bus to the site, she'd only have about half an hour to work. However, Brittany was right; she'd be making up the hours tomorrow, despite her wanting to hang out with Maddy. Responsibilities came first.

"Let's get this wall up."

Because it was easier to construct the frame on the floor, Ashley moved in to help Dallas and Rick lift it into position. Despite the smell of fresh cut wood filling the space, Ashley caught a sniff of Dallas's scent when he took his position next to her.

A hint of cologne mixed with the spice of wood and the tang of his sweat. Though it was sweltering inside, she wished foolishly he'd put on a jacket. Something that would mask the muscles and wouldn't display his abs and narrow waist. At least then she might have been able to pretend he only had a gorgeous face. Instead, she was forced to concede he was gorgeous everywhere.

Well, except for his attitude. That wasn't pretty.

On the count of three, they gripped the wood and walked the frame into an upright position. With Kurt making sure it was level and her and Dallas holding it straight, Rick and Jeff installed more two-by-fours to act as top plates. When the wall was secured to the ceiling Rick climbed down the ladder. He gave the frame a tug, nodded.

"Looks good. Let's call it a day."

Knowing the drill by now, Ashley went outside. After shutting off the generator, she unplugged the cords and gathered the bags of nails and other small tools that were outside. With the compressor off, the hollow belly of her house echoed with footsteps as the men cleaned up the work area and prepared to haul expensive tools to Rick's trailer.

Since thieves loved to break into houses under construction and abscond with power tools, copper wiring, and whatever else they could sell, Rick secured everything in his trailer, which he took home each night.

"What do you want to do with the boxes of siding out back?" she asked Rick as he and Jeff carried the heavy saw across the floor.

"They can come in here. Dallas, once you're done with that"—he jutted his chin toward the compressor Dallas was carrying—"why don't you help Ashley bring in the boxes of siding?"

Her stomach jittered. "I'm sure I can—"

"No problem," he answered Rick, not even bothering to look her way.

Then, barely breaking stride, he angled through the front door with the compressor in his hands. With the muscles in his biceps bulging. With his defined shoulders shifting beneath the tight cotton of his T-shirt.

Ashley's gaze dropped to the floor as she searched for a hammer. Not to hit him, but to try to knock some sense into herself. Yes, he was handsome. And sexy. And if she were a vehicle she'd probably sound like one of those muscle cars revving their engines at the starting line, but she wasn't in the market for a man. Especially one who revved her engine so hot and fast her brain struggled to function in his presence.

God, hadn't sixteen years been enough time to learn her lesson?

"Apparently not," she muttered as she turned on her heel and headed back out.

Seeing the same homeless man standing there Ashley came to an abrupt stop. Her heart bumped against her breastbone. What did he want? It was quiet now so she had no doubt if she screamed she'd be heard. Even the siren in the distance wouldn't be enough to muffle the sound. But though she kept her distance, she didn't shout for help.

"I don't have any money," she said. In case that was the reason he was there, she figured on telling him straight out he wouldn't get any from her. While she suspected most people would say that to any panhandler, in her case it was the truth.

His smile was sad. "I'm not looking for any. I just thought maybe you could use some help."

"It's a volunteer project. Nobody gets paid to work here."

"I know." He stuffed his hands into the pockets of his baggy jeans. "I saw the *Houses of Hope* sign out front. Like I said, I just thought maybe you could use some help."

Ashley had no words. Or none that wouldn't sound rude. Like why he'd work for free when he clearly needed the money? Or wouldn't his time be better spent looking for a paying job? Or even picking bottles.

Shame slid like sour milk through her stomach. She didn't know his story any more than Dallas knew hers and like the construction worker had done, she'd judged on sight. Well, she didn't need to know this man's story to be kind, did she? No. And while she wasn't a 100 percent comfortable around him, she didn't see the harm in his helping. Besides, if he helped her carry in the siding she wouldn't have to do it with Dallas.

"It's fine if you'd prefer I didn't," he said, already turning away. "I won't bo—"

"Wait!" When he turned around again she offered a friendly smile. "I'd appreciate some help. Thank you."

His face completely changed. Underneath his wiry eyebrows, his blue eyes shone with pleasure. The mouth that she'd only ever seen tipped down in sadness curved into a smile. He even stood a little taller. For the first time she could envision the man he'd once been, or could be.

Ashley moved to one end of the opened box of siding. "If you can grab the other end, we'll move this inside for the night."

They were moving the first box when Dallas came round the corner.

"We've got this, thanks," Ashley said when Dallas stepped forward.

Ashley didn't miss the way Dallas's gaze raked over the homeless man's dirty clothing and disheveled appearance. But he kept his tongue as Ashley and the man moved the boxes.

"Thank you," Ashley said to the man.

His smile touched her heart. "You're welcome." He grabbed the backpack he'd set down in order to help her and left as quietly as he'd arrived.

"Who was that?" Dallas asked the moment the man was out of sight.

"I don't know his name, but he's been around before. Mostly, I think he just wants to help."

Dallas scoffed. "More than likely he's scoping things out. Seeing what's worth coming back to steal later. Trust me; I've seen it more than once."

Ashley gaped. "I don't believe you. You find out this house is for me and suddenly I'm the dirt beneath your shoe and now you're accusing a homeless man of theft when he hasn't done a thing to earn your scorn? How's the view from your glass house?" she demanded.

Dallas's gaze went cold as steel. "I don't live in a glass house. But I do live in one I've paid for myself."

She sucked in a sharp breath. "So you're judge and jury? You know nothing about either one of us and yet you stand there and pass judgment?"

"It's been my experience—"

"Save it. I don't need your condescension or your holier than thou attitude." And before she was submitted to more of it, she spun on her heel and marched away.

Chapter Six

"Ash, if you were that tired you should've cancelled," Jess chided.

"I'm sorry," Ashley said after she finished yawning for what had to be the tenth time. "It was a long week."

"They're all long weeks." Jess set her hand on Ashley's capris-clad knee. "I worry about you. You're exhausted."

There was no point arguing. The bags she'd seen under her eyes spoke for themselves.

"It's just for a little while. Once the house is finished I'll have more spare time."

"No, you won't," Jess scowled. "Knowing you you'll just take on more shifts at *Coffee Time* or find another part-time job so you can pay down the mortgage faster."

Ashley sipped her wine. It touched her that her friend worried. It was nice to know someone did.

"If I do, I promise not to take on more than I can handle."

"That's what you always say but you're stretched too thin, Ash. See?" She pointed one of the fingers holding her glass of wine when Ashley yawned again. "It's barely eight and you're practically falling asleep."

"Saturdays are always the worst, you know that, and I worked longer today to make up for Brittany missing Friday.

It's why I texted and suggested we move this to tomorrow."

"I know. But it had already been too long since we'd done this. I didn't want to wait any more. But I should have and I'm sorry. You need to sleep."

"I'm fine. I'll have time to nap tomorrow."

Jess narrowed her eyes. "You work at *Coffee Time* tomorrow."

"Only a few hours."

"Which, if they ask, will turn to a full shift."

"Not this time," Ashley said. Mostly because she'd already agreed to take on that extra shift Thursday. Despite what Jess believed, Ashley didn't work every waking hour. She still had a daughter who needed her time.

"You better not, or I'll lock you in this apartment until you don't fall asleep sitting up anymore."

Touched, Ashley smiled. "Brittany and I have a home spa day planned tomorrow night. Manis and pedis."

Jess helped herself to another sprig of grapes. She smiled as she tugged a plump red one off its stem. "That'll be nice."

"Yeah, but with the construction, I'm not sure there's much point to a manicure."

Ashley leaned back in the soft cushions, examined her hands. Despite the cream she slathered on, they were dry and rougher than they'd ever been. And as for a pedicure, well, who'd see her toes but Brittany?

"How is the construction going? I drove by earlier but from the front I didn't see much change."

"Oh, you should have come around back. We started on the vinyl siding yesterday." Her smile stretched across her warm cheeks. Wine always heated her face and turned her cheeks red. "It's so pretty. My bedroom and master bath are framed, too."

"Then next time I'll be sure to stop. You must be so excited."

Ashley finished her wine. "I am. Seeing the rooms take shape makes it that much closer to being a reality."

Jess looked around the lamp-lit room that acted as both dining and living area. "I won't be sad to see the last of this place."

"Me either." Ashley sighed.

Jess popped another grape in her mouth. She studied Ashley as she chewed. After swallowing she asked, "How come you haven't said anything about the hot guy I saw on site when I drove by?"

"I don't remember any hot guy," she said. She busied herself pouring more wine to hide the lie.

"Uh-huh. You didn't notice the guy in the tight-fitting gray T-shirt, stubble, and ball cap?"

Ashley set down the bottle and gaped. "You noticed all that just by driving by?"

"Honey, when a man looks like that I slow down and take notice."

Ashley took her glass and settled back into the cushions. Hard to fault Jess when she'd done the same. Even today, despite still being mad at him and his superior attitude, when he'd first stepped out of the truck she'd had a foolish moment when everything inside her sizzled. All because of the way he'd leaned over his truck box as he'd reached for his tools. And then when he'd strapped on the belt…

"You know exactly who I'm talking about," Jess stated.

"Yeah, I know. But, trust me, his personality isn't nearly as appealing."

"He's a douchebag?"

Ashley snorted. Leave it to Jess not to pull punches.

"I'm not sure I'd go that far. But he's got a chip on his shoulder, that's for sure."

She sipped more of her drink, hating that she let his opinion get to her. Frowning, she said, "He got all superior when he found out the house was for me. Suddenly I was the dirt under his work boots."

Remembering how she hated when Brittany exaggerated she retracted. "All right, he wasn't that bad. He remained civil."

And earlier that afternoon he'd been sure to check she was properly strapped and harnessed when they'd climbed the scaffold to install the siding all the way up to the fascia.

"But?" Jess prodded, nudging Ashley's thigh with a bright red painted toe.

Taking a sip to buy some time, Ashley considered her answer. She and Jess had the kind of friendship where they shared everything and while she really wanted to confide her feelings, she hesitated. She'd been out of sorts since meeting Dallas yesterday.

She'd caught herself stealing glances over her shoulder. Her heart had kicked up every time she'd heard his voice or met his gaze. It was damn embarrassing to feel sixteen again at her age.

But she also held back because Jess made no secret of the fact she thought Ashley needed to date. That she needed a life of her own beyond being a mom and a provider. Jess wouldn't see all the reasons Dallas was bad for her. She'd simply see him as opportunity for Ashley to break a sixteen-year drought.

"Ash, come on. What's the problem?"

Ashley set down her glass. Folding her legs, she wrapped her arms around them and pressed her forehead to her knees.

"He makes me feel like a teenager again and I don't like it."

"Ah, Ash."

The couch groaned and dipped as Jess shuffled closer. Her hand rubbed soothing circles over Ashley's shoulder.

"It's really not a bad thing, you know."

Ashley raised her head. "How do you figure that?"

"Because you're thirty-one and it's high time a man has an effect on you."

Maybe. Probably. "But why does it have to be Dallas?" She groaned.

"Dallas?" Jess's eyes widened with glee. She resettled herself on the other end of the couch. "I like it."

Yeah, so did Ashley. The problem was it wasn't only his name she liked. And she shouldn't like anything about him, not with his attitude.

"Unfortunately, in his case, beauty is only skin deep."

Jess winked. "Nothing wrong with that if it's only his skin you're after."

"Jess! I'm not looking for a one-night stand."

"Who said anything about one night? Why can't it be two? Or ten?"

Ashley's insides clutched at the thought of sleeping with Dallas. Of seeing more of his gorgeous body. Naked.

Flustered, she reached for some grapes. "This is all moot anyway, since I told you any interest he initially showed cooled when he learned the house was for me. Besides, I wasn't exactly friendly either."

"So you apologize," Jess said with a shrug. "No big deal."

Yeah, no big deal. Except she still wasn't sure it was a good idea. Actually, she was sure. Things would be safer and easier if they kept their distance.

But not nearly as much fun.

No! No, no, no. It was that kind of mentality that had gotten her into trouble sixteen years ago. What harm was there in liking an older boy? What would a little kissing hurt? Why not meet him at his place when his parents were away? She'd loved him. She hadn't seen the dangers until it was too late.

But she was all grown up now. And so was Dallas. Which made things infinitely more dangerous. Because now she did see the warning signs. And, like then, she was struggling to heed them. Because, like then, her body had other ideas.

Naughty ones.

"He's probably a player. Any guy who looks that good knows it and won't ever be faithful to one woman. Probably can't hold down a job either. It's probably all about having fun for him."

Jess unfolded from the couch and went to the small desk next to the TV. Snagging a pad of paper and a pen, Jess settled back onto the couch.

Using one of the textbooks Brittany had left sitting on the coffee table as a base, Jess settled the pad over it and began to write. At the top she wrote "Reasons to date hunky construction worker," double underlined it, and under that drew two long columns. One for the "pros" and the other for the "cons."

"Seriously? Isn't that a little juvenile?"

Jess arched a dark brow. "As opposed to how you've been acting?"

Touché.

"Fine. Whatever."

Ashley finished her wine. With another wide yawn, she scooched lower on the couch.

"In the 'cons' column put down his superior attitude and his quickness to judge."

"Hang on," Jess said as the pen flew over the page. "I'm still filling in the 'pros' column."

Since Jess hadn't met Dallas, Ashley didn't know how she could possibly have that many things already written on the good side.

"Did you happen to get his last name?"

"No. Why?"

"We could see if he's on social media or we could do an online search."

"Stalk much?" Ashley asked.

Jess grinned. "Only when I need to."

"I didn't get his name, but he was driving a truck with a *Granger Construction* logo on it."

"Perfect. Let's start there."

Pulling out her cell, Jess's thumbs flew over the screen. Ashley knew it wasn't good when her friend's lips pursed. It was soon followed by a very satisfied grin.

"Looks like I can add gainfully employed to the pros column. And business owner."

"What?" Ashley took the phone Jess turned toward her.

Sure enough. On the home page for Granger Construction was a photo of Dallas. He wore the same gray T-shirt she'd seen him wear at the house but in the photo he was without his usual ball cap. His sandy-brown hair was cut short. The top was swept back and up, lightly gelled so it stood in place. It gave an unobstructed view of his gorgeous blue eyes. Before she started to drool, she handed the phone back to Jess.

Her friend kept filling the "pros" column.

Ashley would let Jess have her fun. No matter what Jess wrote it wasn't going to change Ashley's mind.

While Jess continued to happily fill out the sheet, Ashley checked her phone. It was only nine. Brittany had another hour until she had to be home. Yawning so hard it brought tears to her eyes, Ashley wondered how she'd manage to stay awake another hour.

"That's it." Jess put the pad and book onto the coffee table. "You're going to bed."

"I'm fine. Besides, I can't go to bed yet. You know I can't fall asleep until Brittany's home."

"I'll stay until she gets back. That way you can get the sleep you need." She held up a well-manicured hand. "I promise to wake you if she's not back on time."

She hated to do it. It made her feel like the worst kind of friend. But the truth was she was having a hard time keeping her eyes open.

"Ash, go. It's fine. Besides, Brittany and I haven't caught

up in a while. This will give us a chance for a little girl time."

"Okay, and thanks." Only because she knew Jess truly didn't mind. "I'll make it up to you."

"Nothing to make up. Besides," she added as she stretched her long legs across the couch, tossing a wink Ashley's way. "I'll be able to work on this list without outside interference."

"I'm allowed to have a say when it concerns my life."

"Not when this is something that can make it better."

She'd never say it couldn't get worse because life sometimes had a way of proving her wrong.

Since she wasn't one for too much makeup, it didn't take long before Ashley was curled onto her side, the sheet tucked under her chin. She glanced at her alarm clock. Ten after nine on a Saturday night and she was in bed. Alone.

Maybe Jess had a point.

Things could definitely stand to get a bit better.

"WHAT'S ALL THIS?"

Ashley couldn't believe her eyes. French toast, fruit, and a cup of steaming coffee waiting for her on the table. Served with a smile. A real one.

"Auntie Jess told me how tired you were last night and I know you worked a little longer yesterday because I missed Friday, so I wanted to make it up to you."

"But it's only—" She checked the clock on the microwave. "It's only nine o'clock."

She'd slept nearly twelve hours. Which was why Sunday

was her favorite day of the week. She felt incredible. Even without coffee.

"I got up early. I wanted to surprise you."

With pride swelling in her chest, Ashley gathered her daughter close and hugged her tight. "Mission accomplished."

They settled across from each other at a small bistro table Ashley had found at a garage sale and refurbished. Brittany had her long blonde hair piled in a messy bun on top of her head. Her normally heavily lined eyes were clear of makeup.

It tugged at Ashley's heart, made her a little melancholy for the days when her baby girl would toddle out of her big girl bed and climb into her mother's lap for morning cuddles. Proud as she was of the young woman Brittany was becoming, Ashley missed her little girl.

And in just over two years her daughter would be in college. It hurt Ashley's heart just to think about it.

Changing the subject to something that didn't make her want to cry Ashley asked, "So, what are you up to today?"

"I have an essay to finish for English. I'll want to get that done 'cause Maddy and I are going to hang out until supper."

"Ah, now I understand why you're *really* up early."

Her daughter smiled. "But I also wanted to make up for Friday."

"Well, either way, I appreciate this." Ashley sipped her coffee.

"You haven't forgotten about our spa night?"

"No, Mom," Brittany answered with a tone Ashley remembered from her own youth. A tone that clearly implied

"I'm not stupid, you know."

"Just making sure. We've both been so busy lately. I've missed our time together."

"I know. Me too."

Ashley finished her piece of toast, pulled a banana and some grapes from the bowl of fruit sitting between her and Brittany.

"How's chemistry going?" she asked as she peeled the banana. "Any better now that the teacher is helping?"

Brittany lowered her gaze. "Not really." She ran a piece of French toast through the puddle of syrup on her plate. "But he's offered to help more if I need it."

"Well, that's good. Take him up on it if you need it."

Eyes still on her plate, Brittany just nodded and cut another piece of toast.

Ashley reached across the table, covered her daughter's hand with her own. "There's nothing to be embarrassed about. I'm proud of you for realizing you need help and being brave enough to ask for it."

Brittany's cheeks turned deep red. "Thanks."

When she quickly stuffed the last bit of toast in her mouth and began clearing the table Ashley grabbed her wrist.

"You cooked, I clean. That's the deal, remember?"

"I can do it. Finish your breakfast."

"Cooking and cleaning? Should I be worried?"

Though it was said in jest there was a part of Ashley that tensed and braced for bad news. Usually when Brittany wanted something she buttered Ashley up first. Wide smiles, more hugs than usual. But then, Ashley had been the same. And when she'd found out she was pregnant…

Ashley's gaze snapped to the sink. Brittany had the water going and was squeezing blue dish soap into the stream. No, she couldn't be. Brittany didn't have a boyfriend. But then, Ashley hadn't had one she'd told her parents about either.

Ashley repressed the rising panic. She and her daughter had a close relationship. She'd brought up the topic of birth control many times in the past year but every time Brittany had immediately refused, said it wasn't necessary. That she wasn't ready. That she wasn't interested in anyone.

As though she felt her mother's gaze boring into her, Brittany peered over her shoulder, rolled her eyes. "No, Mom, you don't have anything to be worried about. It's just a little extra tutoring."

"All right," Ashley said with a smile. She poured another coffee and leaned back in her chair. "Then I won't worry."

"You're up early."

Dallas poured the final scoop of oats into the last of the eight buckets he had lined up before him.

"Sorry to rob you of the chance to haul my ass out of bed."

"Would have been satisfying, given all the times you did it to me growing up."

"I didn't like it any more than you did."

"Could've fooled me."

Dallas tossed the metal scoop into the bag of feed. "Is that how you remember it?"

"I remember you standing over my bed, ripping covers

off, and hollering at me to get up." Ryker stood hipshot. "I remember getting water tossed in my face and even literally getting dragged out of bed by my ankles."

"Because you slept like the dead. Usually by that time I'd already turned on the light and come in three times telling you to get up. I didn't have all day to baby you, Ryker. There was work to be done. You of all people should understand that now seeing as you dragged me back here to help you."

Ryker's face, which hadn't exactly been friendly to begin with, went to granite. Dallas didn't know what his brother's problem was, other than the fact that Dallas was breathing. Ryker had seemed to take exception to that ever since their mother died.

But, like then, Dallas didn't have time to coddle his brother. He had to finish feeding the horses, muck their stalls, and then build the horse shelter for the pasture that Ryker wanted. Then he still had to swing by the office and make sure everything was in order for the coming week.

Dallas lifted two of the buckets off the barn floor and headed down the dimly lit aisle. Though the doors at both ends of the barn were open, dawn had yet to brighten the sky and the only lights came from the few scattered bulbs overhead.

"It's all black and white to you, isn't it?"

Dallas let out a heavy sigh. Apparently, his brother hadn't dislodged the burr up his ass he'd clearly woken up with this morning. Dallas set the buckets down, turned. Ryker's hard glare bore into him like a laser.

"What are you talking about?"

"Jesus, don't pretend you don't know. Mom gets sick, suddenly you're Nurse Sally telling us when we can and can't go in and see her. In our own house! Then when Dad buries himself in work, you turn into some fucking general running us like your soldiers. And the minute you can walk out of here with your conscience clear that you did your time, you're gone."

Dallas jammed his hands onto his hips. "Should I have held your hand while I tried to get you up? Would that have made it all better?"

Ryker stalked down the aisle. Fury swirled in his eyes and tightened his jaw.

"You could have been human through it, dammit! You could have stepped from behind your metaphorical clipboard long enough to see you weren't the only one dealing with shit. I know you were given a lot of responsibility and maybe you didn't want it, but what about the rest of us?"

"What about you? Yeah, maybe I gave you a lot of chores and forced your ass down to do your homework, but someone had to. And I still had to go to school, help run the ranch, and raise you four when Dad was so far into his grief he couldn't see straight."

"So it's still all about you."

"Goddammit, none of that was about me!" Dallas kicked over one of the buckets.

Grain and oats went flying. The bucket skidded across the cement floor. Shit. Now he'd have to clean up the mess.

Ryker didn't seem to care. His scowl was etched into his face.

"Everything was about you. What you saw fit. What you

wanted to do. You never asked us. You just demanded. You never took a minute to look past your own agenda to see what we might have wanted. What we needed. That's what you did then. It's what you do now."

Ryker gave Dallas one last glare before he turned away. His brother was almost out of the barn before he shouted, "And don't forget that horse shelter before you leave."

Since the damage was already done Dallas gave the up-ended bucket another kick. Then another 'cause his blood was still running hot. The action spooked the horses. Feeling threatened, they kicked at the walls of their stalls.

"Sorry, guys," he soothed as he walked over and retrieved the empty bucket.

But as he refilled it, then began to go stall by stall feeding the mares their breakfasts, all he could think of was that working the Diamond G with his brothers was starting to feel like more of a punishment than his community service.

Chapter Seven

DALLAS WASN'T ONE to frequent trendy coffee shops. Typically, he was happy brewing a simple pot at home and filling his thermos. Not only because those fancy coffees were overpriced, but because other than a little creamer, he liked his coffee simple. Just as he liked most things simple.

But every so often nothing hit the spot quite like an iced coffee. Since *Coffee Time* was on his way to the office from the ranch and he figured he'd be at his desk at least an hour, he decided to stop. A shot of caffeine was just what he needed to clear off his desk and ensure he was ready for the coming week.

Even though he was pretty sure what he wanted, he perused the large chalkboard menu as he approached the counter. Deciding he didn't need a sugar rush to add to his caffeine fix, he opted for a regular iced coffee. Stepping up to the till he lowered his gaze to place his order.

And looked into a pair of familiar gold eyes. Eyes that still held some of the anger he'd last seen in them.

"Ashley."

"Hello, Dallas."

She didn't look as surprised to see him as he was to see her. But then she'd likely spotted him while he was looking at the menu.

"I didn't realize you work here." But it explained why she needed a house given to her. There was no way she could afford one working minimum wage at a coffee shop.

"Now you do. What can I get you?"

Ouch. But, as it wasn't completely undeserved, he didn't take offense to her unfriendly manner.

"A regular iced coffee please."

After giving him his change, she scrawled his name on the cup with a black marker and walked it to the barista. Her shoulders were stiff and her movements sharp. Since this wasn't the place to have a conversation, he quietly stepped to the side to await his order.

It didn't, however, stop him from looking at her. Her black slacks showcased the curve of her hips, her small waist. Not to mention what it did to her ass. He wanted to run his hands over those curves. Clamp his hands onto her hips and pull her against him. Feel the fullness of her breasts—

"Iced coffee for Dallas," the barista called, even though he was the only one standing there.

He reached for the drink, suddenly uncomfortably hot. He didn't know if he should gulp the coffee or pour it over his head to cool himself off.

Or you could stop staring at her.

Well, yeah. But where was the fun in that?

Smirking, he poked a straw through the plastic lid just as another employee stepped out of the back room carrying a fresh cash register tray. She smiled at Ashley.

"You're free to go as soon as you cash out."

"Perfect."

Ashley, who had yet to look Dallas's way since she'd given him his change, quickly took her tray and disappeared into the back office. Likely she figured he'd be long gone when she came out. Wouldn't she be surprised?

Walking back to the order counter he said, "I'm a friend of Ashley's. Can you tell me what she normally orders when she wants something? I thought I'd surprise her." He pulled out his wallet.

The young girl frowned. "She can get whatever she wants for free."

"Well, I'd still like to buy it, if you tell me what she likes."

And hopefully the gesture would help toward repairing the rift between them. Because they were going to be working together for the next month or so, maybe even longer now that he was putting in time at the ranch.

The ranch. He shook his head. Yeah, he needed to make things better with Ashley because he already had one job where he didn't feel welcome and appreciated. He didn't need another.

When she stepped out the front door of the coffee shop ten minutes later he was waiting. Rising from his seat, he snagged both their drinks from the round outdoor table.

"Ashley."

She looked over.

Shock registered on her face. "I thought you'd left."

"I wanted to talk to you. Make a peace offering." His mouth curved as he handed her the tall cup of iced tea.

He thought it was a good sign she accepted the drink rather than throw it in his face.

She took a sip, arched a brow. "Lucky guess?"

"Nah, I asked."

"I'm not sure why you bothered, but thank you."

He caught her elbow before she walked away. "Do you have a minute?"

He gestured to the plastic table and the red umbrella that helped shade the late afternoon sun. It wouldn't be as cool as sitting in the air-conditioning but since nobody else was out there, it would give them more privacy.

"Actually, I have plans so I should—"

"Please. I promise I won't take up much of your time."

Her shoulders drooped in surrender. "Fine."

Geeze. He didn't usually have to fight so hard to get a woman to talk to him.

He followed her to the table, positioning his chair so he wasn't right next to her, but he wasn't across from her either. It amused him more than insulted him when she moved her feet under her chair to keep from touching his.

Though he'd promised not to take up a lot of her time, Dallas didn't rush into his apology. Instead, he watched her for a few moments while he sipped his coffee. As it had been at the *House of Hope*, her wavy hair was tied back in a ponytail.

Far as he could tell, and he was no expert, the only makeup she wore was some mascara to darken her lashes. Not that she needed more. In fact, Dallas was a believer that where makeup was concerned, less was more. He preferred women who looked natural. He was a sucker for the girl next door.

Ashley fit that description. Simple ponytail. No flat iron to smooth out the natural wave of her hair. She kept her bangs hovering just above her brows, which were a few shades darker than her hair. Her lips were naturally pink and the only color he'd ever seen darken her cheeks came from her emotions. Currently, there was a hint of pink to them. Could be a natural reaction to being outside but he suspected some of it had to do with him.

"I just wanted to apologize for the other day. You were right. I was hasty in my judgment."

She raised her brows.

He leaned back in his chair, took a slow pull on his straw. "You look surprised."

"I guess I am. I didn't figure you for a guy who ever admitted he was wrong."

Amused, Dallas responded, "Now, who's being judgmental?"

She tipped her head. "Sorry."

"Don't be. Might not be right or fair, but we all judge based on our experiences."

Honey-gold eyes met his. "You have lots of experience with homeless men and single mothers?"

"You're a single mother?" The words tumbled out before he could stop them.

Her back stiffened. "Let me guess, that's something else you have a problem with?" Shaking her head she came to her feet. "Thanks for the lovely chat." Sarcasm dripped from every syllable.

Again he stopped her, this time by boxing her in between his body and the table. "I didn't mean anything by that. It just surprised me is all."

Her chin rose. "Surely you saw Brittany at the site on

Saturday."

"The teenager? Well, yeah, but you were both already there when I got there and it's not like I was watching to see who you left with." He shrugged. "I thought she was just another volunteer."

"Well, now you know."

And now that he did, he kicked himself. Not only for putting his foot in his mouth but for not seeing the resemblance. Thinking back, he could see they looked quite a bit alike.

He took a deep breath, stepped back. "I'd hoped to apologize so working together this coming week wouldn't be as uncomfortable as yesterday and Friday was." He offered a crooked smile. "I don't think I gained anything."

She looked away before meeting his gaze again. "I had Brittany two months before my seventeenth birthday. Let's just say I've had more than enough judgment aimed my way so I tend to be defensive."

He raised his palms. "I was just surprised. I didn't mean it as anything negative."

"Okay." She exhaled loudly. "I really do have to go. I promised Brittany I'd go home right after work."

He reached over, lifted her iced tea off the table and held it out to her. "So we're good?"

She paused for a moment before answering.

"Yeah," she said as she reclaimed her drink. "See you tomorrow."

"See you tomorrow," he murmured as he grabbed his drink and turned toward his truck.

He lurched to a stop when a god-awful squeal blasted

through the mostly empty parking lot. Turning, he saw it was Ashley's old car that sounded like a stuck pig. He saw her teeth graze her bottom lip as her mouth moved. His own twitched when he recognized the expletive she'd just uttered.

Though the squeal faded as she drove away, his curiosity lingered. There was more to Ashley than he'd first assumed. The idea he'd had of the person benefiting from the *House of Hope* was crumbling. The two days he'd worked with her proved she wasn't afraid of manual labor. Now he knew she also worked at the coffee shop and was raising a daughter on her own.

Was the father in the picture? Her parents? Surely at not quite seventeen she hadn't raised her daughter completely alone?

Of course none of it was his business. But as he set his iced coffee in the cupholder of his truck and buckled his seat belt, his mind stayed fixed on Ashley.

She remained in his thoughts as he sat at his desk at Granger Construction, looking over blueprints, making lists, and sending emails. Even after he'd gotten home and showered off the day his thoughts circled back to her.

He'd seen her physical strength at the *House of Hope* but this afternoon he'd gotten a glimpse of her mental strength as well. And a little peek into her life.

A peek that, along with her beauty and sexy little body, left him wanting more.

DESPITE HAVING STAYED up too late last night going

through the classifieds and employment-related search engines online, Ashley was in a good mood when she parked behind Rick's truck at the construction site. Even the cursed generator rumbling in the backyard couldn't dampen her excitement.

She'd found a lead on a job and with any luck would have a replacement for the one she'd lost at Eugene's Small Engine Repair. To make things even better, she saw more studs had gone up when she stepped into the house. Ashley stopped to admire them. Over there was her kitchen and that short wall, what Rick called the pony wall, would separate her dining room from her living room.

It was still nothing but bare two-by-fours but when Ashley looked at it she saw her completed kitchen. Saw the cupboards and countertops, a bunch of bananas ripening on the counter, the gleaming sink.

She saw herself sitting at the kitchen table having her morning cup of coffee while the sun streamed in. She moved to where she envisioned the table would be and for a moment the generator, the hammers, the air compressor fell silent.

It was just her in her sunny kitchen, her favorite mug in hand. Without having to smell whatever the neighbors were cooking for breakfast. Or worse, had cooked the previous night for supper.

It couldn't come fast enough.

And it would get there even faster if she stopped daydreaming and got to work.

For the next hour, she worked alongside Rick and Jeff as they finished framing the kitchen and pantry. Thank goodness she was mostly the one holding the wood in place and not the one manning the nail gun. Because ever since Rick had told her that as soon as Dallas arrived, she'd be back working outside on the siding with him, she'd struggled to concentrate.

Though, in truth, she'd have struggled anyway.

She'd been struggling to think of anything *but* Dallas since she'd looked up and seen him standing inside *Coffee Time*. Shortly after the initial shock of him being there had worn off, all the anger she felt toward him had rushed to the surface. What had been equally upsetting, however, was that it wasn't just anger that rose hot and fast.

It was lust. She'd taken a look at his blue eyes, the backward-facing ball cap and scruff, and all her woman parts had steamed like an espresso machine making a latte. Which had made her even angrier. He'd made his opinion of her clear. It should have been more than enough to cool the desire.

And maybe it would have, given time. But then he'd waited for her, bought her favorite drink, and apologized.

She hadn't had a prayer after that.

Brittany had noticed her mother's distraction and commented several times when Ashley zoned out during their spa night. Ashley had just claimed to be tired but when she had finally called it a night a few hours later, once she had bright red toenails and fingernails, she'd lain awake tossing and turning and dreaming of blue eyes and a gravelly voice.

And now, here she was doing the same thing again. Only instead of tossing and turning, her gaze kept lifting to the back door. It was like being a teenager all over again. With excitement dancing in her belly. With her heartbeat racing.

Wondering what he'd look like today, what he'd say. If they'd accidentally touch.

At her age, that was just pathetic.

Yet it didn't stop her belly from clenching when he finally strode through the back door. Of course, the low slung tool belt didn't help. It reminded her of a meme she'd seen once of a hot-looking shirtless repairman with the caption, "I don't know what he's fixing but mine just broke."

His gaze scanned the space, lingered on her a moment, then met Rick's.

"Small crew today," he commented.

"That's usual for a Monday." Rick came to his feet. "Jeff and I'll keep framing. Thought I'd get you and Ashley back on the siding."

Blue eyes fixed on hers. "I've got no problem with that."

His low voice poured over her. Ashley's toes curled in her work boots.

"All right. I'll let you two get to it." He turned to Jeff. "I'll be right back; I need to make a quick call."

Jeff hooked his hammer into his tool belt. "That's fine. I could use a coffee."

Jeff strolled to the makeshift table made of two sawhorses and a sheet of plywood. He poured some steaming black brew into the cap of his thermos.

"I'm ready if you are, unless you need a break too?" Dallas asked.

"Actually I have a quick call to make as well. But it won't take long."

Since the quietest place to make a call was the front yard where she was furthest away from the power tools, Ashley went there. She pulled her phone and the paper she'd written the number on from her back pocket.

A man picked up on the third ring. "Frank's Hauling."

"Yes, hello. My name is Ashley Anderson. I'm calling about your ad for a part-time bookkeeper."

He must have been driving because between the background noise and the poor connection she missed everything he said but the last word.

"I'm sorry, I didn't catch any of that," she said.

"Yeah, sorry. I'm out in the country and between the lousy cell service and the shape of this gravel road I can barely hear you either. What I said was that you just missed it. I filled the job about an hour ago."

Ashley's hopes sank. "Oh. I see. Well, thanks anyway."

"Yep. No problem."

Ashley disconnected the call. She stood staring at the screen, her insides in a knot. Now what was she going to do? That had been the only ad for a part-time bookkeeper.

"Damn."

"Bad news?"

She looked up. Dallas held his hands in apology.

"I didn't mean to eavesdrop. Rick sent me out for more nails. I couldn't help overhearing."

"It's fine." Ashley slid her phone into her back pocket, crumpled the paper in her fist. "It was just a job I'd hoped to apply for but it's been filled already."

He angled his head. "Not happy at the coffee shop?"

"I'm not leaving *Coffee Time*. This was to replace one of my other ones."

His brows arched. "*One* of your other ones? How many

do you have?"

She sighed. "Some days it feels like a dozen."

"What else do you do?"

"I do part-time bookkeeping for a number of small businesses. One of them will be closing next week. I need to replace it."

Frowning, he asked. "How many?"

Ashley placed her hands on her hips. "Well, there's the small engine repair company on Mondays and Thursdays and the landscaping company on Tuesdays and Fridays. Then on Wednesdays there's the body shop. On top of the small engine repair shop on Thursdays I also have the bowling alley. Fridays I work for a small independent bakery."

Confusion filled his blue eyes. "How do you have time for all that?"

"They're all small businesses so they don't take more than a few hours at a time. To fill in the rest, I work at *Coffee Time* and volunteer here."

He shook his head. "Wouldn't it be easier to just have one full-time job?"

"Sure it would. But I've never been that lucky and honestly most of those places I work at are flexible. If I can't come in that day or need to come in later or earlier, I can. That wouldn't be as easy with a full-time job."

He still looked confused. "So you manage all that, raising a daughter, and volunteering here?"

His shock annoyed her. Mostly because it reminded her of their first meeting when he'd made the comment about how *he'd* paid for his house.

"Well, I need to pay my bills. I can't exactly stop raising my daughter and the deal with *Houses of Hope*, a house I'll have a mortgage on by the way, is we also have to put in a minimum number of hours. So, yeah, I have no choice but to manage all that." Hearing her own bitchiness, she cringed. "Sorry. I'd hoped for better news. I didn't mean to take it out on you."

"Hey, no worries. In fact—"

"Dallas!" Rick stood in the open front doorway. "You bringing those nails?"

"Yeah, coming."

Ashley took a step back. Having seen the boxes of siding and scaffolding already at the side of the house, she gestured in that direction. "I'll meet you over there."

But as she trudged over her mind wasn't on the pretty blue siding. Nor was it on the good-looking man she'd been looking forward to working alongside.

Instead, all she could think about was that next week she was out one job and she had no idea how'd she manage if she couldn't find another before then.

Chapter Eight

DALLAS WASN'T ONE to trust things that came too easily. Not when nothing in his life had ever come that way. He'd fought tooth and nail to get what he had and there were many days when he still did. When he felt it was him against the world.

He recognized that feeling in Ashley. Had seen the defeat weigh down her shoulders when the call hadn't gone as she'd hoped. It made him feel like an ass because while she'd been working all those jobs and raising a daughter, he'd assumed she was living a life of leisure and getting a house handed to her for free.

While he'd already apologized for his assumption, it didn't make up for how he'd made her feel. But there was something he could do that would.

He caught up with her just as she was pulling a vinyl slat out of the box.

"Hang on a sec," he said as he took it from her hand and set it back on the ground.

Her hands fell to her sides. "Dallas, let's just get to work."

"This won't take long, I promise. But I have a solution for your problem."

"You won the lottery and want to share?"

His lips curved. "No. But I have a job for you. My dad was recently admitted to the hospital and we don't know how long he'll be in there."

"Oh, my God. Is it serious?"

"Yeah," he answered as guilt settled over him. Other than a quick text to Cam early that morning to see how Joe was doing, Dallas hadn't given his dad much thought.

"He's had a heart attack and is in a coma. We don't know how long he'll be like that. It's a waiting game at this point."

She touched his arm. "I'm so sorry."

So was he. That didn't stop him from appreciating the fact the news had drawn her to touch him.

"Thanks. Anyway, he does the bookwork for our ranch and none of us have the knowledge or desire to learn how to do it."

"None of you?"

"Me and my brothers. There's five of us in all, but Hudson is off on active duty in the Middle East so there's four of us left to help run the ranch. Anyway, with Dad out of commission and his office a mess, from what I hear, we could use a bookkeeper."

She looked like a child who was being offered candy but was too shy to take it.

"The hours are flexible," he added. "We just need someone to cover while he's laid up."

She pursed her lips. "So it would be temporary?"

"Yeah. But if you find something permanent before he gets better, that's fine too. In the meantime, though, it'll help us both out."

"But you said it was a ranch. How far out of the city?"

"Actually it's outside Last Stand."

Her eyes widened. "That far?"

"It takes just over an hour. Sometimes it can take that long just to cross the city, depending on traffic."

Ashley shook her head. "I don't trust my car to go that far. As I'm sure you heard the other night," she said looking embarrassed, "it's not in the best shape. It's why all the jobs I have are within a half hour from home."

"Tell you what. I'll follow you out the first time. That way if it breaks down you won't be stranded. If it doesn't, or even if it does, my brother Ryker can have a look at it. Don't worry; he's qualified. He and my dad run the ranch but he's also a certified mechanic."

"I can't afford that. It's why I haven't fixed that squeal to begin with."

"Then he can just look at it. See what it needs. Give you an estimate. At least then when you decide to fix it you'll know what you're looking at for price and you won't get gouged by another mechanic. Then the next time you come to the ranch, we can carpool in my truck. That way you won't waste gas or have to worry about your car."

She shook her head. "I can't ask you to do that."

"You're not. I'm volunteering. Besides, it's not like I'd be making a special trip. I have to go anyway."

And if the times she could get away didn't mesh with when he'd told Ryker he'd be there then he'd just have to modify his schedule and his brother was going to have to adjust.

Because he could see the uncertainty on her face he said,

"Just think about it."

And before she could argue, he grabbed a vinyl slat and got to work.

HAVING WORKED WITH Dallas before and feeling confident in what she was doing, they fell into an easy rhythm. She was grateful he seemed to prefer working in silence, as she'd have been hard pressed to make small talk. Her mind was still spinning from his offer.

On the one hand it was the answer to her prayers. A job with flexible hours that would allow her to keep all her other commitments. A ride where she wouldn't have to worry about her car leaving her stranded.

But the other hand held all kinds of dangers. Well, one really. A sexy, hot man who made her feel like a woman again. A man who'd already slid into her dreams. Sharing the confines of a vehicle for a few hours each time they went to Last Stand?

It would make working and sweating in the Texas sun feel like a cool dip in a pool.

Dammit, she shouldn't have thought of a pool. Now she yearned for it. What she wouldn't give to jump in and cool herself from the relentless sun. Her bra was damp, her T-shirt stuck to her. Even though her ponytail was looped through the back of a ball cap, her neck felt as though it was being torched.

Ashley finished attaching her end of the slat. She wiped the sweat running down her temple.

"I need a drink."

She put down her hammer, moved to the shady part of the yard where she'd left her water bottle. Even as she gulped it down she wished she had another to pour over her head.

Dallas joined her. His gray T-shirt bore wet spots of sweat, but it only added to his appeal. So did the scruff covering his face and the way his throat worked when he drank from his own thermos.

"It's not a cold beer, but it'll do for now," he said, smiling at her.

Oh, man, she was in a heap of trouble. When had a slightly crooked eyetooth become the sexiest thing ever? Not to mention the crinkles at the corners of his twinkling blue eyes. But then, she'd yet to find anything about Dallas Granger that *wasn't* sexy.

At least she could blame the heat for the flush burning her cheeks.

Before she further embarrassed herself she set down her bottle and walked back into the sunshine. She could almost hear the sweat sizzle on her skin. Pulling the phone from her pocket she nearly whimpered when she saw she had less than two hours left.

Thank God.

They made good progress, though, which was one consolation as the sun continued its relentless assault. The other, of course, was having Dallas working alongside her. If she had to suffer the interminable heat and humidity, at least she had his nearness and good looks to distract her from the miserable conditions.

Not that it worked completely. Because every time she

looked his way, witnessed the play of muscles as he hammered in a nail or reached for another length of siding, she only got hotter.

They were almost at the point where they'd need the scaffold to go higher. Ashley was stretching up to attach her end of the slat when Rick poked his head around the corner.

"Ashley, can you come in for a second? I want to run an idea past you."

"Yeah, sure."

Figuring she'd just finish what she was doing first, she was surprised when Dallas came up behind her. He leaned over her, placed his hands on the piece of siding to hold it in place.

"I've got it."

Her mouth couldn't form words. With his arms outstretched like that, his body formed a lean-to against the house. With her nestled inside. If she turned she'd come face-to-face with him. Possibly mouth to mouth.

Her lower body clenched hard. It wasn't difficult to picture, not with the smell of his salty skin filling her senses. With the heat of his body so close to her back. Though she'd never had sex against a wall, or even from behind, she had a damn good imagination and had read enough romance novels to envision it now.

"Aren't you going to go?"

Thank God she had her back to him so he couldn't tell the effect he had on her. Ducking under his arms, though with her height it took little ducking, she scurried away.

She spent the next half hour going over a few things with Rick. He had some suggestions that weren't on the blueprints he wanted to go over with her. It would've been a better reprieve from her hormones if, after ten minutes, he hadn't asked for Dallas's input.

Together the three of them discussed modifying the hall closet and moving the access to the laundry room.

"I think this will make a better use of space. What do you think, Dallas?"

"I agree. Flows better too. Otherwise it would feel a little blocked in."

Ashley was more of a visual person so she had trouble seeing it until Dallas sketched out what they meant on the back of a napkin.

"Yes, I see now. You're right, that is better. Thanks."

She smiled at both Dallas and Rick but only Dallas's return grin made her breath catch.

When Rick called it a day they went about hauling tools to his trailer and securing the house. Since Dallas was parked behind the house as usual and she was behind Rick at the front, it surprised her when Dallas didn't immediately go around back.

"Ashley, hold up."

She stopped, turned. And caught Rick's grin from the corner of her eye.

"Have you made a decision about the job at the ranch?"

"I thought you told me to think about it."

"Well, I was hoping you had by now." His mouth curved mischievously.

A grin like that should be illegal. It fried all common sense.

"Please?" he added. "I really don't have time to interview

anyone and you need a job so…"

"How do you know I'm any good? Shouldn't you check references? And I'm not familiar in every accounting program. I may not even know the one your dad uses."

"Actually, I would like to check your references. It's nothing personal," he added.

"Believe it or not, I'm glad you want to check. Makes it feel less like charity."

"Perfect. And as for the software, I can probably find that out. But if your references are what I expect and the program is one you know, what do you say?"

She knew what she should say. A resounding no.

But she'd been feeling in a funk lately, one made especially noticeable when she hadn't been able to keep awake past nine on Saturday night. She was only thirty-one for goodness' sake. While she wasn't the partying sort, there had to be more to life than working all the time.

It was depressing sometimes waking up in the morning knowing exactly what awaited her that day. Nothing exciting ever happened. At least not to her. Which was fine most days. She was a mother. She had a job to do and took it seriously. She wasn't the kind who serial dated, who brought home a new man every few days or weeks. Who went to the bar and got drunk.

And she had no desire to be.

But a little variety in her otherwise dull life sounded like heaven. It would give her a chance to get out of the city, which she never did otherwise. And a ranch? She inhaled sharply. Well, wasn't that every girl's dream? It sure had been hers before she'd discovered she'd been pregnant.

Cowboys in Texas weren't exactly a rare occurrence but they were rare in Ashley's small circle and, as cliché as it was, there was just something about a man with a hat riding a horse.

She studied Dallas. She'd only ever seen him with a ball cap but there was enough swagger in his gait to picture him on a horse. And if he traded his ball cap for a Stetson?

Lord, help her.

"Well? What do you say?"

For the first time since she'd been sixteen, Ashley threw caution to the wind and followed her heart instead of her mind.

Brittany might not have been planned but her daughter was the best mistake she'd ever made. Maybe this would prove to be as well.

"Okay, Dallas. Looks like you might have found yourself a temporary bookkeeper."

His sexy mouth curved. "Well, all right, then."

IT WAS LATER than Dallas had planned when he turned down the long oak-lined driveway to the Diamond G. No doubt, he'd never hear the end of it from Ryker. Well, his brother was going to have to get over it. He still had a business to run and he felt better after putting in a few hours at each jobsite. After seeing they were on time and on budget.

And he'd also checked Ashley's references, which should appease his brother. Hopefully telling Ryker he had one of his problems solved would put his brother in a better mood.

"Yeah, like that's possible," Dallas scoffed as he parked.

He'd grabbed a burger on the fly so he headed straight for the paddock where Cam and a spirited paint were battling for supremacy.

The gelding wanted no part of the man on his back. The animal practically drilled his face into the ground, forcing Cam to lean back in the saddle. The gelding twisted, kicked his hind legs almost straight up the air. He spun first to the left then the right.

With a twist of his lips, Dallas strode for the fence. Propping a boot on the bottom rail, he folded his hands over the top. And waited for the perfect time.

The next time the bronc poised to kick, Dallas shoved his index and pinky fingers in his mouth and let loose a loud, shrill whistle. As expected, Cam whipped his head in Dallas's direction. As though the gelding knew his rider wasn't paying full attention, he twisted and bucked and within seconds of Dallas's whistle, sent Cam flying.

His brother's black hat soared through the air and landed in the dirt, narrowly missing a pile of horse shit. Cam wasn't so lucky. He slid right through the middle of it and when he rolled to his feet, shit was smeared from his shoulder to his waist.

"Bastard," Cam swore as he reached down for his hat.

Dallas was pretty sure his brother was referring to him as much as the horse.

"Just as I was getting somewhere," Cam muttered as he turned his glare first on the gelding then on Dallas. "You better have had a good reason for doing that other than to see me dumped on my ass."

"That's not enough reason?"

Cam shot up his middle finger.

Dallas laughed. "If I'm going to be here more often, I may as well have a little fun."

He looked over to the barn, past that to the pastures and then up by the house. "Where is everyone?"

"Gage is at work and since you didn't show up until suppertime," Cam said as he opted to climb over the fence rather than go through the gate, "Ryker's probably in the house eating another frozen pizza. Geeze, you'd think after being a bachelor this long he'd have learned to cook by now."

"And you have?" Dallas asked.

Cam jumped to the ground. Crossing his arms, he leaned against the rails. "I've never had to. I'm on the road so much. I've got enough gear to haul around without carrying a portable barbecue and cooking supplies. Besides," he added with a knowing grin, "I've never had trouble getting a home-cooked meal when I want one."

"Jesus, Cam, do you ever keep it in your pants?"

"Not if I can help it," Cam answered.

Dallas rolled his eyes. "One of these days that pecker you're so proud of is going to fall off."

"I might play hard, but I also play smart."

Dallas held up his hand. "Spare me the details."

"Are you sure? I have a feeling I can teach you a thing or two."

"I doubt it."

Cam pushed off the fence. "You keep telling yourself

that."

"Where are you going?"

"To clean up and eat. Frozen pizza or not I'm still starving."

He stopped after two strides and turned around. "When you're done mucking out the corral, feel free to unsaddle and take care of my horse. He goes in stall seven when you're done." Cam smirked. "It may need mucking too."

He never bothered to ask if Dallas had eaten or to invite him in to share the pizza. Though Dallas wasn't hungry, Cam didn't know that. And apparently, he didn't care.

Dallas would have chalked that up to payback for getting Cam thrown but it wasn't the first time he was made to feel like an outsider.

Nobody asked him about his business or his life. And other than giving them a hand, they didn't really want him there. Despite what he'd done for them, they didn't give a rat's ass about him.

It hurt, dammit.

He wanted to crack a beer with them, bullshit around the kitchen table. Even if it was over frozen pizza. He wanted to know what was going on in their lives and share with them a little of his. He wanted to be seen as more than just an extra pair of hands.

He looked toward the house. Pressure built in his chest as he pictured Cam and Ryker sitting inside eating and talking together. Or he assumed they were. Truth was even though they didn't include him in their conversations, there really wasn't much said when he was around. He didn't know if that was because he was around or if that was how they normally were.

Shit, he really didn't know much about his brothers or his family anymore. But one thing was clear. If he wanted that to change it was going to have to start with him.

Chapter Nine

ASHLEY DUMPED THE full laundry basket next to the couch.

"Sorry about that. But the machines are much quieter during the week. I can get it all done in about half the time that I can on the weekend."

"No problem." Jess tucked her long legs next to her hip. "You must be looking forward to having your own washer and dryer."

"Oh, my God, yes. It can't come soon enough."

Ashley had had more than enough schlepping baskets of laundry up and down two flights of stairs. Not to mention having to keep her eye on the time so her wet clothes didn't end up in soggy heap on top of the washer.

Jess picked another chip from the bowl and pointed it to the cell phone lying on the end table. "You got a text while you were gone," she said before popping the chip into her mouth.

Ashley glanced at the clock. It was only seven thirty. Brittany was working the closing shift at the drugstore and the one real friend who texted her on a regular basis was sitting on the other end of her couch.

But there *was* someone she'd recently given her number to that could be texting. Butterflies filled Ashley's stomach as she reached for her phone.

"That must be some text."

Ashley finished replying and hit send. "What makes you say that?" she asked, facing Jess.

Jess rolled her eyes. "Oh, I don't know. The fact you're blushing? The fact you haven't stopped smiling since you picked up the phone?"

"I have a new job," Ashley answered. She settled back onto her end of the couch, the phone clutched in her hand.

"New jobs don't make anyone blush."

Ashley grabbed her phone as it announced another text. She was glad for the reprieve. If only for a minute.

"Ash," Jess prompted.

"Okay. I have a temporary job doing bookwork for a ranch out near Last Stand."

"Oh." Disappointment pulled at Jess's mouth. "For a second there I was hoping maybe the texts had something to do with that sexy construction worker."

Ashley's cheeked burned.

"They do, don't they?"

"He offered me a temporary bookkeeping job at his family's ranch near Last Stand."

"That's awful far."

"Yeah, but I won't be the one driving."

"Ah. Now I see the reason for the blush," Jess said, a knowing look on her face.

"It's silly. *I'm* silly. He overheard me calling for a job that I'd found online, but was filled by the time I called. Since his dad is sick and can't look after the bookwork, he suggested I work at the ranch."

She tossed her phone onto the cushions. Saying it out loud made her feel even more like a fool.

"I'm getting myself all worked up when all he did was find a solution to both our problems."

"But you said he's driving you out to the ranch. He doesn't have to do that."

"He's only doing it because I told him I didn't trust my car to get there. Honestly, he sounded pretty desperate for the help. I'm sure it's nothing more than that on his end. Besides, a man who looks like that isn't single."

Jess tipped her head. "Didn't you say he bought you iced tea and waited for you outside *Coffee Time* the other day?"

"So?"

"So." Jess stretched out the syllable. "If he was seeing someone why would he do that? Why would he care if he'd insulted you?"

"Because he's a nicer guy than I gave him credit for. He even offered to have his brother look at my car."

Excitement danced in Jess's eyes. "He did? Well, that's awful chivalrous. And going quite a bit out of his way to help you. Sounds like he's interested to me."

Ashley wanted to believe it. More than she probably should, given that her last attempts at dating had failed so miserably and chipped away at her self-esteem. But there was something about Dallas and how she felt around him that was different than anything she'd experienced before.

"So when do you start?"

Just as Jess asked, Ashley's phone whistled. Jess lunged for it but Ashley was faster. She yanked the phone off the couch, read the text over a few times.

"Well? Are you going to make me wait all night?"

Ashley pressed her hand over her suddenly queasy stomach.

"Looks like I start tomorrow."

DALLAS KEPT AN eye on his rearview mirror. Even though he'd given her directions and knew she could find the Diamond G on her own if they got separated, he'd promised her he'd keep an eye on her to ensure she and her car made it to Last Stand.

Which was why he was currently pulled over on the outskirts of San Antonio with his hazards flashing. Between the start of rush hour traffic and a few yellow lights that had him hurrying through the intersection, he'd lost her.

He tapped his fingers along to an old favorite of Alabama's as he waited for her sedan to come into view. Just as the band proved why it was better with a fiddle player in it, he spotted Ashley's faded car.

Exchanging his hazards for a turn signal, Dallas eased into the lane in front of her. They made the rest of the trip without incident. The clear blue sky stretched unmarred overhead. His aviators protected his eyes from the beating sun. The air coming through his vents was cool and refreshing and when he felt thirsty he had a bottle of iced tea in his cupholder.

Ashley's car held up, which was good. As was the fact that because he'd driven slower than usual with her following, neither of the two highway patrol officers they passed turned around to give him a citation.

All in all, he couldn't have asked for better. Well, Ashley sitting next to him would have better.

Much as he loved country music, he would have preferred hearing her sweet voice. And though he'd taken the time to wash up at the office, he'd have preferred to smell her citrusy shampoo than the clean scent of his deodorant.

But he'd have to wait for the next trip for that. He was looking forward to it already.

Funny, he hadn't looked forward to coming home since he'd left to strike out on his own. For the first time in over a decade, he had a smile on his face when he stepped out of his truck.

He figured the smile wouldn't last, not once he saw Ryker. His brother would find fault with something. He hadn't been as happy as he should have been when Dallas had told him about Ashley.

Considering Ryker hated paperwork like the rest of them he should have been relieved Dallas had found a bookkeeper so fast. Instead, he'd grilled Dallas about who Ashley was, how he knew her, and a whole laundry list of other minutiae.

Until Dallas had given his brother very clear instructions on where he could shove his questions. Dallas wasn't just going to pick some stranger off the street to deal with something as important as the ranch books.

Nevertheless, Dallas had emailed Ryker Ashley's resume then had texted him yesterday to say her reference had checked out.

No doubt it had stuck in his brother's craw that Dallas had actually found someone who was qualified.

Well, Ryker would just have to get over it. Wherever the hell he was. Dallas looked around. He didn't see his brother anywhere. The only thing moving in the corrals were the horses. He glanced over to the machine shed. The big doors were open and one of their tractors filled the front.

It wasn't until he heard a loud curse followed immediately by the clang of a wrench hitting the cement floor that he spotted Ryker's legs sticking out from underneath the orange tractor.

"Sorry about the language. He mustn't have heard us drive in."

Dallas looked over the hood of his truck to Ashley but she didn't seem concerned with Ryker's swearing. Nor did she seem to have even heard what he'd just said.

She stood between the car and the open driver's door. A soft smile curved her lips. Though he couldn't see it, he knew she had a dreamy look in her eye.

What was it with women and horses?

No wonder Cam was so damn cocky. He probably didn't have to do anything more than stand near a horse to get a woman interested in him. But add the shiny rodeo buckle, cowboy hat, and easy grin and he likely had to fight them off.

Dallas shook his head. It wasn't that he was interested in playing fast and loose like Cam did, but it stung his ego that he had to work much harder at getting dates than Cam.

One of the rare occasions when he and Cam had been home at the same time, they'd gone to Last Stand Saloon. Before they'd even made it to a table, Cam had one woman brushing up against him and another winking at him from the bar.

When Dallas had grumbled he didn't see what was so special about him, Cam had laughed and said it was Dallas's own fault. That he looked too serious. Women liked to have a good time. If he didn't always look like he had a stick up his ass, he might get lucky more often.

Dallas frowned, remembering. But unlike Cam, Dallas never had the luxury of being young and carefree as a teenager. And as an adult he had a hell of a lot more obligation than just a horse and trailer. So, yeah, maybe he wasn't as much fun. But he had reason.

Realizing he was standing close to a beautiful woman scowling, Dallas gave himself a mental kick in the ass and focused on what was before him. He'd been looking forward to spending time with Ashley. He needed to get Cam out of his bloody head.

Dallas stopped next to her open door.

"We can go closer if you want."

She looked at him. He'd been right. There was a dreamy look in her gold eyes.

"We can spare the time?"

"Course we can."

He smiled when she all but raced to the fence, leaving her door open. He closed it then followed at a more leisurely pace. No point rushing when he was enjoying the view. Her denim shorts were old and faded but they showcased her ass just fine.

Dallas joined her at the rail. "Did you have horses growing up?"

"I wish. We lived in the city. And even if we hadn't,

there wouldn't have been money for horses." She tipped her shoulder. "Dad was a custodian and Mom worked as a bank teller. There was barely enough for the basics."

"Any of your friends have any?"

"There was one friend growing up that did. Kayla. I used to go to sleepovers at her house and we'd ride for hours."

Her tone turned wistful but there wasn't much happy about Ashley's expression.

"What happened?"

"I got pregnant. As soon as her parents found out they forbade her from having anything to do with me. Didn't want my 'wild ways' to rub off on their daughter."

"That's shitty."

"Yeah. But they were hardly the only ones." She gave another dismissive shrug. "I got used to it."

"You shouldn't have had to." He hated that she'd been treated that way.

"Maybe not. But that's life. It doesn't always play fair."

He thought of his mom dying and what had been thrust upon him when his dad fell apart. "No, it sure doesn't."

"But then there are moments like these. Green grass, rolling hills, clear blue sky. Horses cropping in the pasture, birds singing in the bushes, and I can't help but think it isn't all bad either."

Her smile was soft as she looked at the animals. The sun turned her pale hair into spun gold. Her breasts stretched the soft yellow cotton of her T-shirt.

No, it sure as hell wasn't bad at all.

"I can get a bucket of oats. That'll bring them over, let you pet them."

She pushed away from the fence. "Thanks but I should probably get to work. You aren't paying me to stand around and admire your horses."

Maybe not, but if it kept the smile on her face he'd consider it.

Still, she had a point. They both had a lot to do this afternoon.

"I'll show you to the house."

They turned and Dallas had to bite back a groan. Cam was riding toward them, white teeth gleaming under the brim of his Stetson as his gaze zeroed in on Ashley. From the corner of his eye, Dallas saw Ashley's smile was nearly as big as Cam's belt buckle.

Shit. He should have taken her to the house as soon as they'd arrived.

"Well, if I'd known there was a pretty lady waiting I'd have come back sooner," Cam said. He tipped the brim of his tan Stetson in greeting. "I'm Cam."

"Cam, this is Ashley, the bookkeeper I hired to help make sense of Dad's office. Ashley, my brother Cam."

His brother leaned forward, braced his forearm on the pommel. "It's always a pleasure to meet a lady who's both pretty and smart."

Ashley ducked her head. "Thank you," she answered.

Seeing the blush ride her cheekbones soured Dallas's mood. Clearly, she wasn't immune to Cam's charm. But a man like Cam was the last thing Ashley needed in her life. He didn't know the first thing about commitment and a single mother didn't need some rodeo cowboy who was only interested in having a good time.

Dallas put his hand on the small of Ashley's back. "Come on, I'll show you where the office is."

But once again he was waylaid by one of his brothers. This time it was Ryker blocking his path to the house. Only he wasn't in the jovial mood Cam was. Dallas was pretty sure it had nothing to do with the grease smearing Ryker's right cheek. It could be partially due to the red welt on his forehead, likely from the wrench and curse Dallas had heard when he'd first gotten there.

But Dallas suspected most of it had to do with him since Ryker's scowl was directed firmly at his face. Luckily, their parents, and Dallas when neither could any longer, had drilled manners into him so when Ryker did shift his attention to Ashley, his brother no longer looked as though he wanted to commit murder.

And he had the decency to put the rag hanging out of his pocket to use. He wiped off the grease and his scowl before he extended a hand. Hell, he looked downright civilized when his mouth tipped into a smile.

"Ashley, right? I'm Ryker."

"Hi." She shook his hand.

"I was just about to show her—"

Temper flashed through Ryker's green eyes when he turned them on Dallas.

"Actually, you and Cam are going to the east wheat field. Irrigation pipe broke there this morning and a few more looked about ready to calve. I only had time to shut off the pump because Dad's lawyer was coming to talk about invoking his power of attorney."

Which explained some of Ryker's foul mood.

Dallas turned to Cam. "You couldn't do it?"

"I've been out checking fences and pastures." He turned to Ryker. "You were right. We need to move the cattle before they overgraze where they are."

Ryker scowled. But at least this time he didn't do more than mouth the curse word.

"Gage has the day off tomorrow. We'll move them then. I've got my hands full today trying to get this tractor fixed so we can cut the hay. Cam, go with Dallas. We should have all the pieces we need in the shed. And while you're out there, check the ditches. More than one rancher has already complained of problems with beavers."

Since beavers were known to dam up the irrigation ditches and ruin the banks Ryker wasn't just sending them on a make-work project. Damages from those rodents could cost thousands. Besides, unlike Cam, Ryker didn't seem the least bit interested in Ashley as anything other than someone who could help solve one of his problems.

Ryker faced Ashley. "I'll show you the office."

Dallas hated to ask, hated to put more on Ryker's plate since he could see by the lines of strain bracketing his brother's mouth that he was under a lot of pressure. But he'd promised Ashley if she drove he'd get Ryker to look over her car. And Dallas had run the favor past him when he'd texted to confirm her references had checked out. His brother had agreed.

Plus, Ashley really needed to know what was wrong with her car.

"Hey, Ryker," Dallas called before his brother got too far. "Are you still going to be able to do me that favor?"

For a moment Ryker looked confused. Then his brows straightened and his shoulders drooped. He cast a quick glance at Ashley's sedan.

"Yeah," he agreed on a sigh. "I'll have it done before you leave."

"Thanks."

Ryker gave a sharp nod, turned around.

"If I'm right," Dallas called after him, "you can find what you need on the seat of my truck."

Other than acknowledging him with a dismissive wave, Ryker kept on walking. Ashley gave Dallas a tentative smile then hurried off after his brother.

"What favor is Ryker doing for you?" Cam asked as he dismounted.

"Ashley's car's squealing and she doesn't trust it to get far. I told her if she followed me out today, Ryker would have a look at it. I suspect it's only a worn belt so I bought one in case it is."

"The next time we come, we'll just take my truck."

Cam hooked his thumbs in his belt, grinned at Dallas with a knowing look in eyes. "Convenient."

"Efficient. No point wasting gas."

Laughter rumbled from Cam's throat. "Please tell me that's not what you told her. Nothing more romantic than telling a woman you'll drive to save gas."

Dallas rolled his eyes. "This isn't about romance, Cam. We needed a bookkeeper, she needed a job, and since we're both coming here anyway it only makes sense to take one vehicle."

He went around to the box of his truck, lowered the tailgate. He wasn't a plumber but there were basic tools he had that would work for the broken pipe.

"So, if it's not about romance you won't mind if I ask the lady out?"

Dallas's head whipped around so fast he almost gave himself whiplash. "Don't even think about it."

Cam arched a brow. "So you are interested in her."

"I'm interested in not seeing her hurt."

"And you think I would?"

"I think your lifestyle would. She's a single mom working multiple jobs to make ends meet. She's a hearth and home kind of woman, Cam." Dallas grabbed some tools from his toolbox, closed the lid. He peered at his brother over his shoulder. "That's the complete opposite of what you are."

Unfazed by Dallas's comments, Cam stroked his mare's neck. "It's been my experience that even hearth and home kind of women get tired of the drudgery. Some of them even come looking for what I am."

Dallas jumped from the bed of his truck, slammed the tailgate. "Ashley isn't like that."

"She looks all grown up to me. I think she can make up her own mind."

Was it wrong to want to smack his brother upside the head with his wrench? "Leave her alone, Cam," Dallas warned.

"I will if you just spit it out."

"Spit what out?"

"That you like her and want her for yourself."

"I never said that."

"I know. That's the point. You prefer to bark out orders. It's tidier and simpler that way. God forbid, you actually do anything that proves you aren't as unfeeling as you come across. But in this case, you want me to back off you're going to have to give me a better reason than I'm all wrong for her."

Dallas scowled. "That's enough reason."

"I guess that'll be up to her." Clicking his tongue, Cam pulled on the reins. "Come on, Cady. Let's get you taken care of."

Shit. He didn't know what he wanted. He was attracted to Ashley. Hell, any man with a pulse would be. She was pretty and smart and hard working. She had a hell of a figure.

But he wasn't sure he was the right man for her either. Cam wasn't wrong when he'd accused Dallas of being closed off. Dallas was. He'd had to close himself off when his mom had gotten sick. He'd have fallen apart otherwise. The only way he'd been able to step up and take care of his brothers was by shutting down his emotions.

He'd gotten up every morning and put one foot in front of the other. Did what needed doing. Because there hadn't been an alternative.

He'd left himself open once since then. Yeah, that hadn't turned out any better. Worse, in fact. Because his mom hadn't had a choice in hurting him. Olivia had. And she'd still done it deliberately.

So he'd gone back to casual dating. Nothing serious. Nothing that left him vulnerable like that again. He'd been doing it so long it was habit now. It was who he was.

But if he didn't say something, Cam was going to set his sights on Ashley and while Dallas might not know what exactly he wanted to do about his feelings just yet, he didn't want Cam, or any man, near her.

His chest tightened. He wasn't sure he could force the words from his mouth. But remembering how she'd looked when his brother had ridden in on the horse, Dallas had no choice.

"Fine," he said to Cam's retreating back.

"Fine, what?" Cam asked. He wasn't about to give an inch.

"I admit it. I'm interested."

Cam grinned. "That wasn't so hard now, was it?"

Dallas rubbed his chest as his brother strode into the barn. "No, that wasn't hard at all," Dallas mumbled.

Chapter Ten

ASHLEY FINALLY HAD the papers organized. If stacks were considered organization. Joe Granger might have been in charge of the bookwork, but that didn't mean he'd been on top of it. There'd been at least a month's worth of mail and receipts to sort through, which was now divided into piles that filled the desk. Anything she'd been unsure of, or wasn't straightforward, she'd tossed onto the floor.

She was sitting amid those papers now, trying to ignore the cramp in her knee when she heard a voice over her shoulder.

"Making progress?"

Ashley shrieked. The papers in her hands went flying before she realized it was only Dallas.

"I'm sorry. I figured you'd have heard me walk in."

She turned as he crouched down beside her, his deep blue eyes on her. He smelled of sunshine and soap. Dark gold skin shone in the vee of his open western-style shirt. His sandy-brown hair was damp along his hairline.

"You changed," she said, then mentally kicked herself for saying something so stupid.

"I was hot and sweaty."

Ashley had to look away before she said something else stupid like, "I wouldn't mind seeing you hot and sweaty."

"So you've done what you needed to do?"

His lips curved, revealing his crooked eyetooth. "Well, it has been three hours."

"Three? Already?" Dismayed, Ashley looked around. "I'd hoped to have more progress than this."

Dallas held up a palm. "Nobody expected you to get it all done today. Besides, it already looks better than it did before."

"Most of it's organized at least." She looked at him again. "You're ready to go?"

"Almost. Actually I wanted to show you something outside."

"Oh." Ashley looked at the papers around her. "Can I have another fifteen minutes? I at least want to put this away so none of you are tripping over it. I still need to sort through it."

"Sure. Need any help?"

"No, that's fine. I've got it."

And she needed him to leave so she could breathe. Having him this close felt as though her lungs were closing off. Unfolding her legs, Ashley winced at the pain in her knee.

His eyes darkened with concern. "You okay?"

"Yeah, just sat on the floor a little too long. Got a cramp in my knee. It'll be fine."

His gaze lingered on her bare leg. Or she thought it did. Maybe it was just wishful thinking. Like the idea of running her fingers through his short hair, over that bronzed skin.

"You're sure?"

That her knee hurt? Yes. That she was strong enough to control her hormones around him? Not so much. Nevertheless she nodded.

"Then I'll meet you on the porch in fifteen."

Ashley waited until he'd rounded the corner before she scrambled to gather the papers. Ashley fastened what was left to sort through with a binder clip and attached a sticky note to it with the words "to sort" on it.

The other stacks she secured with binder clips and added sticky notes to those too so if Ryker needed to find something he'd know the payable versus the receivable pile. And it also ensured if things got moved or knocked over before her next trip out, she wasn't starting from scratch.

Ashley grabbed her purse. Having been shown where the bathroom was, she made a mad dash down the hall.

Though the house was air-conditioned, she still felt a little stale after sitting in the office for hours. She wasn't sure what Dallas had planned but since he'd taken the time to wash and change, she wanted to at least freshen up.

Since she wasn't one for much makeup, she brushed on fresh lip gloss, added another layer of mascara. She debated taking out her ponytail but if he was showing her something outside, having her hair up kept her cooler.

She wished she had a skirt or something prettier to change into but her denim shorts were going to have to do.

"It's not a date," she told her reflection before she got too ahead of herself.

Chances were he just wanted to talk about her car and show her what Ryker had found wrong with it. But, no matter how many times she told herself that as she walked toward the front door, it didn't lessen the pounding of her heart. Because why would he change and wash up to show her that?

Which begged the question. If it wasn't the car, what exactly did he want to show her?

DALLAS KNEW HE'D had the right idea when Ashley stepped onto the porch and saw the saddled horses waiting. Her eyes widened in delight.

He figured she had to be close to his age but she looked especially young with her hair in a ponytail, no makeup but for the gloss shining on her lips. His gut hitched. He wouldn't mind wiping that gloss away with his own mouth.

"I thought you might like a ride before we leave."

Some of the light dimmed from her eyes. "I shouldn't. I should get back home."

"I thought your daughter was going to a friend's after school?"

"She is. But you've got lots to do and I should just get going."

"Well, here's the thing. You'd actually be helping me. The horses need to be exercised and I can't ride two at once."

He tipped his head, added a hopeful smile. "Please? We don't have to go far."

Dallas knew by the way she kept glancing at the horses she was tempted. And not wanting her to find an excuse, he pressed on.

"I know it's been a while since you rode but you don't have to worry. Peaches is a sweet horse; she won't give you any trouble."

Ashley gestured to her shorts and T-shirt. "I'm not really dressed for horseback riding."

"I've got you covered." He reached for the sunscreen he'd set on the railing of the porch. "So you don't burn. As for your head," he removed his ball cap, handed it to her. "That should keep most of the sun off your face."

"What about your face?"

He jutted his chin toward the Stetson he'd left hanging off the pommel of his saddle. "I've got my cowboy hat. I figured it would be too big for you so I gave you this one because it's adjustable."

Her attention stayed fixed in the direction of his pommel. He reached out, touched her arm. "What do you say?"

She finally turned her gaze toward him. She still looked a bit uncertain. And the temptation was still there. But he saw something else. Something that made his blood simmer. For a heartbeat or three they just stood there on the porch, staring at each other. Her skin hot beneath the hand he had yet to move away. Because damn it felt good to touch that silky skin.

She cleared her throat. "I say yes."

"All right." He lowered his arm. "I'll go grab us some water bottles from inside while you put on the sunscreen."

In the kitchen, he grabbed four water bottles and raided the fridge and pantry for a few snacks. Since his stomach was growling, he imagined Ashley was hungry as well.

When he stepped back onto the porch, though, the last thing on his mind was food. Ashley had one leg propped on the rail and was slowly rubbing lotion onto all that bare skin. And bent over as she was displayed her perfect ass.

Dallas's mouth went dry. Heat slammed into his groin. He wanted nothing but to step up behind her, snug up his hips to hers, run his hands over those curves and bury his face in her neck.

He was rock hard in less than five seconds.

She peered over her shoulder at him. "I'm almost done."

He would be too if he kept staring and fantasizing. Lowering the grocery bag he'd filled to hide his hard-on, Dallas walked past her to his horse. He moved the provisions into the saddlebags he'd thought ahead to bring.

He hadn't lied about exercising the horses. Although it was a great reason to keep her there longer, they did need to be ridden. The fact that she loved them was a bonus. Just as the time alone with her would be.

Hearing her step from the porch, Dallas turned.

It was like being struck across the chest with a two-by-four.

God, she was beautiful. Fresh face smiling at him from beneath the rim of his ball cap. Her long, wavy blonde ponytail pulled through the back. Her legs glistened from the sunscreen, drawing his attention to the firm length of them. He wanted to drop to his knees and slowly run his palms from her ankles to the cuffed hem of her shorts riding high on her thighs. And then, just to torture them both, slip his fingers underneath and—

He yanked his gaze from her legs. He needed to shift his attention or he wouldn't be able to ride.

"Okay," he said, forcing his mind off her body and what he'd like to do to it. "You remember how?"

She smiled. "Isn't it like riding a bike?"

He chuckled. "Something like that." He stepped to the palomino mare. "Come and meet Peaches."

Even though Peaches stood at sixteen hands, Ashley showed no fear as she approached the horse. She did, however, show she knew a thing about animals. She strolled closer. Reaching out, Ashley let the mare sniff and get used to her before she splayed her hand on the hide and rubbed gently.

"Hi, pretty girl," she cooed as she spoiled the mare with long, firm strokes and some scratches along her mane.

Peaches turned her big head, nuzzled Ashley's shoulder. Ashley pressed her cheek to the animal.

"We're going to get along just fine, aren't we?"

They made a picture standing there, each already half in love with the other. He almost hated to break it up.

"She's pretty tall. Do you need a hand getting up?" he asked.

Not that he couldn't get a stool if she needed it, but why when he was capable of helping? Which just so happened to give him an excuse to touch her again.

"Are you calling me short?" she asked. Her teasing tone matched her mischievous grin.

His lips twitched. "No, ma'am."

"Uh-huh. I think I can manage."

But though she grasped the pommel—barely—she couldn't get her foot up high enough to fit in the stirrup.

Smiling, though he wisely kept his mouth shut, Dallas stepped over. Cupping his hands, he offered her a boost.

She slid her foot into his hands and reached for the pommel. Once she had it, he lifted her until she was able to swing her other leg over the saddle. Her grin stretched her cheeks.

"This is awesome."

"We haven't gone anywhere yet."

"It doesn't matter." She inhaled deep and let it out slowly. "It's already perfect."

He had to agree. Especially when his hands brushed her calves as he adjusted her stirrups.

"Feel okay?"

At her nod, he moved back to his mount, grabbed the black Stetson from the pommel and put it on. He swung up into the saddle, looked over at Ashley. She was staring at him.

"What? Is something wrong?"

"Nope," she squeaked. "All good."

Since she seemed fine, he decided to take her at her word.

"There's a trail that starts behind the machine shed." He gestured to the left. "We'll start there."

Clicking his tongue, Dallas turned Smoky in that direction. Though he suspected Peaches followed as much from wanting to keep up with her corral mate as from any guidance on Ashley's part, she nevertheless fell into step beside him.

Ryker rolled out from under the tractor as they sauntered by. His cold glare knocked the temperature down ten degrees. Dallas ignored him. He'd done what his brother had asked, had put in the amount of hours he'd promised *and* was exercising two of the horses so Cam wouldn't have to. If his brother was pissed because he wasn't doing more he could pack sand.

"We should go back," Ashley whispered once they were past the machine shed.

"Because of Ryker? Don't worry about him. Besides, you put in your time today. You spent over three hours in that office."

"I know, but taking a ride when I could be working feels wrong."

Dallas looked at her. "Don't let Ryker wreck this for you. You deserve a little time off. Besides, you're off the clock."

They followed the trail past the corrals and along the hay fields. His brother hadn't been wrong; the hay was definitely ready to cut. Deep green and thick. If the rain held out, they'd be sure a good crop of bales for feed.

"You did a lot of this growing up, didn't you?" Ashley asked.

"Riding with a pretty woman at my side or riding in general?"

Dallas wasn't usually the teasing sort but he couldn't help it with Ashley. Mostly because he loved seeing the blush spread across her cheeks.

"Riding in general," she answered.

"When you live on a ranch, you're always going to have reason to ride but the ones for fun stopped about the time my mom got sick."

"I'm sorry. I didn't mean to bring up a painful subject."

He shrugged. "It was a long time ago. Anyway, if you're going to be around you should probably know some of this. That way you won't think Ryker's glares have anything to do with you."

But it didn't make the telling any easier. Dallas rarely

talked about his past. The few friends he had from Last Stand already knew his history and the ones he had in the city didn't need to know. As far as women went, he'd told Olivia, but she'd been more interested in his life and business in San Antonio. Luckily, he'd learned the reason for that before it was too late.

He'd ensured the relationships he'd had since never lasted long enough or got deep enough for his past to come up.

"Mom got sick when I was fourteen. Cancer. At first it wasn't so bad. The treatments made her tired but not too sick and she was mostly able to function. But shortly after my fifteenth birthday the treatments stopped working and she got sicker. Since it was terminal, she made the decision not to try anything else. Her health declined quickly after that.

"Dad was a mess. Mom wanted to die at home but he couldn't handle it. He poured himself into the ranch. Work was all he did. Being outside and busy was his way of not having to be around it, I guess.

"As the oldest I had no choice. Gage was only nine. I did what I could to help Mom, to keep the boys on top of their homework and chores."

Dallas stared off over the hills and the grand old oak trees. He could still smell the sickness, feel the despair and the anger building.

"We tried to hide it from Mom, but the hurt and resentment between us kept building. I was mad at Dad for not stepping up the way he should. For making me do it. Which, in turn, led to my brothers hating me."

"But you were just a kid yourself," Ashley argued.

"They didn't see that. They just saw me as someone who rode their ass all the time. Who went out of his way to make their lives miserable."

But they never saw the dates he cancelled when one of them was sick, or the times he stood in the back of the gym cheering them on at one of their basketball games.

"By the time I left at twenty, there was no love lost between us. We hardly spoke. And when we did it was to snap at each other. Dad was coming around by then and Hudson was about to graduate high school. I figured Ryker was old enough to look after Cam and Gage since he was already older than I'd been when I was saddled with the same responsibility. More, actually, 'cause Ryker only had Gage and Cam to worry about. He didn't have to play nursemaid on top of that."

Dallas rolled his shoulders. God, he hated talking about the past. "Anyway, all that to say if you feel tension in the house, it has nothing to do with you." Which was all he should have said rather than blather on about his damn, sad history.

"It says a lot about you, you know."

Dallas looked over. "What does?"

"That you're helping again when they need you."

Dallas let out a sharp bark. "Trust me, Ryker didn't give me much choice."

She gave him a knowing look. Uncomfortable with it, Dallas shifted his attention back to the trail.

"There's a creek coming up. It doesn't have much in the way of shade but we'll stop there."

She didn't say anything else and neither did he. He was

regretting having revealed so much. Yes, he'd wanted her to know that Ryker's scowls had nothing to do with her but he could have given her the *CliffsNotes* version. Instead, he'd rambled on, consumed by his own memories and the bitterness that was always there, just below the surface.

Luckily, however, once they stopped riding, he had more pleasurable things to occupy his mind.

Dallas swung down, looped the reins over the pommel and patted Smoky's rump, knowing the horse wasn't going anywhere. It was too damn hot to trot off on a whim. Sure enough, the gelding aimed for the trickling creek and the clear water waiting.

Moving behind Peaches, Dallas ran his hand over the animal's hips so as not to startle her. When he reached Ashley's side and looked up all thoughts of his past vanished.

Her skin was flushed from the sun. Her shoulders glistened. Though her thigh was right there within easy reach, he jammed his hands on his hips instead.

"Need a hand down?"

"I think I've got it," she answered.

It was hard to be disappointed when she swung her right leg over and treated him to another tantalizing view of her butt. Since her back was turned, he allowed himself the luxury of gawking. And tried to look innocent as a lamb when she turned around.

"Thirsty?"

"Very."

Dallas followed Peaches to where Smoky drank at the water's edge. He dug out the water bottles, granola bars, and apples from his saddlebags.

"I figured you might be hungry as well," he said when he returned.

"Thank you." She accepted the water and snacks.

He tipped his chin to the patch of grass she'd sat on. "I should have thought to bring a blanket. I don't wear shorts when I ride so it didn't occur to me."

Ashley shrugged. "It doesn't bother me."

No, it didn't seem to. She stretched her legs out before her. Dallas's gaze fell hungrily on all her exposed, golden skin.

"Aren't you going to sit?"

"Yep."

He ripped his gaze away, took a seat next to her. But there was no taking his focus off of her. In fact, sitting this close only intensified it. Because now he could smell her sweet skin, could see the beauty mark on her upper thigh. Could hear her soft breathing. He caught the flick of her tongue as she caught a piece of granola from the corner of her mouth.

Uncapping his water, Dallas drank down half the bottle.

He was thirty-one for God's sake. Ashley was hardly the first woman he'd seen in shorts. And it was shorts. It wasn't as though she was sitting there naked.

Not that he'd complain if she were.

But if she were, he wouldn't be able to keep his hands off her. And before he touched her, which, God willing, would be soon, he needed to know there wasn't another man in the picture.

"Can I ask about Brittany's dad?"

She shrugged. "Not much to tell. When Dylan found

out I was pregnant that was the end of the relationship."

"Does he live around San Antonio? Does he ever see her?"

"No. We agreed on child support until she's eighteen, which goes straight into her college account, in exchange for him signing away his parental rights." She looked down. "He's never even met her."

Dallas couldn't believe any man could be so cavalier about his child. Being a parent wasn't anything to fuck around with. Why couldn't everyone see that? Why did some people still insist on using them as pawns? On using them to get what they wanted. Like Olivia had.

"I'm sorry," he said, deliberately shoving his ex from his mind.

"Don't be. I'd rather him not be involved at all than doing it out of obligation. It's healthier for Brittany this way."

Then, as though they hadn't been talking about something that had to be painful for her no matter how she brushed it off, she said, "It's so quiet and peaceful. How can you stand the noise of the city after living here?"

"Noise can be a good thing. Sometimes the ranch can get too quiet."

And too many of those quiet times led to stewing about things that couldn't be changed. But he wasn't going into any more of his past today. Not when he could learn a thing or two about her.

"You don't like living in the city?"

She kept her gaze on the horses that remained at the water's edge, tails swishing lazily. "It has its advantages. Grocery stores are nearby. I don't have a far commute to work.

Brittany's close to her friends." She shrugged. "It works for us."

He tipped his head, studied her. "Because you make it work."

She shrugged. "We should get going," she said as she rose to her feet.

He took their garbage and leftovers and tucked them into his saddlebags. Though she patted and spoke to Peaches, he caught her glance flicking his way and just as quickly shifting away when he looked toward her. He wasn't being egotistical in thinking she was interested. He'd caught enough signs.

With a single-minded purpose, Dallas walked toward her.

Her smile was too wide, too bright. "Sorry to trouble you with this. The disadvantages of being short."

He stopped when the toes of his boots touched those of her sneakers. "Why do you do that?"

"Do what?"

"Dodge compliments. Act like it's a hardship for me to be near you." He grabbed her chin when she looked away, gently brought her head around. "Why do you act like I couldn't possibly be interested?"

"Because why would you be?" She waved her hands toward him. "Look at you. You could have any woman you wanted. Why waste your time on someone like me?"

He didn't know if he was more mad or surprised. "What do you mean 'someone like you'? Have you looked in a mirror lately? You're pretty damn gorgeous."

She rolled her eyes. "Yeah. With my lack of makeup and

thrift store clothes. With tired bags under my eyes. Not to mention my almost sixteen-year-old daughter. It's not exactly what most single men are interested in."

"Then you haven't met the right single men." Dallas stepped closer, spreading his legs so she stood between his. "I happen to like your lack of makeup. It makes you look real. And I never noticed your clothes other than they hug you in all the right places. As for your daughter, I've met Brittany and she seems like a good kid, raised by a hard-working mother."

He brought his body up against hers. He cupped her cheek with his right hand while his left gripped the pommel behind her. Her eyes were wide, her breath shaky. Fueled by her reaction and his desperate need to finally kiss her, Dallas lowered his head.

"You're trembling," he whispered against her lips.

Her fingers clutched his forearm. "I haven't done this in a really long time," she said, her voice barely above a whisper.

He grinned. His tongue flicked her bottom lip.

"Don't worry. It's just like riding a bike."

Chapter Eleven

It was nothing like riding a bike. Even going downhill, her feet raised high off the pedals with the wind blowing over her face, she'd never felt this exhilarated. This alive.

Blood raced through her veins, drummed in her ears. Her heart was a hummingbird in her chest, fluttering wildly, unable to sit still. She hadn't lied when she'd said it had been a long time since she'd been kissed. But it had been even longer since she'd felt this tsunami of sensations with a man.

Even though he was barely touching her—only his lips and the hand that cupped her cheek—she felt more with him than she'd ever felt in another man's arms.

Maybe it was the fact he wasn't touching her. He wasn't rushing to grope and grab. Instead, he was building the anticipation. He was taking the time to tease and savor.

It was as though he was building a fire. He'd struck the match when his long legs cradled hers. The flame had caught when he'd lowered his mouth to hers. Now, with his lips urging hers open, with his tongue sweeping against hers, the fire roared.

Heat spread through her chest, tightening it, making it hard to breathe. Her cheeks burned. Her core pulsed with need. She dug her fingers into his hard biceps.

He hummed low in his throat, slid his hand around the

back of her neck and kissed her deeper. He was skilled; there was no question he had years of experience. His mouth moved expertly over hers, with hers, drawing needy moans she'd never uttered in her life.

Beneath her hands his muscles tightened. But instead of pulling her tighter against him, he drew back.

She almost wept at the loss.

His blue eyes were stormy with desire. His voice even raspier than usual. She'd thought him sexy from the first time she'd laid eyes on him but wearing a cowboy hat added a whole other layer of sexiness.

He ran his thumb over her wet lip. "Still don't think I'm interested?"

Ashley swallowed hard. Standing as they were, both gasping for air, it was a little difficult to deny.

"I—"

"Good."

He banded an arm around her waist, pulled her flush against him and branded her with his mouth. This wasn't a get-to-know-you kiss. This was an I-want-your-body-undermine kiss. His teeth scraped her lips, his tongue swept through her mouth, claiming her. A feral growl reverberated from his chest into hers. The vibrations and the heat coming from his hard body rolled through her.

His jeans brushed her bare legs but it wasn't the soft, well-worn denim that stole her breath. It was the ridge of his erection pressing against her belly. Her nipples tightened. Molten heat converged between her thighs.

Instinctively, she arched her pelvis against him.

Dallas growled, tightened his grip around her, and stole

the little breath she had left with another plundering kiss. For a moment, she surrendered. Body and mind, she let herself be whisked away by the strength of his embrace, the boldness of his kiss. By the simple fact it felt so good to be held in a man's arms. To have, for just a moment, nothing to worry about. To have, just for a moment, something that was all hers.

But then he moved his hand from the back of her neck, over her shoulder. When the heel of his palm skimmed the curve of her breast, reality cut through the fog of want.

This wasn't what she'd intended. Yes, she was attracted. More, she was on fire for him. But she wasn't the kind to jump into bed—or in this case, a pasture—just because she'd been shown a little affection.

Of course, if he thought that, she only had herself to blame. Because grinding against him had surely given him the wrong idea. That she was a lonely single mother who was easily seduced into sex.

Mortified, Ashley pushed him away. She'd have stepped back too for good measure but Peaches remained behind her, unaware of the tension surrounding her.

"I'm sorry," Ashley said, unable to look him in the eye. "I shouldn't have done that."

"You shouldn't have kissed me?"

Ashley licked her lips. His taste lingered, further mocking her. Because what she really wanted to do was yank him back and kiss him all over again. But she couldn't. She wasn't into hookups, no matter the mixed signals she'd inadvertently given.

"I shouldn't have, uh, pressed myself against you that

way." Good Lord, could this be any more mortifying? "It gave you the wrong idea."

"So, you're not attracted to me?"

She sputtered. "I think we both know that's a lie."

"Then how about you stop looking at my boots and explain what exactly you gave me the wrong idea about?"

She raised her gaze. He didn't look mad, thank goodness. But his brows were drawn together.

"I don't do casual sex," she blurted. "I'm not so lonely that at the first sign of attention from a man I sleep with him."

His brows went from a flat line to two perfect arches. "Did I say you were?"

"No, but I pressed myself against you and then you were going to…" She gulped hard. "The other guys I dated—not that we're dating, of course"—she added with her palms out—"they all assumed I was easy. That all they had to do was show a little affection and I'd jump into bed with them." She couldn't look him in the eye any longer and dropped her gaze to her hands. "I'm not like that. And I'm not usually a tease either. So I'm sorry if I gave you the impression I was the type of woman who sleeps around."

His chuckle startled her. Her gaze whipped back to his. Humor lit his eyes.

"What's so funny?"

He crossed his arms over his chest. Corded muscle rippled beneath sun-kissed golden skin.

"You've given me a lot of impressions but that wasn't one of them."

"Oh. Okay." She grimaced. "Sorry, it's just I thought

you were going to—"

Flames lit her cheeks. Could she be any less awkward? Any less obvious she had limited experience? She suddenly felt like a country bumpkin who'd been taken to the big city for the first time and had no idea how to act or what to do.

She dropped her hands to her sides. "Let's just pretend this never happened and go back to being work acquaintances."

Dallas took hold of her wrist, waited until she looked at him.

"I *was* going to touch you. But not because I think you're desperate or lonely and want to take advantage of you. But because you're a beautiful woman and I'm attracted to you." He tugged her gently forward. "I'm not only attracted, Ashley, I'm interested. So if it's all the same to you, I'd rather not go back to being acquaintances. I'd much prefer to take you on a date."

Her foolish heart leapt at the idea but she stomped it back down. She'd been disappointed too many times in the past.

"I don't see the point, Dallas. I'm hardly your type."

He tipped his head. "Okay. What's my type?"

Well, crap. She'd stepped in it now. But she was in so deep already, what was a little more?

"Tall, leggy, perfectly made-up. The easy-breezy type that has evenings free to go out for dinners or to the club. That has a wardrobe for every occasion and looks like a runway model even when she's grocery shopping."

For a moment, shadows darkened his eyes. "I dated a few. Learned the hard way that wasn't my type. Besides"—he gestured to the jeans and button-down he wore—"I don't get much fancier than this and I'm not one to go to clubs. I'd much prefer a beer on my deck."

Yes, she could see that. His long legs stretched out before him, his ball cap on backward, a cold beer to his lips. If she had any artistic skill she'd paint the picture and get rich selling it. What woman wouldn't want that image hanging on her wall?

"You have at least three jobs that I know of, on top of working on your house, so I know you have a strong work ethic, which is important to me. You took the job here partially to help me out, which tells me you're kind and compassionate. You balked at having Ryker look at your car so I know it isn't in you to take advantage of people." He leaned forward, grinned. "See that? You're exactly my type."

Damn that sexy smile and charm! And, Lord, that hat was going to be the death of her.

She shook her head. "And I also happen to have a daughter and very little free time on my hands."

"I don't have much in the way of spare time either and as for your daughter, I have no issues with her. She seems like a pretty good kid."

Ashley's heart warmed. "She is."

"So, how about I get to know both her and her mom better? I can drop by tomorrow night with pizza, if that works for you."

Takeout pizza? Her mouth watered. She hadn't had that in months!

"Don't overthink this," he said when she hesitated. "Just say yes."

She'd be a fool to resist both a man that good looking and pizza. "Okay," she conceded.

"Perfect." He leaned forward, kissed her breathless once more.

When he drew back his eyes were full of mischief. "And for future reference, unless you have your hand on my buckle and are begging me to take you to bed, I won't ever assume that's what you're after."

Then, as if he hadn't just said something that put the most vivid image in her head, that once again ignited every erogenous zone in her body, he grabbed her by the waist and lifted her onto Peaches's back.

He trailed his hand down her bare thigh as he stepped back and walked to his horse. With his hand on the pommel, one foot in the stirrup, he looked over.

"You may not be tall, Ashley, but there's not a damn thing wrong with your legs."

DALLAS THOUGHT ABOUT Ashley and her legs the whole way back to the ranch.

And the kiss.

He blew out a long, slow breath. Damn, that was some kiss. It had never dawned on him her response was due to loneliness or desperation. There'd been chemistry between them since their first meeting and it had only intensified since. He'd expected heat but when his mouth had claimed hers, he'd been knocked back by the blast.

Her taste, the sounds she made, the way she'd gripped

his biceps. The way she'd ground against him.

Probably best not to keep thinking about that. Riding was already uncomfortable and he was only half aroused.

But Ashley had that effect on him. She'd caught and held his attention from the beginning. And the more he got to know her, the more drawn in he was.

Because he hadn't lied to her about his type. Despite her preconceived notions, he wasn't into the flighty, good-time girl. Oh, sure, there'd been a time in his twenties when that was all he was after but it wasn't any more. Now he wanted a woman with substance. A woman who wanted more out of life than a good time.

Cam strolled out of the barn, shirtless, just as they rode up. Dallas scowled. He wouldn't put it past his brother to have seen them coming, run inside and taken his shirt off, then waltzed right back out just as they were arriving.

His cheeky grin and wink confirmed Dallas's suspicions.

Cam reached Ashley's side before Dallas had a chance to dismount. He hated to see Cam's hands on her, but at least his brother was gentleman enough to release her the moment she was on the ground.

"How was the ride?" he asked.

"Good, thanks," she said. She didn't look at either Dallas or Cam.

With Smoky's reins in one hand, Dallas took Peaches's in his other. "We should get these horses looked after. I promised Ashley we wouldn't be too late getting back."

"Actually," Cam said, his humor dimming. "Gage called while I was putting away the feedbags. He's on his way over and he told me to tell you to stay. Some kind of family meeting." His gaze locked on Dallas's. "He sounded serious."

Dallas's stomach dropped. Shit. Had something happened to their dad? As an EMT who was in and out of the hospital a few times a day, Gage would be privy to any change in Joe's condition.

"I can get myself home," Ashley said.

He wanted to tell her to wait. But that was selfish. Without knowing what Gage wanted to talk about, it was stupid to have her sit and wait for him when she could be home.

Dallas sighed. "Okay. And you don't have to worry about your car breaking down. Ryker fixed it. It was just a belt that needed replacing. While he was at it, he changed the oil and gave it a quick once over."

She grimaced. "That was awful nice of him but I wish he hadn't gone to so much trouble."

"It's what he does," Dallas said, knowing she was worried about how she was going to pay for it. "Besides, you're still doing us a huge favor by tackling Dad's office."

"Can you ask Ryker what I owe him? I'd like to pay him for what he did."

Dallas was about to dismiss the idea when Gage's Jeep came tearing up the driveway, leaving a wide wake of dust behind him. Dallas and Cam exchanged glances. Whatever Gage had to say, he was in an almighty hurry to do so.

"I'd offer to help with the horses but I suspect you'll be faster without me getting in your way."

A car door slammed. Dallas looked over. His brother was still in uniform. He motioned toward the house before climbing the porch steps and disappearing inside. Yep. He was in a hurry.

Dallas handed both sets of reins to Cam. "I'll join you shortly. I just want to walk Ashley to her car."

Ashley looked at Cam. "It was nice meeting you."

"You too, darlin'." Cam touched the brim of his hat. "See you next time."

Apparently, even news of their dad didn't dampen Cam's flirtatious ways. Neither did it seem to worry him as he sauntered toward the barn whistling, the horses clomping docilely behind him.

Dallas opened Ashley's door. "Sorry I can't follow you back, but Ryker assures me your car is solid. You shouldn't have any problems."

"Thanks, I'm sure it'll be fine." She took off the ball cap, held it out to him. "I had a great time. Thank you."

Instead of grabbing his hat, he grasped her wrist, tugged her closer. With his other hand he cupped the back of her neck. He grinned when she shivered.

"I had a great time too," he said before lowering his mouth for another kiss.

"Hey, Dallas!" Ryker called from the porch. "Let's go, Gage is waiting."

Ashley pulled away looking embarrassed. "I'll see you tomorrow."

"Okay. Text me when you're home, so I know you made it safe."

She blushed. "I will."

Despite Cam waiting for him in the barn and Ryker and Gage waiting in the house, Dallas stood and watched Ashley drive away. Mostly because she was the best thing to happen to him in forever and it felt damn good to feel like that again.

But also because whatever news awaited him in the house wasn't going to be good. With a sick feeling in his gut, Dallas turned and went to help Cam with the horses.

DALLAS WASN'T AFRAID of change. He appreciated new and better ways of getting things done. He understood to move ahead he had to be flexible and willing to try new things.

But some things he wished hadn't changed.

Back when he'd been a kid, even when his mom had called him and his brothers in for a meal or bedtime, he hadn't minded going inside. Well, not too much. Like any young boy, he'd rather have played outside, but at least when he'd climbed the wide porch steps he'd done it knowing a warm smile, a good meal, and genuine affection awaited him.

He missed that. God, how he missed it. He hated the dread he felt now. Hated that instead of leaping up the stairs, his boots slapped each one and each step was heavier than the last. Because there hadn't been warm smiles in that house for over a decade.

Now it was angry glares, cold, stilted conversation, and years of anger and resentment smoldering between them.

His mom would hate what had become of her family and knowing that, but unsure how to fix it, weighed heavily on his heart. But he couldn't fix it alone, dammit, and none of the others seemed inclined to want to.

So here they were, gathering around the table, sour expressions on their faces and nothing to say to each other, let alone anything nice.

It was shameful. And he was sick of it.

Maybe it was having to explain it to Ashley, or having her witness his family's issues, but suddenly he was done.

Dallas scraped his chair back.

"Now where are you going?" Ryker demanded.

"To make coffee. It won't hurt us to actually sit around the table like civilized people."

"That's never mattered to you before," Ryker accused.

Dallas filled the carafe with water, poured it in the machine. "It does now. Besides, I'm here and I'm listening." Dallas looked at Gage as he scooped coffee grounds into the filter. "You can start if you want."

Gage studied him for a moment, then shook his head. "It can wait."

Dallas could practically hear Ryker seething as he flicked the switch and reached into the cupboard for mugs. Then, and only a little because it was hard to break the habit of picking Ryker's ass, Dallas searched through the pantry until he found a package of cookies. He dumped them on a plate and set it on the table. He set the cream and sugar next to it, along with a handful of spoons.

"Are you done playing Suzy Homemaker?" Ryker grumbled.

Cam reached for two cookies, stuffed one in his mouth. "Doesn't look like it," he said around a mouthful.

Dallas ignored Cam's smart-ass remark and Ryker's scowl. He'd started something and he intended to keep it going. Apparently, change wasn't going to happen on its own.

He looked at Ryker. "Thanks again for working on Ashley's car. I know you're swamped so I appreciate the time."

It wasn't the first time he'd ever said something nice to one of his brothers, although he honestly couldn't remember the last time he had, and it shocked them into silence. They stared at him while the machine popped and sizzled on the counter and the smell of fresh coffee filled the kitchen.

"Let me know how much I owe you. I didn't expect you to do it for free."

Ryker frowned. "Why are you paying for it?"

"Because it was my idea for you to look at the car."

The coffee maker sputtered its last drops so Dallas grabbed the carafe, went around the table and poured each of them a mug before setting what was left back on the warming plate.

"I'd charge him a couple hundred," Cam said as he poured milk into his cup.

Ryker looked as though he'd been considering more. Whatever Ryker wanted, Dallas would give it to him. Well, within reason. But they weren't gathered round the table to discuss Ashley's car.

Dallas sat, turned to Gage. His youngest brother was quiet and watchful as usual.

"So what's happened with Dad?" Dallas asked.

Gage looked from Cam to Ryker. "Do you know if Dad was seeing anyone?"

"Dad? Seeing someone?" Ryker turned his stunned face toward Gage. "Not that I noticed. I mean, it's not as though he ever brought a woman here."

"No," Gage agreed. "And no phone calls either. At least not to the landline. I don't know about his cell."

"Why are you asking?" Dallas inquired.

Gage blew out a breath. He looked a little sick. "I found out today it was a woman who brought Dad in."

"I just assumed it was the ambulance," Ryker said. "How was it you didn't know it wasn't by ambulance until now? You work there."

Gage's jaw tightened. "It wasn't my first priority when I found out Dad was brought in unconscious. And I've been busy. You aren't the only one who works hard, Ryker."

"Nobody's accusing you of slacking off," Dallas soothed. "And it's not only up to you. I never thought to ask either."

Gage nodded, but he didn't look less angry.

"So a woman brought him in?" Dallas prodded.

"Yeah. I don't know much else. She told the nurses he'd collapsed and stopped breathing. That she'd performed CPR, then brought him into emergency."

"Could she have even brought him in on her own?" Cam asked. "I mean, Dad's not a small man. And if he was unconscious he'd have just been dead weight."

"I can't see her doing that on her own," Gage answered.

"So was someone else with her?" Ryker asked.

"The nurse who talked to her said she was alone," Gage replied.

"So we still have more questions than answers," Dallas complained.

"She didn't leave her name or anything?" Cam asked.

"Nothing. She told the triage nurse *his* name and address, which is how they knew to contact me. But she wasn't able to give them any more information, as far as medications or anything he might be taking. According to the report, she said they were just talking when he collapsed."

"Did she say where they were talking?" Dallas asked.

"No. The nurse said she was pretty upset so when the woman asked if she could go to the washroom and get herself together, the nurse thought nothing of it."

"Let me guess, she never came back?" Dallas surmised.

"Nope."

"She couldn't have cared much about him to leave without sticking around to see how he was." Ryker growled.

"So, we know nothing about her or why Dad was with her?" Dallas asked.

"We know a little," Gage countered. "She's young, brunette. Nurse figured her to be mid- to late-twenties."

Cam sucked his breath through his teeth. "That's pretty fucking young for a man Dad's age."

"It doesn't mean Dad was having an affair with her," Dallas said.

"No? Then what were they doing together? And where the hell were they?" Ryker looked to Gage. "You said she drove him in?"

"Yeah."

"In her car or his?"

"Must have been hers. I already checked the hospital lot. Dad's car isn't there."

"Which doesn't mean anything," Dallas said, dreading where this was all leading. "She could have driven him there in his car and drove it back to her place."

"Or his car is still wherever they were 'talking,'" Cam

said, putting finger quotes around talking, "and she drove him in hers."

Dallas rolled his shoulders. He knew his dad had loved their mom. It was why he'd fallen apart so completely with his wife's sickness and death.

Dallas had never assumed his dad wouldn't eventually meet another woman or date; the truth was he'd simply never thought about it. But now he had no choice but to. And he didn't like the betrayal he felt realizing his dad had found someone else. Especially one young enough to be his—

"Holy fuck," Dallas swore.

"What?" Gage asked.

"This could be a hell of a lot uglier than Dad dating someone a third his age."

"Yeah?" Ryker growled. "How?"

Dallas pushed aside his half cup of coffee. Suddenly he wasn't feeling so good.

"She could be his daughter." Dallas turned to Gage. "Is it possible she confronted him with paternity and the shock gave him cardiac arrest?"

All color leached from Gage's face. "I guess so. Yeah."

"It can't be," Ryker argued. "Because if she is his daughter then—"

"Then it means Dad cheated on Mom," Dallas stated.

Chapter Twelve

DALLAS HESITATED AT the door to his dad's room. He hadn't actually been inside to see Joe since his dad had been admitted last week. He'd come, as he'd been ordered to, but other than checking in with the nurses to see if there was any change he hadn't hung around.

He hated seeing his dad attached to machines, with hoses and tubes sticking out of him. He'd had enough of seeing his mom like that at the end.

Not that he held the same feelings for his dad that he'd had for his mom. He'd loved his mom when she'd gotten sick. Loved her even more when she'd died.

He wasn't sure what he felt for his dad. Okay, that wasn't true. He knew exactly how he felt. Angry. Not only because Joe had fallen apart but because when their mom had asked to see him, he'd always been out in the fields or on the range, or doing something else with the ranch. Anything else.

She'd needed him, dammit, and he'd failed her. Just as he'd failed his sons. It was because of Joe's absence, steeping himself in his work and grief, that Dallas had had to take over. And because of that, he'd lost what was left of his childhood and his relationship with his brothers.

And when Joe had finally smartened up and decided to

be a dad again, though it had been too late for Dallas and Hudson by then, he'd never once acknowledged those god-awful years when he'd been absent. When Dallas had had to keep the family together.

He'd never once said a goddamn thanks.

Dallas pressed his forehead to the closed door. He should just leave. He wasn't in the right frame of mind to pay a bedside visit to a man who'd had a heart attack and remained in a coma.

But when had his dad ever shown him any compassion, any leniency? It sure as hell hadn't been when Dallas had been struggling to keep his grades up, keep his brothers in line, and manage some sort of a household.

Dallas clenched his jaw, stood up straight. Grasping the handle he pushed the door open.

His boots sounded especially loud in the stillness of his dad's room. So did the pounding in his ears.

He stopped at the bedside. Wires snaked from the heart monitor, up under the sleeve of Joe's hospital gown to the circular discs Dallas could see taped to his dad's chest. A plastic tube blew oxygen up Joe's nostrils. There was an IV line taped to the back of his hand and a clear catheter tube that snaked from under his gown to a bag, ensuring Joe didn't wet the bed.

Dallas tried not to be swayed by any of it. The man had failed him, his wife, and his other sons. And though he didn't want to feel empathy for what his dad was going through now, Dallas couldn't deny it was there. Which only made him angrier. The man didn't deserve it. Especially not if he had a daughter out there.

"You proved you were a selfish son-of-a-bitch a long time ago but I swear if I find out you cheated on Mom…"

Dallas curled his hands into tight fists. He pressed them into the mattress at his dad's hip, leaned forward so he was within inches of Joe's face.

"I always figured if you ever apologized for abandoning us as kids, if you ever acknowledged how much you failed Mom when she'd needed you most, I'd forgive you. But if it turns out that you cheated on a woman like her, a woman you hadn't bothered to support and console when she was going through the worst time in her life, when she needed you the most"—when it had been Dallas who'd held her hand, wiped her tears, read to her, made decisions with the hospice nurse—"I swear I'll never forgive you."

ASHLEY RUSHED THROUGH her morning work at the landscaping company. She created and printed invoices, prepared a bank deposit, and entered a week's worth of receipts. Luckily, it was all pretty usual and she could mostly run on autopilot because her mind wasn't on her job.

It was on a certain hunky construction worker/part-time cowboy.

A vision of Dallas wearing his cowboy hat and riding a horse filled her mind. As did the memory of his amazing kiss. Smiling, Ashley's sigh filled the small office.

She was still smiling when Jarod, the owner of the company, knocked on the doorframe. It was rare she saw Jarod. Usually, he was out on jobs when she worked and if had something to say to her, or something specific he wanted her to do he either left a note or sent a text.

The bottom fell out of her stomach.

He wasn't going to tell her she was out of this job, too, was he?

He gestured to the stack of mail she had on the corner of the desk. "All done?"

"Yes. Unless you need something else." She'd do anything he needed because she couldn't afford to lose another job.

"Nah, I'm good. I cleaned out my pockets and truck this morning so you're caught up."

"Okay." She braced for bad news. "So what's up?"

He shrugged. "Nothing. We just haven't touched base in a while and since I had to come back here for supplies I thought I'd come say hi, see how everything is going."

"Oh." She released her breath. "Good. Really good. Your sales are up from last week. I've printed up a copy of your weekly sales report as well as an aging report."

She grabbed the papers, handed them to him. "There's only one customer over sixty days in paying their bill and there's a reminder for them in the outgoing mail. The rest are current."

"That's good." His lips twitched. "But surely my sales figures aren't the reason for that smile. It was so bright when I stepped in here I thought I might need my sunglasses."

Feeling the burn on her cheeks, Ashley turned to power down the computer.

Jarod's chuckle carried from the doorway. "That's what I thought. Well, I gotta go. You have a good day."

"You, too."

She finished setting the office to rights, grabbed the stack of mail because there was a mailbox a half-block away, and headed out. She'd dropped off the mail and was putting on her seat belt when her phone pinged with an incoming text. It was from Jess.

"My evening is wide open. Feel like company and a little wine?"

Even though it wouldn't take long to have a quick conversation via text, Ashley hooked up her phone to her headset. As her car was older than Moses, it didn't have Bluetooth capability and she wanted to get to the house site as soon as possible so she could leave earlier than usual to prepare for her pizza date with Dallas. Fastest way to do that was to talk as she was driving.

She dialed Jess's cell, then put her phone in her cupholder. She was pulling out of JJ's Landscaping Services when Jess picked up the call.

"Hey, it's me," Ashley said. "I'm just on my way to the house."

"Did you get my text?"

"I did."

"So what time should I come over?"

"Actually, tonight doesn't work."

"Oh. Okay. You and Brittany have plans?"

"We do," Ashley said. She shoulder checked before changing lanes. "We're having pizza night."

"Real pizza or that frozen crap from the supermarket?"

Ashley laughed. "Real pizza."

"What's the occasion?"

"Who says I need an occasion?"

Jess let out a long-suffering sigh. "Please. You never buy the good stuff."

"I'm not the one buying it," she said, biting her lip.

She must have given it away with her voice because Jess's voice was full of excitement when she responded. "It's a man!" she squealed.

Ashley stopped for a yellow light. "It is," she responded much calmer than she felt. Inside she was a wreck.

"Ooh! Tell me it's that construction worker. Dallas, right?"

"Yes, it's Dallas. He asked me yesterday, when I went to the ranch."

"The ranch! Shoot, I forgot all about that. I told you I'd text you back last night but after yoga I ran a hot bath with a glass of wine and by the time I remembered I knew you'd be asleep. Tell me everything!"

Laughing, Ashley did indeed tell her friend everything as she drove to the house. In fact, she was still talking when she pulled up behind the open back of Rick's trailer and cut the engine.

She couldn't see behind the house so she had no idea if Dallas was there or not. Her stomach fluttered as she pictured him, tool belt slung low on his hips. It was a toss-up which was sexier, the tool belt or the cowboy hat.

She grinned. Maybe one day she'd see him in both at the same time.

"Anyway, Jess, I'm here and I want to put in my hours so I can get home in time to clean up."

"Okay, I can take a hint. But you'll call me later?"

Ashley rolled her eyes. "Yes, I'll call you later."

"And you'll wear that pretty blue blouse I bought you for your birthday?"

"Jess, it's just pizza."

"It's a *date*, Ash. Wear the blouse."

Before she could answer Jess hung up. Not that it mattered. Because despite what she'd said to the contrary, Ashley had already planned on wearing the blouse.

DALLAS CAME ARMED with two large pizzas, some sodas, and flowers. He wasn't sure of the protocol regarding dating women with kids, as this was a first for him, but he'd decided to err on the side of caution. He'd much rather embarrass himself than hurt a woman's feelings.

With one hand full of pizzas, a bag of sodas dangling from his wrist and the flowers hidden behind his back in his other hand, Dallas tapped the door with the toe of his boot.

"Pizza delivery," he called.

Ashley answered the door, grinning. "I knew it was you before you knocked. I smelled the cheese the moment you came up the stairs."

He faked disappointment. "I was kind of hoping you'd be happier to see me than food."

Her cheeks flushed darker than the red boxes in his hand. He considered it a fine start to their evening.

Chuckling, he held out the boxes for her to take. "Don't worry about it. I know pizza is pretty tough to beat."

She took the food, brushing his hands with hers as she

did. Despite the blush, she looked him in the eye. "I'm just as happy to see you." She stepped back. "Come on in."

Since the entryway was barely big enough for one person to stand in, let alone two, she breezed straight into her kitchen. After toeing off his boots, he followed her the rest of the way into her home.

Holy shit. He'd thought the stairwell hot and stifling, but her apartment wasn't much better. Though she had a small air-conditioning unit in the kitchen window and two floor fans circulating, the place was still lukewarm.

Her kitchen was the pass-through type with a fridge and stove on one side and sink on the other. The little counter space she had was filled with a coffee maker, toaster, and kettle.

Ashley set the pizza on the small table she'd already set for the three of them.

"Have a seat," she said as she gestured to one of the chairs that surrounded the table.

She disappeared through the other side of the kitchen, went around the corner. He heard a knock on a door as he set the bag of sodas on the table.

"Brittany, come eat while it's hot."

Her daughter must love pizza as much as her mom because Brittany was on Ashley's heels when she returned to the kitchen.

"You didn't have to wait for us," Ashley said, looking a little dismayed that he was still standing.

"Well, I didn't want to squash these." Dallas pulled the flowers from behind his back as he stepped forward.

He handed the bouquet of yellow carnations with white

baby's breath to Brittany and the pink and white lilies to Ashley. He gave himself a mental pat on the back when Brittany's eyes went round as golf balls. She took the flowers, buried her nose in the blooms.

Then, clutching them to her chest, turned to her mother and said, "I got flowers!"

Ashley, who had yet to do anything but take the bouquet from Dallas, had tears in her eyes as she watched her daughter. He was damn glad he'd gone with his idea to get both women flowers.

Ashley turned her watery gaze on Dallas. "Thank you so much."

He cocked his head. "You haven't even smelled yours yet."

She pulled them close to her heart. "I don't need to. I already know they're perfect."

Dallas had heard the expression of feeling ten feet tall but he'd never experienced it before. It was a hell of a feeling.

If someone could figure out a way to create and bottle it, they'd make a damn fortune.

"I'm glad you like them," he said, including both Ashley and her daughter in his comment.

"They're gorgeous. We should get them in water."

For the next ten minutes while the pizza cooled, Dallas entertained himself watching the women fuss over their blooms. He could have kicked himself when Ashley set hers in a juice jug. Damn. If he'd known she only had one vase, he'd have bought her another. Not that she seemed to care. Long after she and Brittany had joined him at the table, as they plowed through both the loaded and the pepperoni pizzas, Ashley's gaze kept drifting to the counter where she'd left her lilies.

"Thank you, Dallas," Brittany said. "That was so good."

"You're welcome. I'm glad you enjoyed the food and the flowers."

He got a kick out of seeing her eyes light up at the reminder of the flowers. Unlike her mother, Brittany's attention had been solely on the food for the past fifteen minutes.

Dallas smiled across the table at the girl. She was a looker like her mom. Blonde hair, brown eyes, sweet smile. No doubt she had a string of teenage boys looking twice at her.

The thought wiped the smile off his face, made the pizza churn in his stomach. Because he'd once been sixteen. And maybe he'd been too busy and overwhelmed keeping his family together to have much time for girls, but he still remembered how it had felt to be that age and have all those hormones raging wildly inside.

And just what he'd wanted to do with all those hormones.

Dallas gulped down his cola. That didn't bear thinking about. Besides, she wasn't his daughter. It wasn't up to him.

Suddenly, a vision of him standing at the door, scowling down at some horny teenager who'd come calling filled his head. Any ideas the teenager had vanished when Dallas gestured to the gun in the corner and reminded the trembling kid just what would happen if he laid a hand on the girl.

Seeing the boy's face leach of all color was enough to settle Dallas's stomach.

"I'd offer you coffee," Ashley said, "but my coffee maker broke this morning."

Brittany turned a horrified look on her mother. "You didn't buy another one?"

Ashley's mouth pinched. "Brittany…"

The girl rolled her eyes. "Right."

Dallas rose when the women did.

"Nope. We have a rule in this house. Whoever cooks supper, doesn't have to do the dishes," Ashley stated.

"I hardly cooked," Dallas reasoned as he lifted his plate off the table.

"Brought, cooked. Same difference." Ashley snatched his dish from his hands. "Honestly, it's three plates and three glasses. We can handle it."

"Mom, can I dry them later?"

"Sure, no problem."

Brittany grabbed her vase and smiled at Dallas. "Thanks again for everything, Dallas."

"You're welcome, but I hope I'm not chasing you away. You can stay with us."

"You're not. I have homework."

A few seconds later her bedroom door closed.

"I can dry the dishes," he offered.

Ashley shook her head. "Nope. They can stay in the sink until Brittany's done her homework."

Just as Ashley filled the sink with water his phone rang. Since she was busy he didn't feel bad answering the call. But he did move into the living room to take it.

"Granger Construction."

"Hey, Dallas, it's Henry Rawlings. I've got those prices

you wanted for the new cordless drills you're looking at."

Henry was his sales rep at one of the big distribution companies in the city. The ones that sold everything from bolts to rags and everything in between.

"That's great. Can you go ahead and email them to me?"

"Well, I tried all day but our system was down. That's why I'm calling so late. Was hoping it would be up and running by now. But since it's not I figured I'd just call you with them. You got a paper handy? I can just give them to you over the phone?"

Dallas looked around. Seeing a pad of paper on the desk, he grabbed it and a pen. Flipping past the used pages, he set the pad on the coffee table.

"Okay, Henry, shoot."

He wrote down the different brand names along with their prices. Looking them over, he decided on the slightly more expensive ones. He preferred quality over price as nine times out of ten, the old adage of "you get what you pay for" proved to be true.

"I'll take six of the Makita drills. Call me when they come in."

"Will do, Dallas. Have a good night."

"You, too, Henry."

Dallas ripped off the page he'd written on, folded it and tucked it into the back pocket of his jeans. Flipping the pages of the pad back over, he'd just set it back onto the desk when the words scrolled across the top of the page stopped him.

"Reasons to date hunky construction worker"

Underneath that were two columns, "pros" and "cons."

At first Dallas thought it was cute. Especially when a

quick glace showed there was much more written in the "pros" column than the other. With dishes still ringing from the kitchen, Dallas began to read the words.

But he stopped on the second item in the "pros" column. "Business owner $$$"

Dallas went cold. What was that expression? *Fool me once, shame on me?* Yeah, well, he didn't plan on there being a second time to play him for a fool.

Suddenly Ashley was at his side, reaching for the pad. He should have just walked away but he splayed his fingers over the paper, holding it in place.

Dallas turned. Ashley looked horrified. Her eyes were large orbs; her face was pale.

"It's not what you think," she said.

"Really? Because I'm pretty sure it's exactly what I think."

"Okay, yes, it is. But I didn't write it. My friend Jess did. And it was days ago, right after we'd met for the first time."

Dallas wanted to believe her. He really did. But no matter how much he was attracted to her and enjoyed being around her, he couldn't ignore what he'd read. Or what it meant. Or how it dredged up the past. She wasn't the first woman to see a self-employed man and think dollar signs. Although he'd believed her to be different.

"So she thinks you should date me because I have my own business and she assumes I'm swimming in money?"

"Yes. No. Argh!" Ashley scrubbed her hands over her face. "Look, it was the night we'd met and Jess was trying to convince me you were worth taking a chance on."

"Because of my money?"

She threw her hands up. "I guess for her that was part of it. It's not for me. Dallas, I may not be rich, but I've managed this long on my own. I don't care how much money you make. I don't want it."

Well, she had a point. She'd even asked how much she owed Ryker for fixing her car.

"If you need more convincing, keep reading. You'll notice two different handwritings."

Dallas moved his hand. Sure enough there were two different styles. The one had written gainfully employed, the bit about his business. Despite his misgivings, his lips quirked when he read—hot, sexy, turns Ash on.

He doubted she referred to herself in the third person.

Under that, in a neater script was written—kind, sweet, willing to help, cares for his family, hard working.

The cold he'd felt upon seeing the title seeped from him. And it wasn't only because he wanted to believe her, but because he had the proof of her words right in front of him.

It was more than he'd ever had with Olivia.

He shifted his gaze to the "cons" column. There were only four things written. Two were in the fancier, loopier handwriting—superior attitude, although it had since been crossed out, and quickness to judge.

In the tidier writing was written—too good to be true and has power to break my heart.

Once again he raised his gaze to hers.

"I added my own things since I've gotten to know you better," she said. "And after today I can add more, like… made my daughter feel special and gives me something to look forward to."

It wasn't easy to trust, not after Olivia, but he couldn't deny what she was saying.

"I guess I can see why you didn't cross off 'quick to judge.'" He grimaced. "I'm sorry I jumped to conclusions. Again."

Her shoulders relaxed. The worry faded from her eyes.

"I can see why you did." She reached over, ripped the list from the pad and tore it up. She dumped the bits of paper onto the desk. "Can we just forget about the stupid list?"

Instead of answering he took her hand, led her to the couch. "I was engaged once.

"Her name was Olivia and we had, or at least I had, this whole life planned out in my head." He hated that thoughts of what she'd done still had the power to hurt him. "But I found out she mostly just wanted my money."

He shook his head. "I'm no millionaire. The business is solid but it's not like I can retire. But she knew I could afford to support her and she had visions of living a grand old life while I worked and she spent what I earned."

"I can see why the list would upset you."

He shook his head. "I guess I'm not as over the past as I thought I was." He offered her a smile. "See? I'm hardly too good to be true." He turned her hand over, rubbed his thumb over the soft skin. "But I would like to date you." His lips twitched. "If you still need help deciding we can make another list."

She flushed, but didn't look away. "I don't think I need one."

Dallas stretched his arm along the back of the sofa, skimmed his fingers down her toned arm. His blood surged when she shivered.

"Does that mean you already have an answer?" he asked as he continued to gently stroke her arm.

"I'm scared."

His thumb stilled. "Why?"

"Have you ever dated a single mother before?"

"No. But—"

"Nothing about this is going to be simple. I have a very busy schedule and when I do have free time I want to spend some with my daughter."

"I understand that. I'm busy too."

Ashley shook her head. "You say that now. But what happens when I say no to getting together for the third time because of my schedule, or cancel because something's come up with Brittany?"

"And what happens if I have to cancel? Or if I'm needed at the ranch and can't make time to see you?"

"I'd understand."

He tipped his head. "But you don't think I can?"

She raised her hands. "I'm just going by my experience."

"Look, I'm not saying it'll be easy, with our schedules, but I'd like to try, see where this goes." Dallas leaned over, kissed her softly. "What do you say?"

"You make it hard to resist."

"So stop resisting."

Despite the clinging heat and the fact his shirt was sticking to his back, he wrapped his arm around her. Leaning in, he kissed her deeper, longer. He forgot he was trying to convince her to give them a chance and just lost himself in the moment, in the feel of her mouth on his.

He wasn't sure he'd ever get enough of her and the way she surrendered to him. The way she kissed him back with equal hunger, the soft sounds she made in her throat, or the way her fingers curled into his shirt.

His heart gave a warning kick, reminding him of the dangers of getting too close to a woman, too much under her spell. Yeah, that hadn't ended so well last time. But it was different with Ashley. She'd already proven herself to be twice the woman Olivia was. Even with that damned list.

Not that he was completely letting his guard down. A man didn't get that severely burned without learning to be a little cautious. But he was asking her to give him a chance to prove he wasn't like the other guys she'd dated. So the least he could do was give her the same opportunity.

When his lungs started to burn, Dallas broke the kiss. Ashley looked a little dazed when she opened her eyes. No doubt he looked the same. She had that effect on him.

"Is that a yes?" he asked.

She licked her lips. The action turned his already overheated body into an inferno. And made his jeans uncomfortably tight.

"It's a yes," she said, her voice as raw as his.

For the second time since arriving he felt ten feet tall. But before his ego could overinflate too much, her eyes cleared and instead of desire he saw worry.

"Don't break my heart, Dallas."

He wondered that she didn't know she held the same power.

Chapter Thirteen

DALLAS'S PHONE VIBRATED for the fourth time in the hour. What the hell was going on today?

He'd been delayed getting to the *House of Hope* in the first place by subcontractors who either failed to show up on time or suddenly decided to cut corners. Then he'd had to look over and sign the payroll checks; dicker on the phone to two of his suppliers to get the price they should have just given him to begin with.

It better not be another issue with a subcontractor or heads were going to roll. He'd just submitted two quotes on a couple new projects and he'd included a timeline based on his current works in progress being completed. Which wasn't going to happen if the tradesmen had to redo their shoddy workmanship or if they didn't show up in the first place.

Dallas stood from where he was cutting sheetrock. He dropped the knife onto the stack of white drywall sheets and pulled his phone from his pocket.

"Granger Construction, Dallas speaking."

"It's Ryker."

Dallas bowed his head. Well, that'll teach him to not look at his call display.

"What's up?" he asked.

"Can you come tonight? Cam and I have started cutting

the hay but Gage has plans in San Antonio and I've got to go out to Riverbend Ranch. Axel Wolf's tractor broke down and his usual mechanic can't get there until tomorrow. I told him I could look at it after supper."

Which meant if Dallas didn't go, then it would only be Cam cutting hay and they'd only get done half of what they otherwise would. And being a carpenter with several outdoor projects on the go, he was on top of the weather forecast.

They were forecasting rain next week. Which meant they had to get it cut, raked, and baled before then.

"Yeah, I'll be there as quick as I can. But, Ryker, you've got to get on finding a hired hand."

"No shit, Sherlock. But I've been a little busy. You have any luck?"

Dallas cringed. Truth be told he'd completely forgotten.

"Yeah, that's what I thought," Ryker grumbled. "I'll tell Cam to expect you."

No thanks, nothing. Just the call ending in his ear.

"You're welcome," Dallas muttered before shoving his phone back in his pocket.

"Dallas, Rick needs help holding up a panel of sheetrock." Ashley stopped in the middle of the open back doorway. "I tried but—Oh, hi, Roy."

Dallas spun. He'd thought he'd been alone in the backyard but the homeless man was there, quietly picking up scraps of wood and drywall and tossing them in the bin. Automatically, Dallas's gaze went to his truck and toolbox before he remembered he'd locked them both.

Ashley must have understood what he was thinking. When he turned back to her she was frowning as she stepped from the doorway into the sunshine. He assumed she was coming to see him so was taken aback when she walked to the homeless man instead.

Her eyes were bright as he'd ever seen them. "Dallas, I'd like you to meet Roy. As of today, he's an official volunteer with *Houses of Hope*."

Shock filled Roy's brown eyes. "I am?"

"He is?" Dallas said at the same time.

"He is," Ashley affirmed with a sharp nod. She looked to Roy. "Or you will be once you sign the required paperwork."

Roy looked pained. "That'll be a problem."

No kidding. Because what was a homeless man supposed to put down for an address?

"It won't," Ashley promised. She gave Roy a reassuring smile. "Trust me. Rick's got it all worked out."

Roy looked about as convinced as Dallas felt. Although Dallas doubted the man held more reservations than he did. It was one thing to let Roy clean up a little outside but to trust him with the tools? With Brittany when she came to volunteer? His eyes narrowed.

With some more cajoling and reassuring, Roy finally went inside.

"Are you sure this is a good idea?" Dallas asked.

"Yes. I'm very sure."

"How can you be? Do you even know anything about this guy?"

Her back stiffened. "Do you?"

It was the day they'd first met all over again. Hands on her hips, she faced him, fearless and strong, sure of her convictions. Only this time instead of getting angry in return, his heart stumbled. Because the woman was something.

Despite the fact this could very well lead to their first fight, she clearly wasn't going to back down. In fact, she literally went toe-to-toe with him.

"No, I don't," he conceded. "And that's why I don't like it. He could be a thief just waiting for the right opportunity."

"Yes," Ashley scoffed. "Because we'd never notice him running down the street dragging a generator."

He bit back his smile. "There are smaller things he could steal. But besides that you and a few other women work here. Not to mention your daughter." Dallas gave her a pointed look. "I understand wanting to help someone but you can't do it at your own risk. Or Brittany's."

Her eyes went soft. "I appreciate your concern, but Roy is not a threat."

"How can you be so sure?"

A car lumbered down the back alley. Ashley waited until it had passed before continuing. "Because I've talked to him. Because he's had a chance to steal many times over and hurt one of us if he so wanted. But he hasn't." Ashley took a deep breath. "Look. I may not be homeless, thank God, but there were months along the way where I was one paycheck away from it. Heck, most months I still am. And had I lost my apartment, had I had to live on the street, would that have made me a bad person? Someone to be feared or mistrusted?"

"No, but—"

Ashley held up her index finger. "But nothing. The point is we don't know his story and it doesn't matter to me. What matters is the kindness I see in his eyes. And he doesn't smell of alcohol or have any signs of someone strung out on drugs. I think he just wants to feel useful and needed."

"Isn't there any other place he can do that?" Dallas asked.

Ashley squeezed his hand. "I know you're worried, and it's sweet of you. But it'll be fine, you'll see."

Dallas blew out a frustrated breath. There was no point arguing. It wasn't like this was his project and he had a say. But that didn't mean he had to like it.

And it didn't mean he wouldn't be keeping an eye on the man. Just in case.

ASHLEY SLID THE pot she'd used to boil the spaghetti into the soapy dishwater.

"How'd the tutoring go with Mr. Sherman?"

"Good."

"Just good?"

Brittany shrugged a shoulder. "Yeah."

Why was it teenagers could go on and on with their friends but couldn't string a sentence together for their parent? But then Ashley remembered she hadn't been so different.

Of course, her parents had never encouraged her to talk either. When she'd tried they'd often looked bored, or pretended they were listening while their eyes stayed glued to the TV or whatever else held their interest. It didn't seem to matter if it was magazines, crossword puzzles, or *Wheel of Fortune*. Everything was more interesting to them than their daughter.

Which was how she'd gotten pregnant at sixteen to begin with. All the signs were there for her to have a teenage pregnancy. Neglectful parents, only child desperate for attention.

It was Ashley's greatest fear that her daughter would end up the same. It was why she made a point to have mother/daughter time. Why she always asked Brittany how her day was and actually listened to the answer. She shut off the TV or put down her phone when her daughter wanted her attention. She never wanted Brittany to feel as though she was invisible. As though she didn't matter.

"So you'll be good for your finals?"

Even though her daughter wasn't looking directly at her, Ashley saw her roll her eyes.

"Yes, Mom. Don't worry."

Ashley rinsed the pot, set it into the other sink for Brittany to dry, then drained the water. Wiping her hands on a tea towel she said, "Okay, I just want to make sure. Because Mr. Sherman has been giving you a lot of his time. I'd hate to think it was for nothing."

"It *wasn't*," Brittany grumbled. "Can you just let it go?"

The pots rattled as she slammed the clean one in the cupboard.

"Easy!" Ashley scolded.

"Sorry," Brittany responded in a tone that clearly implied the opposite. Then she hung her tea towel on the fridge handle and stomped away.

Ashley leaned against the counter, bowed her head. Other than mornings, it wasn't very often Brittany acted like the typical moody teenager. But when she did, it was exhausting.

She'd love nothing more than to sit down with a glass of iced tea and lose herself in a steamy romance novel. Unfortunately, she'd rushed straight home from the new house to have supper with her daughter instead of stopping on the way for groceries, which meant she had to go get them now.

Ashley's feet weighed a ton as she picked her purse from where she'd hung it on the back of a kitchen chair and walked to the door.

"I'm going for groceries," she called. "Do you need anything that isn't already on the list?"

No answer. Ashley shouted again. Still nothing.

Doing a little stomping of her own Ashley backtracked to Brittany's door. She knocked and opened the door.

Brittany yanked an earbud from her ear. "What?"

Ashley strangled the door handle. It was the safer alternative.

"I'm going for groceries. I *asked* if you needed anything that wasn't already on the list."

"No, Mom."

"How about 'no, thanks, Mom,'" Ashley corrected.

"No, *thanks*, Mom," her daughter responded. "Now, can you shut the door?"

Sighing the sigh of every beleaguered parent, Ashley shut the door. In her car, she took a moment to rest her forehead on the steering wheel and calm down. Otherwise, she was liable to get to the store and bite someone's head off for having the audacity to look at her.

It was a good thing Dallas had said he had to go to the ranch tonight. It was a little soon in their relationship for him to see her this frazzled. It would likely send him running. And she didn't want that to happen. Not when the man could kiss the way he did.

Which made her wonder how well he did other things.

It hadn't escaped her notice that, other than work, they'd have the following weekend to themselves when Brittany was away on her horseback riding trip. Ashley hadn't told Dallas about that yet. Mostly because she hadn't decided just what she wanted to happen in her daughter's absence.

But the possibilities were enough to brighten Ashley's mood.

She felt like a different person walking into the grocery store twenty minutes later. Instead of dwelling on moody teenagers, she was thinking of a certain part-time cowboy and all the fantastic ways they could spend the weekend.

It was those kinds of thoughts that had her mind in the clouds and the reason she bumped into someone else's shopping cart.

"Oh, I'm so sorry!" she exclaimed.

It wasn't until she raised her gaze from the metal carts that she recognized who she'd bumped into.

"Mr. Sherman!"

His mouth curved under his gray mustache. "Hello Ms. Anderson."

"I'm so sorry. I wasn't paying attention."

"That's all right. I get distracted down the cereal aisle myself. Too many choices."

Since that was safer than saying she'd been thinking about seeing her new boyfriend without a shirt on, Ashley didn't correct him.

"Actually, I'm glad I bumped into you, no pun intended," she added with a smile. "I wanted to say how much I appreciate you giving Brittany all the extra tutoring in chemistry."

His brows were as bushy as his mustache and they came together like one furry caterpillar.

"I haven't been tutoring Brittany. In fact, she's one of my best students."

Though they weren't anywhere near the freezer section Ashley's blood went cold. It *had* seemed a little strange to her that her daughter was getting extra help in a subject she'd had straight *As* in on her last report card, but Brittany had said she didn't understand the new material and didn't want her marks to fall before the final.

"So she's not struggling?"

He shook his bald head. "Not at all. As I said, she's one of my best students."

Fear washed over Ashley. Her knees went weak. She tightened her hands on the cart's plastic handle to keep upright. Brittany had lied. Multiple times, over many weeks.

Ashley choked back a whimper because if Brittany hadn't been with Mr. Sherman getting extra help then where had she been all those afternoons?

And with who?

Chapter Fourteen

JUST AS DALLAS finished looking over an invoice that had come in, Sherry waddled in and slipped a paper under his pen. It was a short type-written paragraph. Dallas's gaze whipped up as his heart dropped to his boots.

"You're not quitting, are you?"

She settled her hands over her belly. "Not until I have to," she said. She'd already told him she wasn't planning on coming back after the baby. "But you can't keep putting this off."

She gestured to the paper she'd set down. "It's an ad for my position. I think I covered everything but wanted you to look it over before I send it in."

Dallas read over the brief ad. "Looks good to me." He handed it back to her. "Thanks."

"You're welcome. I know you've been extra busy with your dad and the ranch but I don't want Granger Construction suffering because you don't have a qualified office manager when I leave. And," she added as she rubbed her swollen belly, "I really don't want to have this baby here so the sooner I can get someone trained, the better."

He shuddered at the idea of her having the baby there alone when he was out on a job. Or nearly as bad when he was there.

Born and raised on a ranch meant he'd seen his share of births over the years and while he'd had to help with more births than he could count, he *never* wanted to help a woman deliver a child. The thought scared the shit out of him.

"Agreed. So how soon can this get posted?"

"Deadline for print is today at noon for it to go in Friday's paper. Otherwise, the online sites are pretty much instantaneous."

"Perfect. Go ahead and post it."

He straightened the stack of invoices he'd just looked over and handed them back to her.

"Are you heading to the *House of Hope* for the rest of the day or the ranch?"

He checked his watch. It was two thirty.

"The house. Gage is on days off as of today so he'll help Cam with the baling."

"And you can keep whittling down those hours."

Tired as he was with his crazy schedule, he was no longer in a hurry to rush through his community service. And he no longer resented going over there either. A vision of Ashley filled his head. Yeah, no surprise there.

The office phone trilled.

"I'll get it," Sherry said. She turned to leave.

"I'm right here. I've got it."

He picked up the phone with one hand and a pen with the other. Dragging a notepad closer, he said, "Granger Construction, Dallas speaking."

"Dallas, thank God." A woman breathed in his ear. "I didn't know who else to call and I'm at my wit's end."

"Um, okay?" He signaled to Sherry that he had it. She

nodded and went back to her desk, closing his door behind her. "What's this regarding?"

He'd spent the morning overseeing his projects. They remained on schedule, thanks to nagging his subs, and on budget from some hard negotiations with his suppliers.

Unless Mr. Finkel from the probation office suddenly became a woman, it wasn't him. And he'd have no reason to call anyway as Dallas was fulfilling the terms of his probation.

Thinking it could be the hospital calling, he sat up straighter. Had something happened to his dad? Maybe they hadn't been able to get a hold of the rest of his brothers and had tracked him down instead?

He tightened his grip on the pen. Despite his feelings toward his dad he didn't want the man to die.

"Sorry. My name is Jess Langston. I'm a friend of Ashley's."

His first reaction was relief. It wasn't about his dad. But then her words fully sank in and he was terrified all over again.

"Is something wrong with Ashley?"

"I don't know. I can't find her."

Dallas dropped the pen, shoved the chair back, and stood. "What do you mean you can't find her?"

"She hasn't texted me back since last night, so this morning I called the body shop where she was supposed to work and they said she called in sick. So I bought some soup to take to her for lunch but her car wasn't there."

"Did you check the *House of Hope*?"

"I did. Rick said he hadn't seen her but she did call to say she wasn't going in today. Dallas," her voice cracked, "this isn't like her. She never misses work."

Dallas tried to keep his own worry down. One of them panicking was enough.

"What about other friends?" His gut rolled. "What about Brittany?"

"Well, legally the school isn't supposed to tell me anything but my sister is the secretary at the high school. She said Brittany is there. Has been all day."

Dallas bowed his head. Thank God.

"She also said Ash stopped by there shortly after classes started this morning. Though she couldn't tell me what it was about, she did say she was there for about half an hour talking to the principal. And she looked distressed."

What in the hell was going on?

"Okay. She can't be far, then."

"That's what I thought but where is she and why isn't she answering my calls?" She sniffled in his ear. "Have you tried calling her today?"

"I texted her this morning but when she didn't answer I just assumed she was busy with work." And then he'd gotten busy and he'd just decided they'd see each other that afternoon at the house.

"Shit," he muttered as he rubbed his brow. "You have no idea where she could be?"

"No, that's why I'm calling you. I'd hoped maybe you two had decided to play hookie for the day. Although that wouldn't explain her having gone to the school."

"Let me try calling."

With the landline in one hand, Dallas pulled up his list

of contacts and dialed Ashley.

"It's ringing," he conveyed to Jess.

But that was all it did and after the fourth ring it went to voice mail.

"Hey, it's Dallas. Listen, your friend Jess just called me. She's worried about you. *I'm* worried about you. Can you call one of us back, please, so we know you're okay?"

"I heard," Jess said before Dallas had a chance to say anything.

"I'll text her too."

Cradling the receiver between his shoulder and cheek, Dallas went back to Ashley's contact information and shot off a text basically saying the same thing his voice mail had said.

"When was the last time you drove past her house?" Dallas asked.

"When I went over on my lunch break to bring her soup. I'd go again but I have clients booked all day. Other than lunch, I've only been able to squeeze in calls and texts in between clients or when I've had to wait for color to set."

Dallas didn't know what in the hell that meant until she clarified she was a hairdresser.

"Gotcha. Well, I can drive past her place now, see if she's there."

"Thank you," Jess sighed. "And you'll let me know either way?"

"I've got your number now. As soon as I get there I'll call you."

Dallas hung up, punched Jess's contact information into his phone, and grabbed his wallet and keys from his desk drawer.

"Everything all right?" Sherry asked when he marched from his office.

"Not sure yet," he answered. "I'll see you tomorrow."

He hurried out the door and across the gravel parking lot to his truck. He threw his wallet and phone on the passenger seat and cranked the engine. He hoped to hell she was home. Because if her best friend had no idea where she could be, how the hell was he supposed to find her?

IT WAS TRUE what they said. *You can run but you can't hide.*

Not that Ashley had been running. She'd been scrambling to figure out what Brittany was up to and why she'd lied about it. Though she'd been tempted to barge into her daughter's room after returning from the grocery store last night, she'd refrained.

She treasured her relationship with her daughter and didn't want to ruin it by going in angry and tossing accusations around.

So she'd gone to bed, fretted all night, and that morning had set out to see what she could learn on her own before she confronted Brittany. So she'd gone to the school to see if they knew of any other activities her daughter was in, or if anything was going on that she didn't know.

The principal was as baffled as Ashley. Brittany was a good student, had many friends. She never missed class and was always pleasant. There was no change in her behavior or habits and, no, they hadn't noticed her spending unusual amounts of time with anyone she didn't normally associate with.

Walking out of the school she'd been both relieved and even more worried. If it wasn't anything at school, then what was going on? She'd gone to the drugstore where Brittany worked next. She'd left there no further ahead. Brittany hadn't missed a shift and they hadn't seen any change in her behavior.

Though she'd been tempted to make calls to Brittany's friends' moms, she'd refrained. The last thing she wanted was to tarnish her daughter's reputation unnecessarily. Instead, she'd just texted them a reminder of the horseback riding weekend and how excited Brittany was that the girls were joining her.

She figured if anything was amiss or they were worried about something it was an opening for them to say so. But, like the school and her job, Maddy and Emily's moms answered back positively. Their girls were excited and wasn't it going to be a great time for the three of them?

No further ahead, and sick as to what Brittany was lying about, Ashley had gone to a park. The ducks swimming on the pond hadn't been any help. Neither were the smells wafting from the two food trucks parked nearby. Normally, she loved the smell of barbecue, but not today. Today it stuck in her throat and made her want to gag.

Which was why she didn't linger long. Without being able to afford the gas to drive aimlessly, she eventually found her way home. Now she was sitting in her warm living room, smelling boiled cabbage from the apartment across the hall, and staring at her black TV screen. She hadn't even bothered to turn it on for background noise.

Not that she needed it. There was enough with the traffic outside and the sound of her phone either trilling or beeping with incoming calls or texts. She looked at them in case any were from Brittany. Since none were, she didn't bother answering.

She didn't want to talk about the fear clawing at her throat. Because she foolishly hoped if she didn't speak about it, it wasn't true. Which was foolish in itself because she had to talk about it with Brittany.

Tears filled her eyes. History repeated itself, but she really hoped it wouldn't in her daughter's case.

She ignored the heavy footfalls coming down the hallway until they stopped in front of her door.

"Ashley." *Knock, knock, knock.* "It's Dallas."

Ashley hugged herself close, bowed her head. *Not now.* Opening the door to her new boyfriend when she was a ball of anxiety on the verge of tears was not how she wanted to start their relationship.

Knock. Knock. Knock. "Come on, Ashley," he said in a soothing tone. "I know you're home. I saw your car in the lot."

Shoot. Well, she couldn't very well ignore him now. Although she'd already done that with his calls and texts, it was easier to find excuses for those. She'd been driving. The phone had been at the bottom of her purse and she hadn't heard it. Of course, that meant lying, which was an even worse way to begin a relationship.

So either she opened the door and risked scaring him away with her drama or she ignored him and risked losing him by avoiding him.

Damned if I do. Damned if I don't.

Bracing for the inevitable, Ashley pushed off the couch and slogged to the door. She didn't bother faking a smile but she did blink to clear the tears before she unlocked the door and faced Dallas.

His gaze darted over her face before scaling down the length of her body. Some of the tension left his shoulders as his eyes met hers.

He placed his hands in his front pockets. "Hey."

Tall, strong, and handsome, he filled her doorway. He hadn't shaved that morning. Golden stubble darkened his jaw and cheeks. His backward facing ball cap made his clear blue eyes stand out even more. He looked like a male model standing there, which, of course, only made her more aware of her own shabbiness.

There were messy buns, and then there was the mess she could feel half falling down her back. Though he'd seen her without makeup before, her eyes were sure to be red and puffy given she'd been crying and the bags under her eyes were likely double their usual size after last night's lack of sleep.

Well, if she was going to give him one reason to run, she might as well give him ten. Although, it could have been worse. She could have been wearing ratty shorts and a faded T-shirt, which she'd have changed into upon coming back from the park if she'd had the energy. Instead, she still wore the yellow tank top and navy capris she'd worn when she'd left that morning.

"Hi," she answered.

"Your friend Jess called me. She's worried. You weren't answering her calls or texts and she said you hadn't gone to work today." He tipped his head to the side. "You didn't answer my calls or texts either. Are you okay?"

Hearing the concern, seeing it in his eyes, Ashley had to fight a fresh onslaught of tears. Looking away, she spun on her heel. Not trusting her voice, she signaled for him to follow.

Stalling, she veered into the kitchen, poured them each a glass of water. He stood by the table, his gaze watchful. It did little to settle her nerves.

He accepted the glass she passed him but instead of taking a drink, he set it on the table. Then he took her glass and did the same with hers.

Before she could ask why, he stepped forward, wrapped his arms around her, and pulled her close. It made her feel safe. Cherished. And in that moment, she didn't feel quite so alone.

Ashley's eyes filled with hot tears. Her throat closed. She pressed her cheek to his chest and hugged him back.

The ticking of the kitchen clock marked the time passing but neither of them was in a hurry to break the embrace. Ashley could've gladly stayed within the comfort of his arms forever but it wasn't going to solve anything, no matter how good it felt.

With a resigned sigh, she drew back. She ran her fingers over his T-shirt where her tears had darkened the light gray cotton.

"Sorry about that," she said with a watery smile.

He grasped her hand, held it there. "I don't like seeing

you sad."

"I don't much care for it either."

She pulled her hand free, once again grabbed her glass. Taking it with her, she settled onto the couch.

"You should text Jess," he said as he took a seat next to her. "Let her know you're okay."

Ashley picked up her phone. She winced when she saw the amount of messages she'd ignored. No wonder Jess had called Dallas.

With her index finger, Ashley typed out a message. *"I'm ok. Dallas here. Sorry I worried you. Will explain later. XX"*

Jess must have had her phone handy because immediately the little bubbles appeared to show she was responding. *"Thank God! You scared me 2 death. Call me when you can. Be home after 6. XO"*

Ashley set her phone down, grabbed her glass. She took a sip though she really wasn't thirsty. Mostly, she needed to keep her hands from fidgeting.

Looking at him she said, "I'm sorry you got involved in this. It never occurred to me that Jess would call you."

His brows drew together. "You'd rather me not know?"

She put down her glass. "I'd rather not scare you off mere days after getting together."

He set his water next to hers. "You think I scare off that easily?"

"Well, you don't know what it is yet."

"No. I don't. And I'm not going to force you to tell me what it is either. But I will say this. You know a lot of shit about my family. It wasn't exactly *Happy Days* that day I brought you to the ranch. You got to see Ryker's sparkling personality firsthand. Yet you still agreed to go out with me."

He leaned forward, forearms on his knees. "I don't know what's going on, but I don't scare easy and I'd like a chance to prove I can be the kind of man that stands by his woman when she's having a hard day."

His woman. She liked the sound of that. But it didn't take away her apprehensions. This wasn't just a bad day at work butting heads with a coworker.

But he'd asked for a chance to prove himself and he deserved that chance. So she told him about catching Brittany in her lies and her fears of what it could mean. And how, hoping to learn something, she'd gone from the school, to Brittany's job, and so far as texting her friends' moms hoping to learn something.

"But I've gotten nowhere," she said.

"No, you've gotten somewhere. You know she hasn't missed school or work and her grades haven't changed." He cupped her shoulder. "Those are good things, Ashley."

"I know. But it doesn't make me feel less sick inside."

She'd never considered drugs, as nothing about her daughter's behavior implied she was going down that road. So, while she was thankful for that, it really only left one possibility. A boy. Which begged the question, why was she hiding him from her mother?

Ashley bowed her head. "My biggest fear was always that she'd end up like me. I wanted so much more for her than that."

"Don't borrow trouble," he said. "You don't know why she lied."

"I can't think of anything else it could be."

"Then it's something you haven't thought of." He squeezed her shoulder. "Trust in the job you've done. Trust in her."

Ashley's jaw trembled. "I'm trying. But I work some evenings and I'm not always home and there've been lots of times when she could've—"

"*Could've* doesn't mean *did*." He moved closer, put his other hand on her knee. "It'll be okay."

Feeling like her chest was being pulled apart, Ashley looked him in the eye. "I can't guarantee it will be. Neither can I promise there won't be more issues like this that come up. This is what my life is like, Dallas. This is what you're getting into."

"That's twice now you've tried to warn me off. Are you having second thoughts?"

She wrung her hands. "No. But it feels selfish bringing you into my drama. Why would you want any of this?"

"If by 'this' you mean a beautiful woman that I can't stop thinking about, then I'd be an idiot not to want to be involved. Besides, I knew what I was getting into when I first kissed you."

He inched closer. He slid his hand from her shoulder to cup the back of her neck. Goose bumps broke out along her skin at the feel of his calloused hand on her skin.

Of course, it could have something to do with the heated look that came into his eyes.

He moved even closer, lowered his head until his lips hovered over hers. "And this changes nothing."

If his words hadn't convinced her his kiss sure did. Heck, it did more than that. It made her heart pound. Made her head spin. Made her ache where a woman aches for a man.

The hand on her neck tightened. The other started a slow path up her thigh, stopping at her hip. Beneath his touch, she quivered. Her blood chugged thick and hot through her veins.

Holding on to his narrow waist, she leaned toward him, her body miles ahead of her head. But then that made sense since her brain had short-circuited when his mouth claimed hers.

Even though she'd gotten pregnant and become a mother at sixteen, she'd never been a sex-craved teenager. Oh, sure, she'd fantasized about it. Who hadn't? But it had always been more about the idea of it. The vision of passionate kisses, loving embraces, and the afterglow, which, she'd learned the hard way, was the biggest fantasy of all. Or at least it had been at sixteen. There was nothing warm or romantic about putting on your panties and jeans on a narrow bench seat of a truck.

But with Dallas it was different. He was all man and muscle and her hands itched to slide up his chest, feel the muscles move beneath her palms. She wanted to see them play as he shucked off his shirt. As he reached for his buckle…

The sound of a key in the lock penetrated the fog of lust she'd been lost in. Ashley leapt back, her hands going to her cheeks. Her skin burned under her palms.

"Brittany's home," she whispered.

Looking smug and not nearly as panicked as Ashley felt, Dallas leaned back on the cushions.

"I figured as much."

Feeling a bit like a hypocrite, knowing she was going to ask Brittany about being with a boy when it surely looked like that was exactly what she'd done, Ashley hurriedly yanked out the elastic from her disheveled bun. She plowed her fingers through her hair, deliberately slid further from Dallas.

Brittany breezed into the living room, stopped when she saw them.

Her gaze danced from one of them to the other.

"Hey," she said by way of greeting. "I didn't expect to see you guys here."

Seeing her daughter instantly brought her mind back to why Dallas was there and what they'd been talking about before they'd made out like teenagers.

Not a good analogy, Ash.

"I was just leaving," Dallas said as he came to his feet. "Good to see you, Brittany." He looked to Ashley. "You can call me later, if you want. I'll be home."

"Thanks," she said.

He winked before seeing himself out.

Brittany waited for the door to close before she turned a grin on her mother. "I don't suppose he brought pizza again, did he?"

Ashley forced a smile. "No such luck."

"Bummer. Guess I'll settle for cereal." She dropped her backpack, aimed for the kitchen.

Though Ashley's stomach was one big knot that kept getting tighter and tighter she called her daughter back. "Hold up, your snack will have to wait. You and I have to talk."

For a moment Brittany looked panicked, which, of course, just made Ashley worry more. She got a 'deer-in-the-headlights' look before she flicked it away with a toss of her blonde hair.

"Sure. What's up?"

Clasping her hands together, she faced her daughter. "What's up is that I know you've been lying to me about the tutoring. What I want to know is why and what you've been doing instead."

Chapter Fifteen

It was too nice a night to sit inside and watch TV. Not that Dallas's mind was on baseball anyway. So, with a beer in hand, he stepped onto his front porch and settled into one of his Adirondack chairs.

It was a nice evening. The wind was light, the temperature hovered around seventy-one degrees. Comfortable in bare feet, jeans, and a button-down he hadn't bothered to button, Dallas took a pull from his beer.

From somewhere within the foliage of the oak trees came the scratching sound of katydids. "Katy did, Katy didn't," he remembered his mom telling him. If a person stopped and really listened, that was exactly what it sounded like they were saying.

He lived on a pretty tree-lined residential street in an older section of San Antonio. A more mature neighborhood also meant his neighbors were mostly retired couples that had time to fuss in their yards. Tidy rows of colorful flowers edged sidewalks and decks, circled ornamental trees. Sunny marigolds sprung from raised flowerbeds. The grass was green and lush from fertilizer and several lawns boasted the distinctive pattern of having been recently mown.

As much as he enjoyed the tidy, well-kept yards, what really drew Dallas to this part of town were the houses.

Older neighborhoods such as this were his favorite because the houses weren't cookie cutter homes. He could walk the entire street and not see two exactly the same. Most new subdivisions were regulated and all the houses ended up looking like one another. Even their landscaping was similar.

But here, creativity reigned. Bay windows, dormers, screened sunrooms, wraparound porches, and the good old days where the lots were bigger. Nowadays, some houses were built so closely together, it seemed as though whenever neighbors opened their windows they could practically reach out and shake hands without stepping out of their home.

He'd done work on a bi-level house where one guy's deck was built higher than the fence separating him from his neighbor. So the poor guy in the bungalow next door couldn't do anything without someone looking at him and the fence was too low to allow the guy in the bi-level any privacy either. Dallas shook his head. That wasn't for him.

Both he and his neighbors had bungalows and the fences were high enough to allow privacy. The only reason he'd chosen to sit on the front porch was because he liked to watch the sun go down.

And because he was hoping Ashley would drop by.

He'd texted her his address from his truck before he'd left her apartment. He'd also offered to go back if she needed him after her talk with her daughter. Either way, he'd wanted her to know he was there for her.

He hadn't liked the sick feeling in his gut when they hadn't been able to find her. When she hadn't returned calls.

He'd taken his first full breath when he'd seen her car in the lot. But it wasn't until she opened the door, until he saw for himself that she was okay, that the last of the fear slid off his shoulders.

Not that he'd enjoyed seeing the tears in her eyes or hearing the pain in her voice, but at least she'd been physically fine. He'd hated the worst-case scenarios that had popped in his head when Jess had first told him she couldn't find Ashley.

Anything was better than those.

And she'd thought he'd run from a little family drama. Hell, his whole family *was* drama. If it wasn't him and his brothers at odds with each other, it was them with their dad. And now some mystery woman, who might or might not be his half-sister, might or might not be his dad's mistress, was in the picture.

Dallas wanted answers. Who the hell was the woman who'd brought in their dad and why had she left without saying anything? Last time he'd texted Gage about it, they still didn't know more about this mystery woman. It was frustrating as hell.

"I hope the invitation was still open for me to stop by?"

Dallas blinked his gaze into focus. All thoughts of his dad, an affair, and everything but Ashley standing at the bottom of his porch vanished. She wore the same outfit she'd had on earlier but her hair had been brushed into a tidy ponytail. The sun caught it, turned it the color of ripe wheat.

It was damn good to see her.

"It sure was," he said.

Standing, he moved to the top step and held a hand out for her. But instead of reaching for it, her hands stayed down at her sides. And instead of looking at his face, her gaze focused on his chest. He looked down, unsure what had her attention. He hadn't eaten in this shirt so it wasn't as though he'd spilled anything.

But then he saw what she was looking at and his lips curved. He'd forgotten he hadn't buttoned his shirt and he hadn't bothered with a belt either so his jeans hung low enough the white band of his boxer briefs was visible. Judging by the flush creeping up her neck and the way her throat kept working Ashley enjoyed the view.

He'd never preened in his life but right then he wanted to take a deep breath just to see what her reaction would be. Or better yet, rip the shirt off altogether since it suddenly felt a little too warm.

His ego inflated a little more when she finally looked at him and he saw the desire in her eyes.

Clearing her throat, she put her hand in his and climbed the stairs.

He kissed her softly. She tasted like ripe strawberries.

"I didn't hear you drive up."

"That's because I didn't. I walked."

Dallas gaped. "Walked? You live, like, five miles away."

"Four and a half according to the app on my phone."

"Geeze. That must have taken you forever." He brushed his knuckles over her cheek. "If your car wasn't working, why didn't you call me? I'd have picked you up."

Just as he was going to drive her back because no way in hell he was letting her walk home. Especially after dark.

She squeezed his arm. "My car is fine. It's at home. I just wanted some time to think."

"Everything okay? How'd it go with Brittany?"

"Can I trouble you for something to drink first? I finished my water bottle about two miles ago."

He saw it then, her fatigue. It was in her voice, in the fine lines around her eyes. He could've kicked himself for not offering her something right away. She'd walked over four miles, for Pete's sake. His questions should have waited.

"Sorry, I should have thought to ask." He opened the door, gestured for her to proceed. "Kitchen's straight through to the back."

Out of habit, he locked the door behind him and followed her to the kitchen.

Peering into the fridge, he said, "I've got beer, water, juice, soda, or milk."

When she didn't answer, he braced his arm on the open door of the black fridge and looked at her.

Her eyes were wide, her mouth a perfect *O* as her gaze roamed the kitchen. Dallas stood up a little straighter. She might not be the first woman to gawk at his kitchen, but she was the first whose opinion mattered. Whose pleasure at appreciating what he'd done touched him as nobody else's ever had.

"You like it?"

"Dallas." She sighed. "Look at it. What's not to like?" Almost reverently she touched the reddish-gold wood of his cabinets. "Are these maple?"

"They are." And he'd built and stained each one himself.

Her fingers skimmed the black hardware, dropped to the creamy granite countertop. She sighed over his copper-colored double bowl undermount sink.

"Did you do all this?"

"I gutted the house when I bought it. Took a few years but I'm happy with the results."

"I should say so. It's stunning."

And he'd never been more proud of the time and effort, the nicks and cuts and frustration as he was seeing it through her eyes.

"Thanks. You about ready for that drink now?"

Laughing, she finally looked at him. "What were my choices again?"

They settled for beer on the back deck. He didn't have much in the way of landscaping other than lawn and the jacaranda and elm trees that had come with the place. He did have the one thing that made the evening perfect, however. A porch swing he'd mounted on the pergola he'd built when he'd added on the deck.

A warm spring night, a pretty girl, cold beer, and a porch swing. Other than his truck, which was parked in the garage, it had all the makings of a good country-western song.

Dusk was setting in and a few lightning bugs blinked from the back corner of yard. The katydids continued their chirping. Usually, he could smell Mrs. Olsen's roses next door but tonight his lungs were full of the citrusy smell of Ashley's shampoo.

It was fast becoming his favorite scent.

Content to sit as they were, with Ashley cuddled into his side, Dallas was no longer in a hurry to talk. He loved the feel of her tucked against him, loved the heat of her palm on his thigh, the weight of her head on his shoulder. And he really loved the softness of her skin as he ran his fingers up and down her bare arm.

"It's so peaceful here," she said.

"Hmm," he agreed, as he continued to rock the swing with his foot, the wood creaking as it swayed.

"I'm glad I came. I needed this."

"It didn't go well?"

Sighing, she eased from his side, grabbed her bottle from the deck. Dallas angled himself to see her better, but kept his arm along the back of the swing. He did it as much to offer her comfort as to satisfy his own desire to keep touching her.

"The good news is it wasn't what I feared."

Dallas peered at her. Though she said it was positive news, she sure didn't act like it. Nor did she look happy about it.

"That's good, isn't it?"

"I guess." She took a sip of her beer. "Ashley's been tutoring after school, trying to earn extra money. Her band class is planning a school trip to Disney World next spring break."

"That sounds like fun." And he still didn't see the problem.

"She didn't tell me anything about it." She bowed her head. "She said she knew I couldn't afford it and that I'd feel bad if I knew about it. She said she didn't want me working any harder or longer than I already do to try to make it happen, so she took on extra shifts at the drugstore and started tutoring so she could pay for it herself.

She shook her head. "I know it's not a bad thing for her to earn her own way but it still makes me feel like a failure. It's up to me to protect her, to give her what she needs, and here she's been trying to protect me."

Her eyes shone with tears. "And how do I repay her for that? I all but accuse her of having sex and lying to me about it."

"Hey, now," he said as he took her hand in his. "You had reason. You found out she'd been lying to you. I'm not a parent but I think it was a reasonable conclusion to assume she might have been."

Ashley looked at him. Misery was written all over her face. He hurt knowing how much she was hurting.

"She doesn't think so. She said I should know her better than that. That I should trust her." Ashley wiped the tear that slid down her now pale cheek. "She's not wrong."

"And neither are you." He shifted closer, cupped a hand behind her neck. "Ashley, you're human. You were faced with certain facts and came to a reasonable conclusion. Just because she's mad at you, doesn't mean you were wrong."

"It feels like it," she said, her voice trembling. "Just because I made a mistake when I was her age doesn't mean she's going to."

"No," he reasoned. "But it doesn't mean she won't either."

He wiped her next tear before she could. It was warm on his fingers.

"From what I've seen, you're a hell of a mother and you've raised a good kid. Give her some time. She'll come around."

The doubt filling her eyes broke his heart. So did the fact she was struggling to keep it together and instead of leaning toward him, she sat there, stiff and alone, with her chin trembling.

"Come here," he said as he drew her close. He wrapped his arms around her, held her tight enough for her to know she wasn't alone.

"God, I'm sorry to do this to you again," she said once she'd stopped crying.

"Don't be. I'm glad you came."

Ashley drew away, looked him in the eye. He was glad to see she no longer looked miserable. Tired, and spent, but not nearly as unhappy.

"You're glad I soaked another of your shirts?" she asked.

"Sure." He winked, wanting to put a smile back on her face. "Gives me an excuse to take it off."

Her gaze dipped to his chest before zinging back to meet his. Color rushed back into her face. She all but leapt from the swing. Clasping her hands before her, she asked, "Do you mind if I use your bathroom?"

Well, shit. He'd only wanted to lighten the mood, not scare her off.

"It's down the hall, second door on your right."

"Thanks."

Since the only hallway was the one that branched off between the living room and kitchen, she wouldn't have any problem finding it. Once the back door closed behind her, Dallas scrubbed his hands over his face.

Nice move, jackass.

Well, at least he could prove he was still a gentleman by driving her home. With a heavy sigh, he pushed up from the swing, grabbed their half-empty beer bottles, and brought them into the kitchen. He poured the lukewarm liquid down the sink then placed the empties in his recycle bin. He was buttoning up his shirt when he heard Ashley coming down the hall.

"I'm in the kitchen."

She came around the corner, clear-eyed and composed. The only sign she was nervous was the way she wrung her hands together.

He met her halfway across the hardwood floor.

"Ashley, I only made that comment about my shirt to try to lighten the mood. I didn't mean anything by it. I don't want you to think I was pressuring you into something you aren't ready for."

"I never thought that."

"Then why—"

"Dallas," she said with exasperation, "when a good-looking man offers to take his shirt off, a woman would rather not be a blubbering mess when he does."

His gut hitched. "So, you weren't upset?"

"The only thing I'm upset about is that you buttoned your shirt instead of taking it off." Biting her lip she looked him in the eye. "I liked the view better before."

It was the first time she'd flirted with him and it packed a hell of a punch. All the blood rushed south of his waist. Every brain cell went with it. Except for the few that commanded him to kiss her.

It probably wasn't wise to pull her against him. There'd be no mistaking the erection pressing against his zipper and he'd meant what he'd said about not pressuring her into something she wasn't ready for.

But the look in her eye when she was flush against him was anything but afraid. And when she wrapped her arms around his neck and lifted onto her toes to kiss him, there was no doubt she knew exactly what she was doing. And exactly what he wanted.

Though the air-conditioning was working just fine, a blast of heat shot through Dallas's body. Everywhere they touched, his body flamed. Which, when he backed her against the counter and pressed into her, was damn near everywhere.

Sweat broke out on his brow, between his shoulders. His heart was about ready to crash through his chest.

Dallas had built his own business from nothing. He'd been in charge of raising his brothers when he'd been barely more than a boy himself. But nothing made him feel stronger and more of a man than having Ashley in his arms. Than hearing her sigh his name. Than having her arch her body toward his.

Her tight nipples pressed into his chest, her heart banged against his. Not to mention the heat, the sweet heat he felt when her pelvis rubbed against him. If she kept doing that he'd do something he hadn't done since he was fourteen.

"Ashley." He gasped as he drew back. Then damn near said to hell with it when her slumberous eyes opened and looked into his.

"You don't have any condoms, do you?" Disappointment coated her words.

His balls tightened even more. Yeah, he had some. And he was damn tempted to run into his room, dump the box on the counter beside her and slowly but surely work his way through them. Okay, the first few probably wouldn't be so slow. But he'd make it up to her.

"I do, actually. And, trust me, I'd like nothing better to use half a dozen about now."

He shook his head. *Smooth, Dallas, real smooth.*

"But?"

"But I haven't even taken you out on a first date yet." He forced his lips into some semblance of a smile. "And I think sex on my kitchen counter is at least a second date kind of thing."

She cocked her head to the side. "Well, technically, this is our third. First was horseback riding, then the pizza, and now this."

She grinned, all bold and feisty and sexy as hell.

"Actually, the riding and the pizza were before we were officially dating and I'm not sure I'd call tonight a date. I didn't even make you supper. So how about we have a real date and then we revisit this?"

"Okay," she conceded, looking about as happy about it as he felt.

Since the last thing he wanted was for her to be disappointed or somehow feel he wasn't interested, though she couldn't possibly think that when he was still uncomfortably hard, Dallas slid his arm around her waist. "I think we're building something good here. We don't have to rush it."

He gave her a slow, languorous kiss to prove it.

"So, you free tomorrow night?" he teased.

Her laughter filled his kitchen and warmed his heart. "I have to work at *Coffee Time*. But I'm free the next night."

He kissed her again. "It's a date. Now let me drive you home."

It was only ten o'clock when Dallas dropped her off but other than a lamp in the living room, the apartment was dark. And quiet. Ashley locked the door, hung her keys on the peg, and toed off her sneakers.

It wasn't unlike Brittany to spend a lot of time in her room doing homework or texting friends, or listening to music but tonight it felt different. More like she wanted distance than privacy.

Even knowing it wouldn't last, it pained Ashley to know her daughter was angry with her. Oh, not that it was the first time, but usually when Brittany was mad at her it was for something Ashley hadn't done. Like not let her to go a party, or not let her stay out past curfew.

Tonight was different. Because this time it was for something Ashley *had* done. And regardless of her reasoning, she'd done more than anger her daughter. She'd hurt her.

Guilt weighed on Ashley as she walked down the short hallway to Brittany's door. She stopped, paused. The only thing she heard was the soft hum of the air conditioner.

Though she should probably leave well enough alone for the night, Ashley tapped on her daughter's door. If nothing else she wanted to say good night and that she loved her.

Not surprisingly, Brittany didn't respond. Undeterred, Ashley inched the door open. The bedroom was dark. The hall light was enough to see that Brittany was curled onto her side, her back to the door.

Ashley's heart tugged. She remembered being a young mom, sharing a room with her baby. Having the crib next to the bed and lying on her side watching her daughter sleep. And sometimes waking up to Brittany's cherubic face staring right back at her.

She'd spent so many hours lying there worrying about their future. Worrying how they'd manage, how she'd be able to raise a child. She'd been so afraid of screwing up. Of scarring Brittany for life if she made a mistake. Over all, she thought she'd done a pretty good job.

Her daughter had good friends, didn't get into trouble, was a good student, and worked to earn her own money. And, Ashley thought with a stab of guilt, wanted to pay for her own school trips.

Tiptoeing into the room, Ashley pressed a gentle kiss to Brittany's cheek.

"I love you," she whispered.

She closed the door quietly behind her, moved into the kitchen where she'd left her purse. Digging through it, she pulled out her Day-Timer and a pen then sat down to do some figuring.

Because, come hell or high water, Brittany was going on that trip. Ashley just needed to find a way to squeeze in more time at one of her jobs.

Somehow.

Chapter Sixteen

Dallas finished screwing in a piece of drywall into what would be Brittany's closet. Taking his measuring tape from his tool belt he measured the next section he needed. Stepping from the frame of the closet he almost bumped into Roy, the homeless man.

"Rick sent me to help you," he said.

He didn't look any more pleased about the prospect than Dallas felt. But it wasn't Dallas's project and after spending time in Ashley's apartment, he just wanted to help her get her house as fast as possible. If that meant working with Roy, so be it.

"You know how to read a tape?"

Roy's brows creased. "Doesn't everyone?"

"No. Some of the kids I take on, and some adults too for that matter, don't know three-eighths from six-eighths."

"I do. I learned to read a tape not long after I learned to read."

Dallas nodded. It was his experience that most grown men over thirty knew how. Because they'd been raised before every kid over the age of six had their own smartphone. They'd learned to play outside, build things themselves, work with their hands and brains. In other words, they'd figured shit out.

"Okay, then. Rick should have an extra tape measure and drywall knife. You ever cut sheetrock before?"

"I have."

"Good. I'm sure you saw the sheets lying outside." He rattled off the size he needed cut. "While you're doing that I'll measure the next pieces we need."

He had the rest of the closet measured and a list of the sizes he needed when Roy came back. They exchanged list for sheetrock and Dallas set the piece in place. It fit exactly. Impressed, Dallas used his cordless drill to secure it to the studs. The rest of the closet went as smoothly.

Once they moved into the main part of the room it took both of them to lift and hold the full sheet. Dallas wasn't much of a talker when he worked but Roy seemed to be. Between whirs of his drill and when Dallas was measuring the next piece, Roy filled the silence with questions.

"I take it you're Granger Construction?"

Dallas positioned another screw. "I am," he answered before drilling it home and moving to the next.

"You from San Antonio, then?"

"Not originally. I've lived here twelve years." He fastened two more screws. "I was raised on a ranch outside of Last Stand."

With his side secure, he moved over to Roy's. The man held the sheet steady while keeping his fingers clear of Dallas's drill.

"You have a big spread?"

Dallas bent to secure the corner. "Big enough."

"You farm any land or just raise cattle?"

Dallas stood, gestured to Roy he was okay to let go.

Then, with years of experience and a practiced eye, finished anchoring the sheet to the studs, keeping the screws twelve inches apart.

He was surprised to turn and see Roy measuring the next piece. Ashley's house had eight-foot ceilings so they could get away with two full sheets before they'd need to cut. Roy already had that figured and was measuring the space that would be left once they added another full sheet. Dallas couldn't deny he was impressed. The man knew what he was doing.

He set his drill down. "You interested in ranching?"

Shadows passed through Roy's eyes. The corners of his mouth turned down. "I used to have my own farm once upon a time. Cows, horses, chickens, and pigs. Hay and wheat fields."

Roy looked out the window, presumably not seeing the two-story house next door but rather the farm he used to have. Since Dallas not only didn't know what to say and really didn't want to get involved in Roy's history, he circled around the man.

"Let's go get the next sheet," he said before he strode from the room.

Thankfully, Roy didn't stay lost in his memories. He was right on Dallas's heels and soon they were back in the room butting the new sheet of drywall up against the one they'd just hung.

"You didn't like ranch life?" Roy asked before passing Dallas the drill. "That why you moved to the city?"

"Nope."

Dallas fastened the next few screws while Roy studied

him. He wasn't going to get into his life story with a stranger.

Roy seemed to realize that. He slipped out, came back as Dallas was driving home the last screw.

He passed Dallas the next length of drywall. "You a baseball fan?" Roy asked.

"Do Texans like barbecue?" Dallas retorted as he placed the section into place. Another perfect fit.

They were still talking baseball and Dallas was on the ladder fitting the last piece over the door when Ashley poked her head in the room.

"Hi," she said, looking anxious as her gaze moved from Dallas to Roy. "How's it going?"

Dallas looked over and down to where Roy stood. The older man stared back at him, still and silent. It was clear he was waiting for Dallas to answer first. Almost like a child waiting for its parent's approval.

It was hard to imagine being that age and life having knocked him so far down he had no self-esteem anymore. That he needed validation from a stranger. For the first time, he found himself wondering what Roy's story was. The man was intelligent and hard-working and definitely had skills, so he shouldn't be standing there looking like a beaten dog waiting for the next kick.

No man should.

Though Dallas hadn't lived in Roy's shoes, he knew the power of words, the good and the bad. He'd mostly only heard the bad from his dad over the last decade, but he remembered, clear as day, the effect his first client's positive words had had on him.

When the wife had seen her new kitchen, she'd squealed with delight practically laid herself on her new island. Satisfaction and pride had welled within his chest until he thought his T-shirt would rip at the seams.

He wanted that for Roy. He wanted to give the man back his pride, his sense of self-worth. And the best part was, he didn't have to lie to make that happen. He only had to speak the truth.

"It's going good. Real good. In fact, Roy can do this without me. He's been cutting pieces like he's been doing it for years. I'll finish screwing in this piece and then I think you and Roy can work on the next room and I'll see what else Rick needs me to do."

Dallas turned to Roy. The man's eyes almost blinded him. And if Dallas wasn't mistaken, he stood a little taller. It felt damn good to know he was responsible for that.

"How does that sound, Roy?"

The man gave a toothy smile. "Sounds good to me."

BRITTANY SAT DOWN on the edge of Ashley's bed. Glumly, she looked at the calendar, Day-Timer, and pad of paper Ashley had spread over her lap. And hadn't been quick enough to hide when she'd heard her daughter heading toward her bedroom.

Of course, with Ashley's room at the end of the hall and Brittany's right next to it, by the time she realized her daughter wasn't going into her own room but rather coming into her mother's, it was too late.

"This is why I didn't tell you about the tutoring," she said. "I knew you'd stress about it and try to jam even more work into your schedule."

Ashley set her pen down across the coils of her Day-Timer. "I'm just looking," Ashley answered with a reassuring smile.

As she had been since last night. With no luck.

Brittany rolled her eyes. "Mom, you don't *just look* at anything. You don't go shopping unless you need something and when you do, you only buy what you went in for. You never window shop."

No, she never did. What was the point when she couldn't afford it?

"So?"

"So, if you're looking at your schedule it's because you've already decided to work more."

Brittany looked down at her hands. "I don't want you to. I'd rather miss the trip."

And Ashley would rather not sleep for the foreseeable future than have her daughter miss out on that kind of opportunity. High school was supposed to be fun, supposed to be where memories were made. While she'd certainly made memories in high school, they weren't exactly the fun kind. She wanted better for Brittany.

"You're not going to miss the trip. And if I do take on extra work, it'll be temporary. Once we have enough saved, I promise I'll cut back." She peered at her daughter, trying to catch her eye. "How's that?"

Brittany raised her head. The glow of the lamp caught the shine in her daughter's eyes. Ashley's heart fell. She just wanted to help. She didn't want to make her daughter sad.

"I'd really rather you didn't but I don't think I can stop you."

Ashley reached across the papers, squeezed Brittany's hand. "It'll be temporary, you'll see."

"Yeah," Brittany sighed. "You say that now." She pushed off the bed. "I'm going to bed. Good night."

"Good night," Ashley answered.

She slumped against the headboard as Brittany left the room, her head bowed and shoulders drooped. She told herself it was okay, that Brittany would appreciate her efforts once she was marching through Disney World with her classmates.

But first they had to get there.

With a long exhale, Ashley sat up, grabbed the pen. There had to be a way to get in more hours somewhere. She'd already told her boss at *Coffee Time* that she was open to more hours and had given him the days and times she could squeeze it in.

There wasn't much more she could do at the other bookkeeping jobs. There was only so much she had to do there and she wouldn't drag out her work just to add hours. That wasn't fair to her employers and it would feel like cheating.

But there also wasn't time in her schedule for completely new jobs as her days were almost full. The best option would be to work a little longer at the jobs she already had. An hour here and there would add up.

She looked down at her calendar again. *Coffee Time* already knew she was up for more shifts and her other bookkeeping jobs didn't need her more. That only left the Diamond G.

It was a possibility. And, even if they didn't need her in the office, maybe she could muck stalls or some other chores. It sounded like they needed the extra help with their dad in the hospital. Maybe they'd jump at her offer.

Of course, that would add more gas, which would take away from her profits. And it would take her over two hours round trip. Damn it. Would it even be worth it? And just as important could she swallow her pride to ask Dallas?

Ashley tapped her pen against her lips.

Truth was Dallas already knew money was tight for her, which was why he'd offered her the job doing the ranch books. And he knew about Brittany's tutoring for the trip, so really, asking him for more hours wouldn't be a surprise.

Which didn't make her feel any better. God, it was mortifying to have to admit to her new boyfriend how broke she was. But what choice did she have?

As for the time, if she went on the days she didn't work at *Coffee Time* at night, then yes, it would be worth it. She was figuring out the exact times she could go to the ranch when her cell rang.

She frowned. It had been dark for hours. And Brittany was home. Who'd be—

It had to be Dallas. Her stomach twittered. She'd never expected to feel the excitement of dating again, especially at her age, but she had to admit it was wonderful. Grinning, she picked up her phone. Her heart kicked hard when she saw it was indeed Dallas calling.

She let it ring another time, more in an attempt to calm

her racing nerves than to play it cool and casual. Ha! There was nothing cool and casual about smoothing her hair and tugging on her tank top when it was just a phone call. It wasn't as though he was standing in her bedroom doorway.

Although, wouldn't that be—

She caught herself as the phone rang for the third time and hurriedly answered it. She could only hope she sounded far less nervous than she felt.

"Hi."

"Hey, there."

His gravelly voice slid into her ear, pushing all her buttons. The heat in her bedroom shot up another ten degrees. Maybe twenty. She'd always thought Sam Elliot had the sexiest voice, but Dallas had him beat. By miles.

"I didn't wake you up, did I? I figured you'd still be winding down from your shift at the coffee shop but if you're in bed I can let you go."

"I wasn't sleeping. Just doing some paperwork."

"This late?"

"Yeah and while I have you on the phone there's something I need to talk to you about."

"What's up?" he asked.

Ashley pulled the schedule she'd worked out closer. "You know about the trip Brittany is saving for?"

"Yeah."

"Well, I'd like to help with that. I've looked at my schedule and the only thing that'll work is spending more time at the jobs I already have." She took a breath, swallowed her pride, and plowed on. "I was hoping maybe there'd be some chores or something I could do at the ranch."

"Chores?"

"Well, obviously the office comes first. But I was thinking once I have it organized and caught up, it won't take me long to keep it that way. And if I'm going to be down there anyway, I may as well do some other work." She held her breath. Her heart raced faster the longer he took to answer. "If it's a problem then—"

"No, it's not. I'm sure we can figure something out. I'll talk to Ryker."

"Are you sure because you sound a little hesitant?"

"I was just thinking about how to make it happen. We both have busy schedules and I might not always be able to go when you can."

"I can take my car. I'm not asking for you to always drive me there."

"I know but—"

"No 'buts,' Dallas. The only thing I need from you is to check with Ryker to see if he needs a little help. I'll look after getting myself there."

His beleaguered sigh filled her ear and made her laugh.

"Fine," he conceded.

"Thank you."

With that settled, she closed her Day-Timer. She stacked it, the papers, and her calendar onto her nightstand before turning off her lamp. Then she lay down and snuggled into the mattress.

"I have another question for you."

"If it's about work the answer is no. You already do enough work for two people."

And wasn't it wonderful he cared?

"It's not," she confirmed.

"Then shoot."

A flush crept up her neck, heated her face. She almost backed down, told him never mind. But then she'd never been a quitter. Besides, she really wanted to know the answer.

"If sex on your counter is second date material, what can I expect for our first date tomorrow?"

His low, gravelly voice whispered over the line. "Guess you're just going to have to wait to find out."

Chapter Seventeen

HE HADN'T DELIBERATELY meant to stay away from the *House of Hope* that day. In fact, he'd been anxious to get there. He hadn't wanted to have to wait until their date that evening to see her smile. To brush up against her. To steal a kiss.

But he'd had a couple guys down with the stomach bug that was going around and he'd had to fill in. By the time they'd knocked off for the day he'd barely had time to finish his surprise, shower, and change before it was time to pick up Ashley.

His gut hitched when the door opened. It was nothing compared to the free-falling feeling he got when he caught his first glimpse of her.

If he were a cartoon character his eyes would have popped from his head, his tongue would have rolled onto the floor, and he'd have little red hearts circling his head.

"You look…" He had to work to swallow his mouth had gone so dry. "You look amazing."

And even that wasn't adequate to describe her. Angel, might have been closer. Although he didn't suppose angels wore blue floral halter-style sundresses that ended just above the knee. And while he imagined they might indeed wear gold sandals, he was certain the celestial ones weren't high and strappy. And he doubted the heavenly ones were designed to show off the length of a woman's legs.

Or meant to bring a man to his knees.

"I wasn't sure what to wear. You didn't give me much of a hint."

He pulled his gaze from her sun kissed legs. "It's perfect. You look perfect."

Her smile shone in her eyes. "Thank you."

"These are for you," he said, extending the mixed bouquet of flowers he'd bought on his way over.

"I couldn't decide on just one kind so I got you a variety. Plus I liked that it was colorful. Reminded me of you."

Her gaze dipped to the flowers as red the color of the roses spread across her cheeks. "I should put these in water. Come on in."

When she turned, her skirt did a little flare that showed off her toned thighs. His breath rushed out like he'd been sucker punched.

"I think I'd better wait here."

She stopped, looked over her shoulder. "Why?"

His gaze slid down her body and back again. God, he only had to look at her and he was hard.

"Because your daughter is at work and if I go in there, we might not get to the restaurant in time for our reservations. Or not at all."

Her eyes sparkled and she laughed. "I'm sure you can control yourself," she said before disappearing around the corner.

It was cute she thought he was kidding. But he wasn't. However he wasn't going to stand in the hallway either so he compromised. Though he followed her inside, he only went in far enough to close the door behind him. He'd promised her a real first date before they got too physical and he meant to keep that promise.

But after…

As soon as she was done with the flowers, he hurried them out the door. He'd chosen a little out-of-the-way Italian restaurant because he wanted a quiet, romantic setting. Besides, he figured it would be a nice change from barbecue or Mexican.

"This is really nice," she said as she spread her linen napkin over her lap.

He'd asked for a corner table with a little more privacy. In the middle of the cream-colored tablecloth, candlelight flickered within the frosted red holder. Soft Italian music drifted through hidden speakers. The savory smell of oregano and Parmesan floated in the air.

"The food's really good, too."

"I'm sure it is. It smells incredible." She fussed with her cutlery. "But you didn't need to do all this. You impressed me the day you brought pizza."

He frowned. "I didn't do it to impress you. I did it because I think you're special and you deserve to be treated that way."

"Thank you. But just so you know, I'm good with barbecue from a food truck, too. I don't need fancy. Although I suppose this will be less messy."

Their server arrived and placed a basket of hot dinner rolls onto the table then took their drink order. Dallas chose a beer while Ashley selected white wine.

By the time their drinks arrived they'd chosen their entrees.

Pulling back the napkin that covered the rolls, Dallas offered one to Ashley before taking one for himself. The yeasty smell made his mouth water.

"You and Roy seemed to get along yesterday," Ashley said as she slathered butter onto her steaming bread.

"Yeah." Dallas shook his head as he remembered. "The man is a good worker, knows his stuff, too. I've had guys work for me who couldn't cut and measure drywall to fit as closely as he did."

Ashley's lips curled into a smug smile. "So your first impression of him was off base, then?"

Dallas lifted his beer, tipped it her way. "Touché."

"I think he's a nice man that lost himself somehow. I'm hoping by letting him work on the house, we'll help him find his way back." She shook her head before sipping her wine. "I know that sounds cheesy."

"Cheesy doesn't mean wrong. I happen to think you're right. I think he just needs a chance."

Her brow arched. Mischief sparkled in her eyes. "I'm right? Should I mark this down in case you never admit it again?"

"Very funny. Just for that I get the last roll." He snagged it from the basket, then cut it in half and handed her a piece.

"Roy mentioned he'd owned a farm. I was thinking of talking to Ryker about him. The ranch needs another full-time hand and he might be interested. I'd offer him a job with Granger Construction but I don't really have enough work for one more right now."

Ashley leaned forward, placed her hand over his. "He'd love that. You're a good man, Dallas."

He scoffed.

"What? You are."

"There's something I need to tell you. Remember that first day at the *House of Hope*? When I asked for privacy with Rick?"

"Yeah."

"There was a reason for that. I had to give him some papers from my probation officer and I didn't want anyone to know."

She slowly set down her glass. "Probation officer?"

He gave her a reassuring smile. "You don't have to worry. It's pretty minor." He told her the story, stopping only when their food arrived. "So, that was partly why I was so short with you at first. I resented the fact I had to be there. And," he added with a grimace, "I also didn't know as much about the program as I do now. I thought it was all for free and I had the misconception that you were just looking for handouts."

Her eyes went wide and her jaw dropped.

Dallas held his hands up. "I know. I've researched it since. I know you'll have a mortgage like everyone else and I know you have to give hundreds of hours of your own time to it. And I know you're not sitting at home watching soaps and eating bonbons in between times."

She gaped. "Is that really what you thought?"

He deserved her shock and more. He wasn't proud of his assumptions.

"It was," he admitted. "And I'm sorry for it."

With pinched lips, she set her fork and knife down, grabbed her napkin. Damn it. He should have kept his damn mouth shut. Not that she didn't deserve to know, but he should have saved it for another time. Hell, he'd wanted to make her feel special and instead had admitted he'd once thought she was a lazy, entitled woman just looking for handouts.

Smooth, Dallas. Real Smooth.

But instead of slamming her napkin down and storming off, she raised it to her mouth and laughed into it. Confounded, he slumped back into his chair.

Still chuckling, she lowered the serviette. "Oh, Dallas, I don't think I've ever eaten a bonbon in my life."

Feeling embarrassed, he grabbed his beer, took a long drink. "So, you're not mad?"

"No, I'm not mad. That was before we knew each other. Besides, you've admitted you made a rash assumption and you've more than made up for it since."

He shook his head. She never failed to surprise him.

"I know better now. I know the kind of woman you are."

One he liked more each time he saw her. One he was fast developing feelings for.

"Did you actually picture me wearing a muumuu with a bowl of bonbons on my lap?"

His lips twitched. "I don't even know what the hell a muumuu is."

They were still laughing when the waiter came by with the bill.

Dallas parked the truck under the pale yellow beam of a streetlight in front of his house. Looking over to the darkened home, Ashley's nerves fluttered. Though they'd teasingly said sex on his counter was second date material, there was too much sexual tension between them to just be going inside for coffee and conversation.

And, truthfully, that wasn't what she wanted.

Up until now, he hadn't really touched her and she craved the moment when he would put his calloused hands on her. When he'd press his skin against hers. When he took her aching breasts into his hands. Into his mouth.

Heat burned her cheeks and ears. Ducking her head, Ashley reached for the handle on her door. Before she could grasp it, however, Dallas leaned over, pulled her hand.

"Nope. You have to wait a bit."

God, if she waited any longer… "Dallas, let's just—"

He grinned. "Nope. I have a surprise. Just stay here. It'll only take me five minutes. Ten tops. I'll come get you when it's ready."

He didn't give her a chance to argue. He hopped out his side of the truck, loped up the sidewalk, and disappeared inside.

She peered after him, trying to see through the living room window. A light from the kitchen turned on. What was he up to?

It couldn't be tidying the house. It had been spotless last time, as was the interior of his truck and his yard. And he couldn't very well be putting out food, not after the meal they'd just had.

A few minutes later, with the cab of his truck stifling,

Ashley opened her door and stepped onto the sidewalk. She wouldn't ruin his surprise, but she needed to get out in the fresh air.

She moved to the rear of the truck, out from under the glow of the streetlight. Tipping her head back, she looked up at the night sky. It was mostly cloudy. Only a few pale stars winked from between the inky clouds.

The static of traffic from a few blocks away carried over but his street was quiet. Not even a dog barked. God, it must be so nice to sit outside in this neighborhood. To not have to fall asleep to the sound of cars and sirens.

"Not many stars to see," he said as he joined her.

"No, but it's still pretty." She turned to him. "You have a nice neighborhood."

"Yeah, I do." His gaze searched hers. "Ready for your surprise?"

Nerves danced along her skin, fluttered in her chest. "I'm ready."

Taking her hand in his, he led them up the sidewalk. "I think you'll like this."

She liked it already. Especially when he pressed his warm palm against the small of her back as he followed her inside.

They walked through the dark living room into the kitchen. With only the light of the fume hood to guide them, he walked them out the back door.

Puzzled, she looked around. There was nothing to see. The yard was black. It didn't explain why he'd left her out in his truck.

He stepped to the side. She heard a click then the yard lit up.

Words escaped her.

He'd strung fairy lights to make a path that led to the back of his yard. There, like something from a dream, was a small square cabana tent complete with white drapes pulled back at all four corners. She'd only seen such thing in advertisements for those all-inclusive resorts in the Caribbean.

Instead of a bed inside there was a blanket spread on the grass with a small mountain of pillows at one end. Above the blanket more lights twinkled from the metal frame. It was stunning and romantic.

She couldn't believe he'd done this for her.

He wrapped his arm around her waist. "What do you think?"

"It's like something out of a dream."

"They'd forecasted a chance of rain today so I didn't set out the pillows and blanket until now. That's why you had to wait."

Touched that he'd go to so much trouble, she tipped her head, looked him in the eye. "Thank you doesn't seem enough."

He pulled her closer, lowered his mouth toward hers. "Thank you is just fine," he said before closing his lips over hers.

Swept away by the romance of it all, Ashley grasped his shoulders. He made her head spin. And not just from his kisses, though those alone managed it. It wasn't the spicy scent of his cologne that filled her senses either. It was the effort he'd put in, all the small touches he'd added to make everything special.

She was still trying to get her balance when he swung her into his arms. "What are you doing?"

"Saving you a sprained ankle. I can't imagine it's easy to walk on grass in those spiky heels."

It was just a matter of tiptoeing but she didn't argue. She'd never been carried in a man's arms and she wasn't about to give up the chance by being practical. Instead, she laid her head on his shoulder, breathed everything in.

Unfortunately, his yard wasn't that long and soon he was laying her on the blanket. Not that it was a disappointment. Especially when he closed the curtains and stretched out beside her, their heads supported by the mound of pillows. The lights twinkled soft enough to add ambiance without being so bright as to blind them.

It was like their own little private villa.

"I'd offer you wine but we both have to work tomorrow and I still have to drive you home." His mouth curved. "I don't really want more community service, despite how well the first one is turning out."

Smiling, she put her hand on his chest. Felt the solid beat of his heart beneath her palm.

"It is working out pretty great, isn't it?"

He skimmed his fingers across her bare shoulders. "I can't think of anything better."

Angling closer, she slid her hand up into his hair. "I can."

His eyes heated. "Yeah? Maybe you should show me."

She didn't stop to consider if she was being too brazen. If they should wait longer. They'd been edging around that pool for days and, as far as she was concerned, it was time to dive in.

Pulling his head toward hers, Ashley flicked her tongue over his lips. His hand jerked, then splayed between her shoulder blades, and pressed her close. Feeling empowered, she took his mouth in a kiss that was supposed to steal his breath but instead stole hers when she found herself flat on her back with Dallas on top of her, his tongue tangling with hers and his hand clamped possessively on her waist.

Her fingers dove into his short hair. Though there wasn't room between them for a whisper he still felt too far away. Or maybe he just had on too many clothes. She couldn't think clearly when he nipped at her mouth like that, when his thumb brushed the underside of her breast.

She'd been touched on the few dates she'd had over the years. Usually right before she backed off and told the guy she wasn't interested. And right after his touch had left her feeling deflated. Or worse, nothing at all.

But with Dallas she felt *everything*. The press of his arousal through his dark Wranglers. The weight of his body on hers.

And still she wanted more. She wanted the heat of his bare skin, his rough and calloused hands claiming every inch of her. She wanted to feel him driving inside her until the pressure building consumed her.

She'd been a girl the last time she'd had sex and that was all it had been, sex. There was more, so much more, with Dallas. Desperate to discover it all, Ashley grappled with his tan dress shirt. Tugging it free from his jeans, her hands dove underneath the fabric.

Yes. There it was. The hot skin, the muscles twitching beneath the rake of her fingernails. The hunger it added to his kiss.

His hand cupped her breast, his thumb zoning in on her aching nipple as, thanks to the flowy material of her skirt, he slid his thigh between hers.

Ashley's fingers dug into his back. She arched into him as she reached for what she most wanted. Her orgasm swept over her, wave after wave of hot pleasure as she clamped her legs around Dallas's. Her muscles were still quivering when embarrassment hit her as hard as her orgasm had.

She could've just died. Instead, she buried her face in his neck, mumbled her apologies. Bracing his hand next to her head he pushed away, looked at her. Ashley couldn't bear to face him. But he caught her arm before she could use it to cover her eyes.

"Don't," he stated. "I know you think what just happened is something you need to apologize for but, hell, Ashley, that was the hottest damn thing. Can you do it again?"

He had to be kidding. But when she summoned up enough courage to open her eyes and look at him, she saw he was serious. Desire darkened his blue eyes like the sky before a thunderstorm. His chest heaved with his short and choppy breaths. And if anything the ridge pressing against her was even harder.

She'd read about women having multiple orgasms in the romance novels she devoured but she'd always chalked that up to fiction. But looking at him looking at her, knowing he still wanted her, Ashley felt herself revving back up.

Only this time she wanted him there right along with her. Reaching behind her she untied the halter on her dress, pulled the top down.

The night air brushed her bare breasts in an erotic caress. Dallas's Adam's apple bobbed as his gaze drifted to her chest. The combination of both beaded her nipples into hard nubs.

"I have to—I just—" He swallowed and on a growl, lowered his head and captured her breast with his mouth.

The Fourth of July wasn't for another two months but fireworks exploded. She didn't even know if her eyes were open or closed. All she saw was bright white light. All she heard was her moan, her plea that he never stop. And all she felt was a keen, aching need to make love to him.

"Dallas." She panted as his teeth closed over her nipple, as her lower muscles made a tight fist. "Dallas," she said again, this time pushing him back a little.

Before he could say anything she reached behind her, dealt with the zipper on her dress and slid it down her legs. Then, in only a pair of ice-blue lace panties, reached for his shirt, hurried with the buttons.

If ever construction or ranching didn't work out for him he could be a male model. Broad shoulders, well-defined pecs, and a washboard stomach frontier women could have done their laundry on.

Though tonight, she wanted to be the only thing rubbing up and down his chest. Hands splayed wide, she ran them up his abs to his shoulders and skimmed them down his arms, taking his shirt at the same time. Then she followed the same path with her lips, tasting the saltiness of his skin.

Goose bumps broke out along his chest. His hands tangled in her hair as he did his own pleading. Pleased with herself she smiled as she pulled his belt free, opened the button, lowered the zipper on his jeans, and spread the fly open.

Suddenly, she could think of better things to do with her mouth.

Ashley pushed him onto his back. Once he'd kicked off his boots, she slid his jeans and boxer briefs down his muscled legs.

My God, the man has a gorgeous body. Every inch of him was hard. And she touched it all, kissed her way down his throat, into his neck, and across those ridged muscles. She'd have done more, had gone lower but when she reached his navel he flipped her back over.

It was hard to be disappointed when he claimed her breasts, removed her panties, and discovered all her sensitive places with his calloused fingertips. He drove her to the edge of ecstasy more than once only to pull back, shift those magical hands to her hair, her face.

She had no idea if he played a musical instrument. All she knew was he played her until she vibrated like a plucked guitar string.

Almost crazy with lust, Ashley wrapped her hands around him and squeezed. And as she circled her thumb over the tip of his arousal, she whispered in his ear how he was as wet as she was.

And only got wetter as she watched him roll on a condom, grab her hips. Then he plunged into her in one long, hard stroke that had her hips rising to meet his.

She didn't let him pull back again. Didn't let him slow down. No, the next time he drove her to the edge, she was going to put her foot on the gas and take them both over. So she wrapped her legs around his, met him thrust for trust.

Dimly, she hoped one of his neighbors wouldn't decide to go sit on their back porch. Though the curtains were drawn it was clear what she and Dallas were doing. The slap of flesh on flesh, the moans she couldn't contain. Especially when he pinched her nipples. Or when he wrapped a hand around the back of her bent knee and lifted her leg even higher until—

"Yes, yes," she chanted as she ground against his fingers. As his hips pistoned even faster.

He caught her moan with his mouth but then let one of his own go as her orgasm ripped through her. As she squeezed him hard. Her fingernails dug into his ass and a moment later he broke right alongside her.

Chapter Eighteen

DALLAS WAS HAVING a damn good day. Everything on site had gone smoothly for what felt like the first time since the incident with Vince and the nail gun. Because of that, he'd felt comfortable leaving them in his foremen's capable hands and had gone over to the *House of Hope* earlier than scheduled.

There he'd talked to Roy about the job at the ranch, and how it included room and board. When the man's face had lit up like Christmas, Dallas had hired him on the spot. Considered it a bonus that Roy said he'd be fine cleaning out the bunkhouse, that no fuss was needed.

So, with a bucket of fried chicken and all the fixings filling the cab of his truck with greasy temptation, with the same smile he'd had since he'd caught his breath after making love with Ashley, Dallas turned down the long tree-lined driveway to his family home.

His smile stretched wider with thoughts of Ashley. How she'd looked so pleased and shocked at his surprise. How she'd felt in his arms. How he'd felt beside her. And even better, inside her.

And though he'd just seen her at the *House of Hope*, he already couldn't wait to see her again. It was crazy the effect she had on him. When he wasn't with her, his thoughts were consumed by her and even when he was with her, he couldn't get enough. Which was why he'd feigned a problem in one of the closets just so he could get her in there for a stolen kiss.

He'd gotten away with one more of those imaginary problems until she'd caught on. But it hadn't stopped her from following him into the third.

Chuckling, Dallas parked next to Gage's Jeep and hauled the food out. He hadn't seen anyone in the yard as he'd driven up and the house was empty when he set the bucket of chicken and the bags of side dishes onto the table. He glanced at the clock on the microwave. Quarter after six. Shit, no wonder his stomach felt as though it had been hollowed out.

He'd go ahead and eat and then head out to the hay fields. He could continue cutting or baling while they came back to eat.

Dallas was halfway through his second piece of chicken when he recognized the rumbling sound of Ryker's truck pulling in. Then, through the open kitchen window came the unmistakable slam of a vehicle door followed by some muttering and gravel kicking.

Unfazed, because Ryker was usually bitchy about something, especially when it came to him, Dallas dragged a fry through the puddles of gravy and ketchup on his plate. He'd just swallowed it down when Ryker stormed in.

Dallas was used to Ryker scowling at him but the hot glare his brother shot his way, combined with the deep grooves around his flat mouth, warned of more than the usual resentment.

Not wanting to be caught at a disadvantage, Dallas wiped his mouth and fingers on a napkin, slid his chair from the table.

"What'd I do now?"

Ryker looked at the food with disgust. "Other than sitting on your ass while the rest of us are out busting ours?"

Dallas came to his feet. "I busted *my* ass all day too. And I brought supper so none of us would have to cook or do dishes because I *know* you've been busy. So maybe instead of jumping down my throat for a change, you can just say thanks."

But Ryker just glared. *Okay, then.*

"So what's got you so pissed off? Other than me eating."

"If you'd check your fucking phone you'd know the goddamn answer."

Dallas tamped down his temper. It wouldn't do any good if they both lost it. "You never called or texted."

"No, I just said that for shits and giggles."

Dallas pulled his phone out of pocket. "You want me to prove it? Fine." But the minute he pressed his thumb on the wake button he saw the missed text. And the missed call. Both from Ryker's number.

Son-of-a-bitch.

"Look, I'm sorry. I don't know how I missed it. My phone is always—"

But then he remembered. He'd taken a call as he was pulling into the chicken place and he'd left his phone on the passenger seat when he'd gone in to order. He hadn't bothered to look at his screen when he'd returned with the food.

He looked now, read Ryker's text. *"Got a sick cow. Vet will have prescription ready at clinic by end of day. Can you grab it on your way? Or let me know and I will, but would save a shit load of time if I didn't have to."*

Dallas set his phone on the table. "Sorry. I would have if I'd seen it but—"

"Save your fucking excuses. I've had enough of them to last a lifetime." Ryker tossed the white prescription bag onto the counter.

"The hell is that supposed to mean?"

His brother dug out a plate from the cupboard. "Exactly what it sounds like."

Something in Dallas snapped. He was sick and tired of coming home only to get shit on. And more, he was fed up not knowing what the hell he'd done wrong. So he'd left? So the hell what? So had Hudson and Cam.

He yanked the plate from Ryker's hand and slammed it onto the counter. "You want to snap at me, fine. But I'll damn well know why."

"Why?" Ryker shoved Dallas back. "You come and go whenever you damn well please and what? The rest of us are just supposed to be so damn grateful when you do show up? Fuck that."

Dallas counted to ten. And when that didn't push back the red clouding his eyes, he counted ten more.

"I've been here when you've asked. *Every time* you've asked. I found you a temporary bookkeeper and today I hired you a ranch hand. He's coming down with me on Friday. So—"

Ryker's fist flew so fast Dallas didn't have time to duck.

It rammed into his jaw like a sledgehammer. His head whipped to the right. Seeing stars he stumbled back into the counter; growled a curse when the edge of it cut into his hip.

Dammit, that was enough. He was through being Ryker's punching bag.

Pushing off the counter, squinting to see through the vision that had yet to clear, Dallas lunged for his brother. Head down, he caught Ryker in the gut, did his own shoving into the counter. Felt a grim kind of satisfaction when Ryker did some cursing of his own. Good. He hoped that hurt.

But his brother wasn't done. He punched Dallas's back, head. Got in a vicious one to his side. Using his brother's chest as leverage, Dallas shoved off with one hand as his other came round and cracked Ryker in the nose.

Dishes rattled. Glass shattered as something hit the hardwood. Blood poured like a geyser down Ryker's face. Ryker didn't notice. Or, if he did, he didn't care. With fury in his eyes, he came at Dallas. Braced, Dallas was ready but Cam and Gage ran in before any more punches could be thrown. Because Ryker was closest, Cam grabbed him, held him back.

"What the hell is going on here?" Gage demanded.

"Don't ask me," Dallas said. Slowly he moved his jaw side to side then up and down. It hurt like a son-of-a-bitch but at least it wasn't broken.

With a scowl on his face, Gage pointed from Dallas to Ryker. "Sit down, the both of you."

Since Dallas's head throbbed in time with his heartbeat, he was only too happy to comply. Ryker followed suit at the head of the table, and Cam, looking amused, settled across from Dallas.

Gage pulled out ibuprofen from the medicine cabinet, shook out four tablets. He dumped two in front of Ryker and two in front of Dallas before pouring them each a glass of water to wash them down.

"I told him I'd found him a hired hand and the next thing I knew I had his fist in my face," Dallas began.

Gage grabbed a towel from the drawer, shoved it at Ryker, who pressed it gingerly to his face. But there was nothing soft or delicate about the glare Ryker shot Dallas over the edge of the cloth.

"Maybe you wouldn't have if as ranch foreman, you'd respect me enough to run it past me before hiring someone to work on my ranch. But no," he continued on, sounding like a man with a bad head cold, "you did your own thing and expected me and everyone else to fall in line. Just like always," he muttered, before tilting his head back and closing his eyes.

Dallas got a rude awakening when the other two didn't jump to his defense. They simply nodded. Well. He could sit there and justify himself, tell Ryker and the other two to suck it up, what was done was done. After all, Ryker had agreed to hiring another hand and Dallas had saved him the trouble. Besides, he hadn't just hired the first man he'd seen on the street. Roy had experience and was a hard worker and—

Dallas blew out a deep breath. And Ryker was right. It wasn't his ranch. He should have run it past his brother first. He wasn't in charge anymore. Hadn't been for years. And his brothers didn't need him to be their father or their boss.

Quite frankly, Dallas was more than ready to just be their brother. And hopefully their friend. He'd been wanting to fix their relationship and he'd had no idea how. It seemed now he did.

Trudging to the cupboards, glass crunching under his boots as he did, he removed two cloths from the drawer.

Dallas pressed one of dishtowels into his brother's free hand. Ryker opened his eyes. He didn't say anything but passed Dallas the soiled cloth. Dallas was glad to see the bleeding was slowing before Ryker placed the clean towel beneath his nose.

After tossing the bloody dish towel into the sink Dallas dug out a pack of peas from the freezer. He wrapped it in the second towel and pressed the modified ice pack to his jaw before sitting again.

Shit, he should have made coffee while he was up but he lacked the ambition to do it. It would mean moving again and until the ibuprofen kicked in, his head thought it best to remain as still as possible.

Cam must have also thought coffee was in order. That or he'd caught Dallas's longing glance toward the coffee maker. Not that Dallas cared which. He was just damn glad his brother was making it. Just smelling the grounds as Cam measured them into the basket made Dallas feel better.

While the coffee maker gurgled and popped, Cam set out three more plates and sets of cutlery. He arched a brow at Dallas's half-eaten meal.

Though he felt the judgment and the need to defend himself, he kept his tone neutral. "Nobody was around when I arrived. I figured you were out haying. I thought I'd eat first, then ride out and take over so you guys could take a break and get some food."

"Take over," Ryker grumbled through the cloth. "That sounds about right."

Old habits died hard and it was on the tip of his tongue to tell his brother where he could shove his shitty attitude.

New beginnings, he reminded himself. "I know that's how it looks to you, to all of you," he said. "And maybe that's how it was. But hell, you're forgetting I was barely a teenager when Mom got sick and Dad fell apart. I was scared shitless." Could still feel it, when he thought back on those years. "All I knew was that Mom was dying, Dad was pretty much nonexistent, and as the oldest it was up to me to keep things together. I didn't have a fucking clue how but I had a friend at school that had been through the foster care system because his mom was an addict—"

"Dad wasn't an addict," Gage stated.

"No, but this kid's mom wasn't capable of looking after her son and his dad had taken off years before." Dallas grabbed his fork, twisted it between thumb and forefinger. "I didn't see our situation as much different. If word got out that Dad wasn't around to cook meals and do the shopping, to keep up the house and make sure none of us were running wild, I was afraid we'd be split up and sent away."

And that fear, that clawing, choking fear, had kept him on his brother's asses. Had ensured they did their damn homework and chores, that they had rules and curfews. That their grades didn't slip.

"So, yeah. I barked out orders, I rode you hard, and I wasn't any fun. *It* wasn't any fun. But it kept us together.

And it kept my promise—"

Choked up, he pushed away from the table. Needing some time to steady himself, he passed the bag of peas to Ryker before grabbing a handful of mugs.

He was glad his back was to his brothers, so they couldn't see his hand shake as he poured the coffee. But then again, maybe they needed to see it. Wasn't that what this was all about? Laying it all out there?

So, not as composed as he'd prefer to be, Dallas passed around the mugs, let them see he wasn't quite steady. Let them hear the tremble in his voice.

"When Mom got to the point she couldn't get out of bed anymore, when she knew her time was coming, she sat me down. Made me promise to look after you. Made me promise to do what she saw Dad wasn't."

And he'd promised her. With tears pouring down his face, he'd sworn to his mom he'd look after her family. When she'd finally slipped free of the disease that had taken her body, he'd stepped up. Pushing aside his own grief, running on a tear-filled vow and enough fear and worry to take ten years off his life, he'd fulfilled that promise.

As long as he'd been able to.

"You never said anything about any of that before."

Dallas looked into Gage's stricken eyes. "I was just trying to keep it together. So if I rode you hard, barked out orders, or made you think I didn't care, I'm sorry. I was flying blind and scared. I did the best I could."

"You cancelled a date for me once," Cam said, shuffling the macaroni salad around his plate with his fork. "I was sick with fever, puking my guts out, and I heard you call and cancel. I never thanked you for that."

Dallas lifted a shoulder. "Like I said, I did the best I could. I tried to always put you guys first." His gaze shifted to Ryker. Now that the blood had stopped, he'd replaced the bloody towel with the bag of frozen vegetables. But he still hadn't said anything.

"I know you resent me for leaving. For leaving you to look after Gage and Cam and help Dad with the ranch. I know you blame me for paving the road for Hudson and Cam to also follow their own paths."

His shoulders dropped under the weight of it all. "I had to go. It was getting to the point that I was resenting it. Resenting you guys. Resenting Dad. Resenting the ranch. But it wasn't until I started to get mad at Mom that I knew I had to make a change. I'd kept the family together for her but if I didn't leave then, if I didn't do something for myself, it was all going to be for nothing."

He took a sip of his cooling coffee. "Ends up it was anyway. Dad hates me for choosing my own business over his ranch and other than a call from you guys when you're desperate, we hardly talk."

Dallas again looked at Ryker. "I'll start by apologizing about Roy. I saw the perfect opportunity to make your life easier. He used to own a farm, he's available right away, and I thought he'd be a great asset, the perfect solution to getting the hay done.

"But," he added when Ryker's gaze narrowed, "I still shouldn't have hired him without running it past you first. I can tell him he doesn't have the job, if that's what you want."

Bruising was already blooming under Ryker's eyes. Dallas winced. Come morning, if not before, his brother was going to be sporting two impressive shiners.

Ryker put down the bag of peas. He leaned back in his chair, crossed his arms over his blood-spattered T-shirt. "This guy have a resume?"

Shit. Just when he thought he was making progress. Resigned to losing all the ground he might have just gained, Dallas told him everything he knew about Roy, including the fact he was homeless and he'd promised him he could live in the bunkhouse.

Dallas shook his head. He might have meant well but he realized how he'd stepped all over Ryker's toes. Had someone else come in and made decisions for Granger Construction without his okay, he'd be pissed too. Hell, he'd want to throw a punch or two.

Why hadn't he ever seen it that way before?

"I can write it all up for you. It's a couple days before Friday. It'll give you a chance to look it over, think it through. If you decide he's not right for the ranch, I'll talk to Roy, explain how I overstepped and made promises and decisions that weren't mine to make."

Ryker's gaze searched Dallas's. "You'd do that?"

"I would. Just say the word."

Although he hated to be the one to take the light from Roy's eyes, he'd do it. His relationship with his brother, with all his brothers, was too important not to.

Ryker turned to Cam and Gage. "What do you guys think?"

Gage shot Cam an incredulous look. It was clear Ryker

asking their opinion wasn't common occurrence. A little weight lifted from Dallas's shoulders, from the entire room. Maybe change was finally happening.

"I say we look at what Dallas writes about the man, weigh the pros and cons. But it's up to you," Gage said.

"Yeah, it is, but you guys work here too and you'll have to work with him. Do you trust a man who has been homeless to stay here, work alongside you?"

Cam shifted his attention to Dallas. "You trust him?"

"I didn't at first, but I've worked with him, seen his skills. He's had opportunity to steal and hasn't. I think he's worth a chance."

Ryker tapped his fingers against the table. "Okay. Write it down. I'll have a look."

Pride tightened Dallas's chest. They might not have been close the past decade and maybe he'd never recognized it before, but his brother was a good man. A solid, dependable one. They all were, he realized, as he looked around the table. Even though Hudson wasn't there, there was no question he fit into that mold as well.

Maybe, Dallas thought with a sudden burning in his throat, he hadn't done so bad raising his brothers and keeping the family together after all. They might have stretched the ties that bound them, but they hadn't broken them.

Chapter Nineteen

Looking in the full-length mirror, Ashley turned her leg this way and that. She'd fallen in love with the teal stitched brown boots when she'd seen them in the display window.

Her mistake had been sighing over them.

The next thing she knew Jess was dragging her into the country-western store and making her try them on. Okay. It hadn't taken much dragging or forcing. And looking at them now, how cute they looked with her shorts, she was sunk.

"Just get them, Ash. They look great and they're practical. If you're going to be spending more time at Dallas's family ranch, you need more than sneakers or flip-flops."

Ashley gnawed her lip. She wanted so badly to buy into Jess's rationalization but...

She pulled her eyes from the mirror. "I shouldn't. Brittany's birthday gift was expensive and even though I saved months for it—"

"Almost a year," Jess corrected.

"Almost a year," Ashley agreed. "Even so, it wasn't cheap. And this is a frivolous expense no matter how I try to justify it." She gave Jess a pointed look when her friend opened her mouth to argue. "You know as well as I do that I can ride a horse in sneakers."

"I know. But the bonus you got from the small engine repair shop is just that. A bonus. It's supposed to be used for frivolity."

Jess lifted herself off the log bench that customers used when trying on boots. She stood next to Ashley in front of the mirror. Her flowery perfume was in direct contrast to the smell of leather that filled the boot section of the store.

Jess slung a friendly arm around her shoulders, tipped her head toward Ashley's.

They couldn't be more different. The up-to-date-on-everything-fashion Jess with her chic wardrobe and modern hairstyle and Ashley, with her denim shorts and tank top she'd bought from the thrift store. She didn't remember the last time she'd had a salon haircut and there was nothing fresh or modern about the ponytail and bangs she trimmed herself.

Even though she'd already committed to putting half the bonus in her checking account, she felt guilty even contemplating such a purchase.

In the mirror, she looked into Jess's eyes. "I feel selfish."

"Good." Jess squeezed her shoulder. "It's okay to think of yourself for a change. Ash, you're a good mom and you've spent the past sixteen years putting Brittany first. It's not a crime to buy yourself a new pair of boots."

"But I already bought the jeans you talked me into and the fancier coffee maker than I'd planned on getting."

"Trust me, you won't regret that coffee maker. The convenience of those pods when you're in a hurry is golden, and you'll still have the regular pot for when you're home."

She'd fallen for that as hard as she'd fallen for the boots.

And the jeans.

"And just like that coffee maker, those boots are practical. They'll go with dresses, shorts, and they'll look great with those new jeans you bought."

Ashley grinned. Yes, yes they would.

Sensing her capitulation, Jess grinned. "Now hurry up and get them so we can go eat. All this shopping has made me hungry!"

RUNNING ON HER shopping high and the fact she now had a few extra hundred dollars in her bank account, Ashley decided to look up Granger Construction. She didn't know Dallas's schedule but figured, as it was four o'clock, he might be in his office to wrap things up before closing.

She could have texted or called, but that would have ruined the surprise. And even though they were going to be spending most of the weekend together, thanks to Brittany's overnight trail ride, she couldn't wait until then to see him.

Of course, after last night's events in his backyard, it wasn't only seeing him she was anxious for. It was kissing him, running her hands over his muscles, through his hair. Feeling his body pressing against hers, inside hers.

A rude honk behind her reminded her a busy intersection wasn't the place for fantasies. She focused on her driving the rest of the way into the industrial area.

Following the mechanical directions coming from her phone, Ashley soon saw the sign for Granger Construction.

She knew he did good work from his time working on

her house but if his other projects were as impressive as his sign, then the man was a genius on top of his other talents. She pulled over to better admire it.

Instead of a basic flat sign, he'd built a miniature gray gazebo complete with matching wooden rails and floor. The roof, with its red tin, was as eye-popping as the railing planter boxes that dripped red petunias. In the entranceway to the gazebo, at the same height as the railing, he'd made a solid cedar gate with the words *Granger Construction* in raised red writing.

She wasn't an expert in branding, but she'd heard the term and couldn't deny Dallas had nailed it. Not only did the gazebo match his company colors, but the thing itself was a standing display of his craftsmanship.

It was silly to be proud considering she'd had nothing to do with it, but she took a picture of it anyway before pulling into the driveway and parking next to a small SUV.

Only then did she realize Dallas's truck wasn't in the lot.

Well, shoot. Her gaze dropped to the cute tray of mixed succulents on the floor of her passenger side. She'd bought it on a whim at a flower shop on her way over, figuring the small green plants would be perfect for his office. They didn't require a lot of care and attention and weren't fussy or too girlie for a man. Plus, she hoped he'd think of her when he looked at them.

Should she just go home, take them with her? Then she could give them to him in person. She chewed her lip as she contemplated but ultimately decided she'd rather leave them here. Maybe she wouldn't see his reaction this way, but she liked the idea of him going into his office and finding them.

Picturing him smiling as he read the small card she bought to go with it sealed her decision.

The office of Granger Construction was a cute A-frame in the same colors as the gazebo. It boasted a wide wooden porch complete with the same railing planters. On the right side of the door was a beautiful round wooden picnic table and on the left three red Adirondack chairs that faced a firepit table. Everything about it spoke of comfort, quality, and attention to detail.

Armed with her tray of succulents, Ashley climbed the short two steps to the entrance and let herself in.

A small waiting area sat to the left, the tall reception desk to the right. Straight ahead were two doors. One was an office, Dallas's she assumed, and through the doorway of the other, what was clearly a break room. Behind the reception desk a row of file cabinets lined the wall. Along with them was a photocopier, a water cooler and just past that, in the corner, a restroom.

Since nobody was at the desk and the door to the restroom was closed, Ashley assumed that was where his bookkeeper was. She was happy to wait. Noticing the red-framed photos filling the walls, Ashley stepped forward for a closer look.

There were decks and garages. Barns, houses, and, yes, gazebos. There were even a few displaying patio furniture similar to what he had outside.

She'd never been the mom that sat in the stands at a sporting event, band concert, or awards night and bragged about her child. Oh, there'd been times when she'd wanted to stand and yell, "that's my girl!" but she never had.

It was the same standing there looking at Dallas's work. She wanted to point at the photos and brag, "My boyfriend built that!"

Not that anyone would hear her. Or see her for that matter.

Ashley glanced toward Dallas's office. Since it was right there she decided to go ahead and put the tray and card on his desk. If the receptionist came out and saw her in Dallas's office she'd point to the plants and introduce herself.

But the bathroom door remained closed even after Ashley stepped out of Dallas's office. Remembering his bookkeeper was pregnant, Ashley couldn't help feeling concerned. Though the front door to Granger Construction didn't have bells over it to announce a visitor, it did have the same kind of front door as a house. Which meant it made more noise closing than a commercial glass door that just floated shut.

Surely the woman must have heard her enter and walk around? Although her sneakers were quieter than her new boots would have been, she'd made noise. And since none was coming from the bathroom, Ashley was fairly certain the woman would have heard her. She gnawed on her lip.

It didn't feel right to just turn around and leave. She couldn't explain it, other than a weird feeling in her gut that told her not to leave without seeing the woman.

She was considering coughing to get her attention when Dallas's office manager shuffled out, hands splayed over the mound of her belly. Tears shone in her eyes.

Ashley leapt forward. "Oh, my goodness, are you all right?" She took the woman's elbow. "Come sit down."

"I'm all right," the woman said. But she didn't argue as Ashley led her to one of the chairs in the waiting area.

As soon as the woman was off her feet, Ashley hurried to the water cooler, poured a cup, and brought it back.

"Thank you."

"You're welcome." Ashley settled next to her. "Can I call someone for you?"

The woman sniffled, sipped her water. "I already did. My doctor says it's probably nothing to worry about but to come in and he'll have a look." She wiped a tear that fell. "My husband is coming to pick me up."

Ashley smiled reassuringly. "Sounds like you're doing everything right."

Realizing the woman had no idea who she was, Ashley introduced herself. Unsure how much of his private life Dallas told his employee, she left it that she was a friend of Dallas's.

"So you're the reason he's been happier lately. Nice to meet you. I'm Sherry." Her lips tipped into a smile that never made it past the worry in her dark brown eyes.

Ashley's heart went out to the woman. She remembered being that close to term and terrified of what was to come.

"Is this your first, Sherry?"

She nodded.

"Are you having cramps?"

"No. That's why the doctor didn't seem concerned." She met Ashley's gaze. "I'm spotting."

Ashley placed her hand over one of Sherry's, which still held the baby bump. "You're about eight months?"

"Yeah."

"I was too when I started spotting. I panicked, thought for sure something was wrong."

Sherry looked shocked. "You have a baby?"

Ashley laughed. "Yeah, if you consider sixteen a baby."

Sherry gaped. Clearly, Dallas hadn't told her the woman he was dating had a kid. Though it hurt, she reminded herself they really hadn't been dating that long. Besides, Sherry didn't need to know all the details of their relationship.

"So nothing ever came of the spotting?" Sherry asked, bringing Ashley's thoughts back.

"No," she said. "He said it happens, no reason why. Brittany was born five weeks later, a day before she was due." Ashley squeezed Sherry's hand. "Eight pounds five ounces. Perfectly healthy."

Sherry sputtered. "Eight pounds?"

Ashley laughed. "That's why they make epidurals." She let her smile fade. "I know you're scared, but it'll be all right."

"Thanks. I'm glad you're here."

"I'll stay until your husband arrives."

Which, ten minutes later, he did. He wasn't as visibly shaken as Sherry but it was clear by how careful he treated his wife he was worried too.

It wasn't until she watched them drive off that Ashley realized the woman had left Dallas's office unmanned. Pulling her phone from her purse, Ashley dialed Dallas's cell.

"Hey, beautiful. This is an unexpected surprise. What's up?"

His deep voice slid over her. Like sinking into a hot bath,

it warmed her all over. Some places definitely more than others.

"I'm at your office. Thought I'd stop by and surprise you on my way to *Coffee Time*."

"Aw, shoot. Sorry I missed you."

There was a lot of background noise and she pulled the phone from her ear because he was shouting to be heard over it.

"That's okay. I figured it was a long shot. But that's not why I called."

"Okay, what's—Hang on a second."

The beeping noise she'd heard, the kind machinery made when it was backing up, stopped. In fact, most of the noise suddenly dimmed. He must have put his hand over the mouthpiece. A few seconds later the sound came rushing back.

"Sorry about that. So what's up?"

"Sherry had to leave. Her husband picked her up to take her to the doctor but they left in such a hurry, she didn't tell me what to do. I didn't want to leave your office unlocked."

"Is she okay? Is it the baby?"

"She was spotting and scared. The doctor told her it was likely fine but to go in anyway. She'd already called her husband by the time I got here."

His breath whooshed in her ear. "Okay. Well, as long as they're both fine."

"I think they will be. But I really need to get going." And by the sound of things where he was, he wasn't coming back anytime soon. "What do you want me to do here?"

"If you can power down her computer and make sure all

the lights are off that'd be great."

Ashley looked up at the dead bolt. "What about the door? You want me to leave it unlocked?"

"It should be fine," he said after a small hesitation.

Ashley figured he was thinking about the employee that had stolen the nail gun. She worried her lip. "I can call *Coffee Time* and see—"

"No. It'll be fine. I'll swing over as quick as I can to lock up."

"You're sure? Because I can always call and say I'll be late." Though she hated to, she would if Dallas needed her to.

"I'm sure."

Who was she to argue? He was the boss. "All right."

"Listen, I hate to rush off, but I really should go."

"No, that's fine. I have to get going, too."

"Okay, then I'll see you tomorrow afternoon?"

Ashley grinned. Tomorrow, after the morning spent at the *House of Hope*, they were dropping Brittany and her friends at the dude ranch in Last Stand and after a few hours working at the Diamond G, would have the rest of the day and night to themselves. It couldn't come fast enough.

"I can't wait," she said.

After they hung up, Ashley went around Sherry's desk. She closed all the programs Sherry had open then powered off the machine. She'd just shut off the photocopier when the phone rang. Did he have an answering machine? She had no idea, but she did have his cell number so if she needed to get a message to him she could.

Though it felt awkward, she answered the phone.

"Granger Construction."

She breathed a sigh of relief when it was nothing but a solicitor. She was just telling the woman thanks but no thanks when a very distinguished man walked in the door. He had a head full of thick silver hair and sharp green eyes. Judging his dress shorts and matching polo shirt, he must have just come from the golf course.

"I'm sorry Mr. Granger isn't in and—"

He waved a hand. "I don't need Dallas. I just came to pay my bill." He pulled an envelope from his pocket as he approached the desk.

Ashley's gaze darted around the desk. "Um. Sherry had to leave suddenly and I've just powered off the computer." She started opening drawers. "If I can find a receipt book, I'll—"

"I can get it later." He set the envelope on the counter. "Name's on there. Tell Sherry to email the receipt same as she has before."

Before she could do more than stammer, he strode right back out the door. Ashley grabbed the envelope, intending to put it in the desk but when she picked it up she realized it was thick with cash.

Well, shoot. She didn't feel comfortable leaving it in the desk, not when the place would be unlocked. And not, judging by the thickness of the envelope, with that amount of cash.

Deciding to take it with her, Ashley tucked the envelope into her purse. She'd give it to Dallas when she saw him tomorrow. After shutting off the lights and ensuring everything was tidy and put away, she turned the sign on the door to closed and hurried out before something else or someone else delayed her further.

"I'M SO SORRY," Ashley said, shoving her wet hair off her shoulder. "I'd meant to be ready before you got here but I got stuck behind an accident. And to add yet another delay, Brittany got tired of waiting for me so she's at her friend's. I hope it's okay but we'll have to stop over there and get them on our way to Last Stand."

Dallas heard most of what she said. But really, only two things stuck in his head. One, she was alone. Two, she'd just come out of the shower.

He'd figured that last one out on his own. And it wasn't only the dripping wet hair that gave it away. It was the forest-green towel she wore. The *only* thing she wore.

The combination of her being alone and naked short-circuited his brain, drove everything but Ashley out of his head. Drove everything beneath his buckle until he was hard, throbbing.

Without a word, he stalked forward. When he'd cleared the entryway he shut the door. Turned the dead bolt. Kicked off his boots.

She arched a brow, quirked her mouth. "Planning on staying, cowboy?"

He tossed his hat to the floor. "I'm planning a hell of a lot more than that."

"I was hoping you'd say that."

Then, with the same hunger in her eyes he felt clawing

through his body, she dropped her towel.

Hell, yeah.

Before he'd fully realized his intent, he had her against the wall, his hips pressing into hers. Through the denim, he felt her softness. Her heat. He rocked against her as he took her mouth in a scorching kiss that left his lungs burning.

A man could live without oxygen, couldn't he? Especially when he had a soft, fresh-smelling female in his arms, grinding her hips against his. In that moment, he couldn't think of anything he needed more than Ashley tugging at his shirt, begging him to hurry.

He was happy to oblige. They'd have later to linger in bed, and again tomorrow morning because he had every intention of having her stay the night at his place.

So he filled his hands with her breasts, teased her nipples into sharp points.

If there was anything hotter than a woman about to have an orgasm Dallas didn't know what it was. Head tipped back, bottom lip between her teeth, and catchy gasps in her throat.

He lowered his head. With his mouth tugging on one nipple, his hand slid from the other, over her taught stomach, down to where she needed him most.

They moaned together. Ashley rocked her hips against his hand as Dallas switched to her other breast. His fingers wet with her arousal, he pressed two inside her. She screamed his name as she shattered and collapsed against him.

It was the hottest damn thing, holding her there as she caught her breath. But he was rock-hard and damn uncomfortable and when he figured she could hold herself up, he dug the condom from his wallet and stripped. When he'd protected them, he grabbed her leg, hooked it around his hip, and finally entered her. She squeezed around him.

"God, yes." He moaned as he buried his face in her neck, as he started pumping his hips.

She was soft, hot, and smelled of citrus. Matching him thrust for thrust, she raked her hands down his back, grabbed his ass. Pinning her against the wall, he lifted her other leg.

While he wasn't forcing her, far from it, a part of him recognized this time was different. And maybe it was only their second time, but he knew right then and there he was claiming her as his. He never wanted anyone else to touch her this way. *He* didn't want to ever touch another woman this way.

It was a feeling he'd never had before, not even with Olivia and he'd been ready to propose to her. But with Ashley, he felt it down to his soul. This was his woman. He was her man.

And almost as though he couldn't make the claim fast enough, Dallas drove hard.

He caught her gasp with his mouth, deepened the kiss as he rocked her against the wall. She shattered first, her cry muffled in his neck as her heat poured over him. Feeling it, drowning in it, Dallas surrendered to his own pleasure.

With both of them shaky, he held her until their racing breaths no longer ricocheted off the walls.

"I think I might need another shower," she giggled against his neck.

He pulled back, grinned. "You know, I think I do too."

DALLAS WAS FEELING damn good as he tucked in his T-shirt and buckled his belt. Though they really hadn't the time to spare, he'd promised shower sex wouldn't take long. His lips curved, remembering how he'd ran his soapy hands over her breasts, down her belly, between her legs. And then, to be sure he'd done a good job, had tasted all those spots with his tongue just to make sure.

She'd come against his lips, and a few minutes later, she'd come again with him buried inside her. So maybe it hadn't been as quick as he'd promised, but hell if he regretted it.

And though Ashley had shoved him and his clothes out the bathroom door so she could finish getting ready, she'd done it with a very satisfied look on her face.

Beyond her satisfaction, though he had no problem seeing to that, what mattered more to Dallas was her happiness. He loved making her smile. Loved surprising her. Loved knowing he was giving her something she'd never had before.

Loved her. He ran a hand down his stubbled cheeks as his heart skipped a little. It was normal to feel afraid, right? It didn't mean he was going to get hurt like he had before. Even though he felt more for Ashley than he'd ever felt for Olivia.

Because Olivia had broken his heart and she'd never had as much of it as Ashley already did. But Ashley wasn't like his ex.

He breathed out a deep breath. If he weren't convinced

of that, he wouldn't be standing in her living room ready to spend the weekend with her.

"Brittany just texted for the fifth time," Ashley said as she hurried into the living room, bag in hand. More than her overnight things, he'd told her to bring a change of clothes so they could go riding.

That was the story they were going to go with as well if Brittany asked why her mother needed an overnight bag to go to the ranch.

Looking at her, his fear faded. She was absolutely nothing like Olivia.

Grinning, he said, "Then I guess we should go. It's never good to keep a lady waiting."

Her smile dazzled him. But then, everything about her did. Especially denim shorts that showed off her toned legs and tight tank tops that did amazing things for her breasts.

While he tugged on his boots, she nudged him aside to get into the hall closet. She pulled out a brand-new pair of boots. The smell of leather rose to his nose.

"Nice boots," he said as she put them on.

"Thanks. I probably should have saved the money instead." She looked down, tapped the heels together like they were ruby-red slippers, "But I really wanted them."

He tipped her chin up. Kissed her. "You deserve to treat yourself once in a while. Besides, your legs look amazing in them."

The guilt that had pulled at her mouth lifted with her smile. She looked down before meeting his gaze. "They do, don't they?"

"Yeah. Makes me want to do this." He slid his hands up

her legs, dipped his thumbs beneath the cuff that rode high on her thighs.

Yelping, Ashley slapped at his hands and leapt out of reach. "I really don't want to explain to my sixteen-year-old why I'm so late. It's bad enough I have whisker burns on my thighs."

He winked. "Not where anyone can see."

Laughing, she opened the door. "I don't have the energy for more of that right now."

He stopped, braced a hand in the doorway and leaned toward her. "I bet I could prove you wrong," he drawled.

Ashley laughed. "I'm sure you could."

But she slapped her hand in the middle of his chest and shoved him instead.

"Come on, cowboy. You can prove it later."

Chapter Twenty

ASHLEY LOVED HER daughter more than anything on earth, but by the time they dropped Brittany and her friends off at the Cartwright Dude Ranch, signed them in and hugged them goodbye, she could have wept with gratitude. A day and a half of peace! No giggling, no screeching, no constant chatter, no drama.

Dallas pinched the bridge of his nose, closed his eyes. "Is it always like that?" he asked.

Ashley couldn't help but laugh. He'd given her four orgasms, had two of his own, and been ready to prove he could deliver more but one hour in a truck with three teenage girls had wiped him out.

"You should see what one of their sleepovers is like."

He dropped his hand, actually looked pained. "You've had more than one? Why?"

God, he was cute. "Because it's what parents do. Besides, if she's at home I know where she is and who she's with."

He leaned over the console of the truck, kissed her. "You're a good mom."

"Thank you."

"You're welcome." His mouth curved. "Now it's adult time."

"Work first," she corrected even though her stomach

flipped at his words.

"Don't see why we can't mix the two." His smile widened. The good kind of trouble glinted in his blue eyes. "Dad might have left some papers in the hayloft. We should probably check it out."

"Papers in the hayloft? Really?"

He put the truck in gear, turned it around and bumped back down the driveway. "Hey, you never know."

She shook her head, laughed. But, if he were to suggest it, she'd definitely follow him up into the hayloft.

MUCH AS THE hayloft called to him, it wasn't the day for it. They had a shit ton to get done and the sooner they got to it, the sooner they could go back to his place. Not that he wasn't going to make time for a horseback ride before they left, but until then, he just wanted to plow through the work. Which was why he took the ATV to the field instead of a horse.

Since he hadn't seen Roy in the yard, he hoped the man was cutting hay. Which would make Ryker happy. Which, in turn, would make life easier for Dallas.

He was bumping along the trail that led through the pastures to the hayfield when his phone vibrated. He geared down, then shut off the engine and pulled out his phone.

"Granger Construction."

"Afternoon, Dallas. It's Paul Jenkins."

"Yes, Paul. What can I do for you?"

He'd built a sunroom onto the man's house and when

they'd finished two weeks ago Paul had seemed pleased. Since his tone wasn't angry, Dallas didn't think the call was about a problem.

"I just wanted to say again how pleased I am with that sunroom. We had guests over last night and they couldn't stop talking about it. I referred them to you."

"Thanks, I appreciate any business you throw my way."

Dallas hated nagging but when it came to business, he didn't mess around. It was his policy that all jobs had to be paid for upon completion. The only reason he'd left the finished job without being paid in full was that Paul only had a thousand owing and as they'd finished earlier than planned and the man preferred to pay cash, Dallas hadn't been too concerned. But since he had the man on the phone…

"So, now that we're all done and you're happy with the sunroom, when can I expect the final payment?"

"That's the reason for the call. I stopped by your office yesterday, paid the balance. Your new secretary took the envelope. In case she forgot to mention it, I just wanted to let you know."

His new secretary? He didn't have a new—

Oh, right. Ashley had been there, had shut things down for Sherry. He frowned. She hadn't mentioned Paul stopping by. In fact, he'd gotten the impression all she'd done was power things off and left. And when he'd gone back later to lock up, he'd double-checked everything. Granted, he hadn't looked in every drawer, but he hadn't seen an envelope on either his or Sherry's desk.

Despite the sweat trickling down his back from the Texas

heat, a shiver skittered down his spine. The boots. She had new boots. And hadn't she looked a bit guilty putting them on? Hadn't she said she should have saved the money?

"Dallas? You still there?"

"Yeah, sorry. I'm just at my family ranch. Listen, thanks for letting me know. I haven't had a chance to cross paths with her yet, so I didn't know you'd stopped by," he lied. Because he had indeed crossed paths with her. More, he'd had sex with her. Multiple times. Not once had she mentioned the cash.

"Then we're good. I won't hold you up. Thanks again, Dallas."

"Yeah, no problem. Bye."

Woodenly, Dallas replaced the phone. It didn't mean anything. Her having new boots was just a coincidence. It didn't mean she'd taken the money.

But as he looked over to the grazing cattle, watched a few lumber along, he couldn't shake the sick feeling roiling in his gut.

If she hadn't taken the money, then why hadn't she mentioned Paul stopping by?

ASHLEY HAD JUST printed off the last of the checks when Ryker walked in the office. He had a smear of grease on his cheek, a rip on the sleeve of his T-shirt, and dirt on his jeans. He'd taken off his hat but the imprint of it remained on his dark blond hair. Without it shading his face his two black eyes were unmistakable.

"You're just in time. I've paid all the outstanding invoices and the checks are ready for your signature."

He looked over the desk. It wasn't clear, but it was much tidier than the last time she'd been there.

"You do fast work."

"The thing that took the longest was organizing it. I did that last time I was here. Now it's just a matter of working through the piles."

He raked his hand through his hair. "Well, better you than me." He pointed to the file cabinets. "You figured out Dad's filing system?"

"Yes. In fact, the problem wasn't that he didn't know how to file. It's just that he didn't do it often. He actually has a pretty organized system."

"That's good." He took the pen she passed him, reviewed the checks as he signed them, then handed her the stack.

"Did Dallas talk to you about me helping out around here once I'm caught up in the office?"

He set the pen on the desk, his expression guarded. "No."

"Oh." Ashley grabbed the pen, fiddled with it as she hurried to explain. "I need some extra cash to send my daughter on a school trip and—"

His eyebrows arched. "You have a daughter?"

"Yes. She's sixteen, or will be tomorrow." She tried not to read too much into Dallas not having said anything about Brittany but Ryker was the second person Dallas hadn't told. Was he embarrassed?

"Anyway, I could use some extra money to help pay for her band trip and I asked Dallas if I could do some chores around here."

Ryker crossed his arms. She thought she saw a flash of anger in his eyes.

"You asked Dallas?"

"I asked Dallas to ask you, actually. The truth is once I get the office caught up, and if your dad still isn't up to running it, it really won't take long to maintain it. Maybe a couple hours each time I come, if that. So I was hoping, as it's a long ways to come out, that I could help around here after the paperwork was done. It would make the drive worthwhile."

And she was babbling. She pressed her lips together.

Ryker studied her. "What did Dallas say when you asked him?"

"He thought it would be fine but said he'd have to run it past you."

The stiffness faded from his shoulders. He lowered his arms and for the first time since she met him, he actually smiled.

"That's fine. We'll work something out."

Relieved, Ashley sank into her chair. "Thank you. Thank you very much. Between the *House of Hope* and my other part-time jobs it would be difficult to fit something else in. This will make things easier."

"*House of Hope*? You're a volunteer there, too? Is that how you and Dallas met?"

Her relief turned to concern. Dallas hadn't told them about the house either? Geeze, did his brothers even know they were dating?

"The *House of Hope* is for me and Brittany. As recipients

we have to work several hundred hours. And, yes, that's where I met Dallas."

"Huh." Ryker nodded. "Cool. Anyway, just leave the envelopes with the checks on the desk when you're done. I'll take them to the post office Monday."

Ashley sat there long after Ryker went back outside. Why hadn't Dallas said anything about her? Was he embarrassed to be dating a single mom? A woman who needed to work six days a week just to make ends meet? A woman who wasn't above mucking stalls if that was what it took to ensure her daughter had what the other kids in her class had?

No, she was being silly. He'd never given her any indication of that. In fact, he was great with Brittany. Had even bought her a sweet sixteen present. And maybe at first he'd seemed like a self-righteous ass, but she'd gotten to know him since and he wasn't that kind of man.

So, she was going to give him the benefit of the doubt. He'd admitted he wasn't close to his brothers. It stood to reason they hadn't had a conversation about her.

Determined not to let her past insecurities ruin a good thing, Ashley put aside her conversation with Ryker and got back to work.

EVEN DALLAS WAS surprised with how good hiring Roy was turning out. Not only did the man know the equipment, because his dad's machinery was at least a decade old and he didn't need to be taught how to drive it, but he had an aptitude for fixing things as well. When the shear bolt on the baler broke because Cam was feeding the hay into it too fast, Roy was right there to replace it from one of the spares.

It was a perk of hiring an older man. That generation tended to be jack-of-all-trades and, whenever he could, Dallas preferred to hire one of them. Plus it had the added advantage that they weren't glued to their phones.

With Cam, Gage, and Roy on hay duty, Dallas saw to the stock, checked fences, and knocked a few repairs off the list Ryker had given him.

The work kept his mind off Paul's call. In fact, he'd managed to forget about it completely until he was saddling up the horses for his and Ashley's ride. Then his mind went back to the fact that Ashley hadn't told him about Paul's visit or the envelope.

He wasn't proud of the fact that he even considered the possibility she'd take the money. But he couldn't discount the facts either. She needed money. Enough that she'd asked if she could muck out stalls for a little more income. Enough that she'd lived with a terrible squeal in her car because she couldn't afford to get it fixed.

Then there was the new boots. And after the shower he'd walked through the kitchen and seen the new coffee maker. The much fancier one than she'd had before.

And at the bottom of all that was the damn pros and cons list he'd seen at her house. The one with the dollar sign next to his business. Maybe if he'd never seen it, if he'd never almost married Olivia before he'd realized all she'd wanted was to trap him, it would be different. But it wasn't. And it wouldn't be until he got to the bottom of it.

"I'm all set."

Dallas finished cinching the mare's saddle, turned.

She'd changed out of her shorts into jeans. But not just any jeans. The dark denim looked brand new. And when she stepped forward, he recognized the brand. Those jeans didn't come cheap. He felt sick. If she'd taken the money to put gas in her car or food in the fridge, he'd understand. But to buy clothes and a coffee maker? Had he really misread her that badly?

No. He couldn't have. He couldn't be that wrong about a woman twice. But Olivia hadn't confessed until he'd backed her into a corner and demanded the truth. He'd given her the opportunity to come clean and she hadn't. Not until she'd had to. If Ashley was indeed the woman he thought she was, she'd admit it before it got to that point.

All he had to do was give her the chance.

"You look great," he said.

And she really did. She wore a pink-and-white plaid western shirt tucked into her form-fitting jeans. Her hair was tied back in a ponytail and her face glowed from nothing more than the coconut sunscreen he smelled. She looked young and innocent. And his gut twisted with the possibility she wasn't as innocent as she appeared.

"Thanks."

Though the mare and gelding stood perfectly still in the aisle of the barn, Dallas tightened his hold on the reins. He felt slimy as hell for what he was about to do, but he needed the truth.

"I like your jeans."

Her smile lit up the dim aisle. "I don't remember the last time I owned a new pair of jeans." She turned for him, showing off more than the rhinestones on the pockets. "You like them?"

"I do," he admitted. "But I thought you were saving for Brittany's trip."

Her smile faltered. "I am. But when some unexpected money came my way, I decided it was time I did a little something for me, too."

Yeah, he supposed being handed a grand in cash would be considered unexpected.

She looked at the horses, pointed to the mare. "Am I riding Peaches again?"

"You are."

He handed her the reins. Together they walked out the barn, the horses clomping along behind them.

"I wanted to thank you again for covering for Sherry yesterday."

"Oh, that wasn't a problem. I'm just glad she's okay."

"Yeah, scared her, though. You could still hear it in her voice when she called me last night. But the doctor said the baby is doing just fine."

For which, he was eternally grateful. He'd have felt responsible if something bad had happened while she was at work.

Out in the sunlight, they mounted the horses. This time when they passed the machine shed toward the trail, the building was empty and his brother wasn't scowling at him.

"She said to say thanks, too. She appreciated you staying with her and closing up. She asked if you had any problems." He peered at her. "I told her no."

Ashley smiled at him. "I really wasn't there that long. It

was all fine. I just closed down and left."

Yeah, and then went shopping. Well, he'd given her opportunity to come clean and she hadn't. And he was a damn fool.

Pissed off he'd been duped again, he pulled on the reins. "Whoa."

Ashley followed suit. "What's wrong?"

"Why didn't you tell me? You had to know I was going to find out."

Her brow creased. "Find out what?"

The fact she wasn't admitting it, even now, threw fuel onto the fire.

"Don't," he warned. "Don't pretend you don't know what I'm talking about. Paul Jenkins called me this afternoon."

She frowned. "I don't know who that is."

"He's only the man who came into my office yesterday and handed you an envelope with a thousand dollars in it. The same thousand you used to go shopping."

Shock drained her face of color. "What? I never took the money."

"He said he gave you an envelope with the cash in it."

"Yes, he did but—"

"Then why didn't you mention he stopped by? And why didn't I see an envelope of cash when I locked up?"

"Because I put it in my purse. I didn't want to leave cash in an unlocked office. So I took it with me. Because I lock my purse in the lockers at *Coffee Time*, I knew it would be safe and then today, first thing when I got to the house I tried to put it in your truck, but it was locked. That's why I asked you for your keys and told you I had something to put in there. I didn't want to be responsible for it."

"Yeah, I remember you asking for the keys. But you never said what you'd put there." And he'd forgotten all about it after his shift because he'd been in a hurry to get home and change and then pick her up to take her to the ranch.

Her eyes flashed. "Did you expect me to announce that I was putting an envelope of cash in your truck in front of everyone?"

"It wasn't there."

"Did you check your glove box?"

Hell. No, he hadn't. But she hadn't told him where to look either. Despite that, the first feeling he'd screwed up royally tightened his stomach.

"No."

"No. Instead, you thought I'd stolen it. Stolen it and gone shopping."

He gestured toward her jeans and boots. "You have to admit I had reason. You do have new boots and jeans, not to mention the coffee maker I saw earlier."

Color poured back into her face. "Because Eugene at the small engine repair shop gave me a bonus to go with my last paycheck. And after I put half in the bank, I decided that, yes, I deserved a little something. A little something, not so long ago, you agreed I deserved. So, yes, I bought myself some boots and jeans and replaced my broken coffee maker."

Her chest heaved. Angry tears shone in her eyes.

"You actually believe I'd steal from you? After I swallowed my pride to ask if I could muck out stalls for extra money?"

Her hands clenched into fists. "I pay my own way. I always have." She shook her head. "I know you thought little of me when we first met. I know you believed that I was just out for a free ride. I thought you knew me better than that. I thought we knew each other better."

Realizing what a huge mistake he'd made, Dallas hurried to explain. "Ashley, I'm sorry—"

"Don't!" she shouted, loud enough to have Peaches startle beneath her.

Dallas reached for the reins, but Ashley held the mare steady.

"Don't." She said it softer but with just as much venom.

And hell if he didn't deserve it.

"You know what's ironic in all this? I found out today Ryker didn't know about either Brittany or the *House of Hope*. I thought you were ashamed of me. Ashamed to tell your brothers the truth about me. That I'm a struggling, single mom. But I gave you the benefit of the doubt. I told myself it was just because you aren't close with them and not because you're embarrassed to be dating me."

"I'm not embarrassed." He pushed his hat up, needing her to see he was being honest. "Cam knows all about you. It just hasn't come up with Ryker or Gage."

"It doesn't matter. The point is I had a chance to jump to conclusions, too, but I didn't. Because I know you. Or thought I did."

"Ashley, you know me. Look I made a mistake but—"

"No." Her eyes were dry. Dry and hard with anger. "What you did was more than a mistake. You accused me of lying and stealing."

"Because when I asked you how it had gone at the office you said all you'd done was close things up. You never mentioned Paul at all."

"Because it slipped my mind! Nothing more nefarious than that. Dammit, I was in a hurry to get to work. You know, the job where I *earn* money."

He winced.

"You can find your damn envelope in the glove box of your truck." She turned the horse toward the house.

Fear, a tight hard ball of it, lodged in his chest. "Ashley, please." He'd beg if it would stop her. Hell, he'd do anything if she'd only look at him.

She bowed her head. Dallas had never felt sicker in his life. Dammit, he couldn't lose her. Not because of this. Not because he was too jaded by the past to see what he had in her.

"I asked you once not to break my heart," she said. Her voice trembled with emotion. "And you did. In the worst way."

"I'm sorry. Please let me—"

Her head lifted. He watched her struggle to compose herself. "Please don't follow me. I'll see Peaches is looked after and find my own way back to San Antonio."

Then she straightened her spine, her gaze anywhere but on him. "Goodbye, Dallas."

Chapter Twenty-One

DALLAS STAYED AT the ranch, mostly with the horses so he wouldn't have to talk to anybody. When he heard the rumbling exhaust of Ryker's truck pulling in, he pushed away from the stall door and strode down the lit aisle of the barn, shutting off the light as he walked out.

"What the hell did you do?" Ryker slammed his door, stalked forward. The yard light caught not only his frown and the scowl on his face, but the bruising of his black eyes. "She cried half the way home."

He'd figured as much but hearing it made him feel even worse. "I'll fix it." He wasn't sure how to mend the trust he'd broken but he was damn well going to try.

Ryker scowled. "You better because otherwise we're out a bookkeeper. Again."

Dallas's head whipped up. "She quit?"

Ryker scoffed. "She did more than quit. When I asked her where I should mail her check, she told me to send it to the nearest homeless shelter. I got the distinct impression she didn't want anything to do with the money."

And the hole just kept getting deeper. But Ashley wasn't the only one used to hard work. He'd keep digging until he'd crawled his way out of the mess he'd created. Until he made her understand. Until he earned her forgiveness.

Fishing his keys out of his pocket, Dallas loped toward his truck.

He hadn't realized Ryker was right behind him until he heard his brother's voice.

"She means something to you, doesn't she?"

Dallas braced his arm on top of the open door, looked over at Ryker. It took his brother a moment or two to look Dallas in the eye. When their gazes met Dallas saw something in Ryker's that hadn't been there since their mom got sick. Interest. As though he might actually care about Dallas and what was going on his life.

Dallas's chest tightened. Oh, he wanted a relationship with Ryker, with all his brothers, and as much as he'd said he was sorry for the past, and meant it, it hadn't prepared him for the olive branch Ryker was offering.

Because he wasn't ready for it. And he really, really didn't want to screw this up.

If he said the wrong thing now, he'd lose his chance at making amends with Ryker. But damn it, the timing was wrong. He wanted to get to Ashley but he didn't want to rush through this with Ryker. Or have his brother think he was brushing him off.

Ryker rolled his eyes. "Whatever." He turned to go.

"Yes, she means everything to me." He waited until his brother stopped and looked at him again. With the words scratching in his throat Dallas added, "But she's not the only one."

It was awkward but he hoped Ryker understood what the hell he was trying to say. Because his throat was so tight, speaking wasn't a possibility.

Ryker's gaze bore into Dallas's. He must have had the same difficulty speaking because he swallowed at least half a dozen times.

In the end he didn't say anything, just nodded. Dallas's heart sank. Shit, he'd blown it after all.

But just as he was lowering his head his brother said, "I'll see you Monday?"

Dallas's head whipped up. He wouldn't say his brother was smiling, but at least he wasn't scowling.

"I'll be here."

Ryker jammed his hands in his pockets. "See you then."

ASHLEY SHUT DOWN her computer, leaving it on the desk, still plugged into her printer. After allowing herself an hour to mope and nurse her anger once she got home, she'd turned on the lights and powered up her computer.

The time for self-pity was over. It was time she once again pulled herself up and did what needed to get done. With that mindset, she'd methodically gone through the classifieds and every employment website. She'd found six possibilities.

But only one had her stopping and reevaluating. Only one had her questioning not only what she wanted out of a job, but also what she wanted out of life.

And how much she was willing to work for it.

She'd stared at the ad as her mind raced and her heart shook. It wasn't that what she had to do was hard, necessarily. At least not physically. But emotionally it meant swallowing her deepest fear and, yes, some pride.

Surprisingly, despite the way she'd felt earlier, it hadn't taken her long to realize she was looking at the solution. Not only because this job would allow her to quit her others and have more time with her daughter, but because it would give her what she'd foolishly and rashly accepted she couldn't have.

What she now believed to the bottom of her soul, she not only could have, but she darn well deserved, as well.

Ashley pulled her resume off the printer, stared at her cover letter. The papers were rock steady in her grasp. Most people didn't go out applying for jobs after nine on a Saturday night. But she wasn't most people.

And this was no ordinary job.

DALLAS WAS STILL trying to figure out exactly what to say when he was standing at Ashley's door.

He'd only ever felt real fear, the ice-in-your-veins kind of fear, twice before. When his mom got sick and when his dad checked out of their lives and it was up to Dallas to look after the family.

But standing there, he felt the same kind of fear. Because, once again, he was on the verge of losing what meant the most. He didn't want to lose Ashley. *Couldn't* lose her.

He took a deep breath, prayed she'd at least give him a chance.

Knock. Knock. "Ashley? It's me. Can we talk?"

It was no great surprise when she didn't open the door.

But if she thought he was giving up that easy, she was in for a shock.

"Ash, I'm not going anywhere. Not until you hear me out, give me a chance to apologize."

He waited, pressed his ear to the door. Nothing.

The door at the end of the hall opened and a couple walked in. Dallas gave them a weak smile when they stared questioningly at him. The man positioned himself between Dallas and the woman as she slipped the key in the lock. They disappeared inside, the dead bolt clicking loudly behind them.

With a sigh that filled his lungs with the lingering spicy aroma of someone's supper, Dallas pressed his back to the door and slid to the floor.

"I stopped at the hospital on my way here," he began. "There's no change with Dad. He's stable but not responsive." Still, Dallas hoped his old man was at least aware that his eldest had been there. And what he'd said.

"My dad made a lot of mistakes in his life. What he did to my mom was unforgivable. He abandoned her when she needed him most. And then he abandoned us. But you know what pisses me off the most? That when he decided to come back, he never apologized for what he did. He never once said he was sorry for not being the kind of man he should have."

And in a coma or not, Dallas had finally let Joe know just how much that still hurt. Maybe if his dad had acknowledged what he'd done wrong, Dallas could find it in him to forgive the man. But to just march on like nothing ever happened? That didn't fly in his books.

Of course if it turned out Joe had had an affair, there wouldn't be a way to make any of it right. But until either his dad woke up, the woman came forward, or they found Joe's car that might give them a clue as to where his dad had been, it was all moot. They wouldn't have any answers until one of those things happened.

But this wasn't about Joe.

"I'm not my dad," Dallas continued. "I can admit when I'm wrong and I can apologize. Even grovel." He closed his eyes, tried to picture her listening. Because, damn, he really needed her to hear him.

"Ashley, I'm sorry. I'm sorry I let you down. I'm sorry I hurt you. I want what we're building together. I want to be there for you and Brittany. I want us to be together."

Despite not hearing footsteps, the door at the end of the hall creaked open. Dallas opened his eyes. He scrambled up.

"Ashley." He gestured behind him. "I thought you were home."

She slowly walked forward. "I had an errand to run." She cocked her head. "You didn't notice my car wasn't in the lot?"

"I parked out front. I was in such a hurry I didn't think to look in the lot."

And instead of confessing to her, he'd confessed to a closed door and an empty apartment. Only—

"I didn't hear you walk up the stairs."

She moved closer, stopping in front of the door across the hall from where he was standing. After Ryker having told him she'd cried half the way home he'd expected to see her puffy eyed and sad. But her eyes were clear. There wasn't any indication she'd been crying. In fact, she looked confident and strong.

Hell, did that mean she'd already decided to move on? And she was good with that? His stomach fell to his boots.

"I followed my neighbors up but when I heard your voice, I hung back, wanted to hear what you had to say." Honey-gold eyes searched his. "Did you mean it?"

"About wanting us to be together? More than anything."

Her sharp inhale filled the short hallway.

Worried she was about to tell him it was too late, Dallas hurried on. "I realize that's probably hard to believe given how I acted earlier. But I meant what I said about being sorry. More than that, I was wrong to accuse you of stealing. And I know just how to prove to you that I do trust you."

When she arched a brow, he plowed ahead. "Come work with me. As my office manager, you'll have run of most things as I'm gone a lot of the day. While most customers pay by check there are some that pay cash. I'll trust you with that, with my books, with everything I've built. And, if this goes where I'm hoping it will, one day we can be partners in life as well as in business."

Ashley's jaw slackened. Her keys fell from her fingers.

A loud thump and giggling came from behind the closed door at her back. Clearly her neighbors hadn't gone very far into their apartment when they'd gotten home.

Dallas grabbed her keys off the floor. "Maybe we can finish this inside?"

She flushed, took the keys he held out. "Good idea."

He said nothing else as he followed her inside. He waited until she'd turned on the lights and invited him to sit. He took a seat on the couch and patted the spot next to him. He took it as a good sign when she settled next to him. The citrus smell of her shampoo filled his senses and for the first time since their argument at the ranch, he felt as though things were going to work out.

"Dallas—"

He took her hand. "Can I go first? I'd like to finish what I started out there." When she nodded he took a deep breath, blew it out. "Remember when I told you I was engaged before I found out she was using me? Well, I never told you everything. She was pregnant."

Ashley frowned. "But—"

"No. I don't have a child out there I never told you about. Truth was she was pregnant. But it wasn't mine."

He still remembered the strange fluttery feeling in his stomach at the thought of becoming a father. And the bitterness when he'd discovered the truth.

"Turns out the deadbeat who was the father had no money to support her or the child and she saw me as her answer. A way to make her life easier."

She took his hand, squeezed. "I'm so sorry."

"There were signs. When I looked back I saw them clearly. How she said she didn't trust her car to be safe enough for a baby. How she didn't want to buy anything secondhand in case it was damaged or unsafe. How it was a good idea to start a child's education fund early so the money had time to grow."

He shook his head. "I know you're not like her, Ashley. In my heart I know that. Always knew it. You're the hardest working woman I know, and you've already raised Brittany on your own. You don't need me. But I let my insecurities overrule common sense."

"I think we both did."

"Maybe." He offered her a self-deprecating smile. "But I think I got you beat." He sighed. "When I thought I was going to be a dad I was excited. Not ready, but excited. Even though Olivia wasn't the woman I'd have chosen for my child's mother, I wanted it."

And when he'd learned it was all a lie? He'd died inside.

"I was planning this life and suddenly everything I knew and believed, everything I wanted, was gone. It gutted me. So when Paul told me about the envelope of cash? I thought back to the pros and cons list. Then when I saw the new clothes I thought I'd done it again. Blinded myself to the facts for what I wanted. Instead, I ruined the best thing I ever had." Dallas laced his fingers with hers. "Earlier this afternoon I recognized that I was in love with you. That I wanted to share everything I have with you. My home. My life. My heart. I promise I'll never make you feel less than again."

She sniffled. "When my parents found out I was pregnant, they kicked me out. When Ashley's dad found out, he left. When the few guys I've tried dating found out I wasn't going to fall into bed with them right away, they never called back." She looked at him with shining eyes. "You're the first to fight for me."

Emotion lodged in his throat. How she'd managed to become the woman she was when everyone in her life had let her down he'd never know. He only knew it made him love her that much more.

"As for working for you? I already applied. You'll find a resume in your mailbox at home and another one in an envelope taped to the door of Granger Construction." She grinned. "I didn't want you to miss it."

Gratitude and relief made him weak. Humbled she'd give him another chance, he pulled her close, wrapped his arms around her.

"What I said back at the ranch was inexcusable. You have shown me in every way that you're trustworthy and honest and I'm so sorry I let my fear get the best of me. As for nobody fighting for you?" He pressed a kiss to her head, pulled her a little tighter. "I promise I always will." And by everything that was in him, he'd never hurt her this way again. "I love you, Ashley."

She held him close, pressed her cheek to his chest. "I love you too."

DALLAS WASN'T THE only person prepared to fight. When her parents had kicked her out, she'd thought, "Fine. Who needs you?"

When Dylan had offered child support but nothing else she'd thought, "Well, at least her child would have an education."

And when Dallas had hurt her, she'd run, told him not to follow her. After all, she'd been on her own half her life, she could keep doing it.

Like Dallas, she'd seen a pattern in people and had assumed the worst. He wasn't alone in that. But she didn't want him to be another person who just came and went in her life.

Ashley set her hands on his chest, leaned back in his embrace. "I want us to build that life together, too."

His blue eyes warmed. His hands tightened on her hips. "So about that. I know it's soon, and maybe too soon for you to even consider, but you're months away from your house being done and I've got more than enough room for you and Brittany at my place."

Ashley's head was spinning. So much had happened and changed in one day and she was scrambling to keep up. Not that they were bad changes, because every single one of them was a dream come true, but it was a lot to process.

Worry creased his brow as he peered at her. "You can even have your own room, if that makes you more comfortable. And the basement is developed so Brittany would have her own space and privacy."

Like she'd done earlier when she'd seen the ad for Granger Construction, Ashley took a deep breath and asked herself what she really wanted. What would make her happy.

"Would she have her own bathroom?"

Dallas's brow smoothed out. "Yeah. And there's a TV down there as well."

Oh boy.

"Well, I'm pretty sure she won't say no to that, but I can't make the decision without asking her first."

He squeezed her hand. "That's fair."

"What happens when the house is done?"

"I'm not going to lie. I hope you stay. But you put in a lot of hours and heart into that house so if you want to live in it for a little while, I'm okay with that." He leaned in, kissed her. "As long as it's temporary."

Ashley already knew she wouldn't. Which tugged at her

heart a little because the house *had* been a dream for so long. But then, that wasn't really true either. She'd wanted a house, a place with roots for her and her daughter. A place to call their own.

And she'd have that with Dallas. In the meantime, she'd continue to work on the *House of Hope* knowing that if she needed it, it was hers. And if, when it was done, she decided she didn't need it after all, the organization would give it to someone who did.

Feeling happier and more at peace than she'd ever felt, she wrapped her arms around Dallas, kissed him long and slow.

Before he could press her back into the cushions she asked, "You're sure you're up for a moody teenager?"

"I know I'm up for trying." He cupped her cheek. "I want this, Ash. I want us. All three of us."

One of the things she'd realized when she'd decided to fight for him was that as much as she wanted the three of them to be a family, she also wanted more. And since it seemed as though she was about to get everything she'd ever wanted...

"How would you feel about there being four of us one day?"

His lips curved. She saw everything she needed to know in his eyes. It was exactly what was in her heart.

"You're up for another one?"

She wrapped her hands around his neck, kissed him. "I am with you."

The End

If you enjoyed this book, please leave a review at your favorite online retailer! Even if it's just a sentence or two it makes all the difference.

Thanks for reading *Cowboy Up* by Michelle Beattie!

Discover your next romance at TulePublishing.com.

If you enjoyed *Cowboy Up,* you'll love the next book in….

The Tangled Up in Texas series

Book 1: *Cowboy Up*

Book 2
Coming soon!

Available now at your favorite online retailer!

About the Author

Award-winning author Michelle Beattie began writing in 1995, almost immediately after returning from her honeymoon. It took 12 long years but she achieved her dream of seeing her name on the cover of a book when she sold her novel, What A Pirate Desires, in 2007. Since then she's written and published several more historical novels as well a contemporary. Her pirate books have sold in several languages, been reviewed in Publisher's Weekly and Romantic Times. Two of her independent self-published works went on to win the Reader's Choice Silken Sands Self-Published Star Contest.

When Michelle isn't writing she enjoys playing golf, reading, walking her dog, travelling and sitting outside enjoying the peace of country life. Michelle comes from a large family and treasures her brothers and sister as well as the dozens of aunts, uncles and cousins she's proud to call family. She lives outside a tiny town in east-central Alberta, Canada with her husband, two teenage daughters and their dog, Ty.

Thank you for reading

Cowboy Up

If you enjoyed this book, you can find more from all our great authors at TulePublishing.com, or from your favorite online retailer.

Made in the USA
Monee, IL
26 August 2019